365 more BEDTIME STORIES

© 1986 Autumn Publishing Ltd

Designed and produced by
Autumn Publishing Limited
10 Eastgate Square, Chichester, England

Text by: John Gatehouse

Illustration by: Bojana Ban

1986 edition published by Derrydale Books,
distributed by Crown Publishers, Inc.,
225 Park Avenue South
New York
New York 10003

Typeset by Tigertype, Alresford, Hampshire
Printed in Czechoslovakia
ISBN 0 517 61793 5

365 more BEDTIME STORIES

DERRYDALE BOOKS
New York

King Muddletop

King Muddletop was a jolly old king, but he was also very absent-minded. He could never remember where he had put things.

One morning the King looked very flustered indeed. "Gadzooks!" he cried. "I've lost my royal crown!"

The King searched the palace from top to bottom. He looked in cupboards and under the royal bed. He searched in the kitchen, behind the fridge, even inside the washing machine. He looked in the garden, around the old oak tree, under the royal statue and inside the water barrel, which tipped over and drenched him in cold water. But still he could not find his crown.

"Call out the guards!" he bellowed crossly. "Someone's stolen my crown!"

The Queen hurried up to him, laughing merrily. "You are a silly-billy, dear! Your crown is on top of your head!"

The King reached up and sure enough there was the crown. "Oh, my!" he chuckled. "What a memory I have. I forgot I put it on this morning!"

5

The Scarecrow

Sammy the Scarecrow had a problem. No matter how hard he tried he could not scare away the crows from the farmer's field.

"Shoo! Go away!" he would shout but the crows ignored him.

JINGLE! JANGLE! JINGLE! JANGLE! went the bells on Sammy's feet and arms as the wind blew harder. The crows turned their backs and pretended they couldn't hear.

Occasionally a cheeky crow flew on to Sammy's pumpkin head to eat the seeds.

When the farmer saw this he was very angry.

"Sammy's no good," he told his wife. "We'll have to get rid of him."

Sammy felt a tear run down his face. "Oh, dear," he sighed, looking at the trees and hedges that surrounded the field. "If the farmer gets a new scarecrow I'll never see my beautiful field again."

"Here, Sammy," said a rough voice somewhere on top of his head. It was the cheeky crow. "Don't you worry now. We crows will help you."

"Help me?" repeated Sammy who was by now very puzzled. "You don't even like me."

"If the farmer gets a new scarecrow it might really be frightening and scare us away," explained the crow. "Then we'd have nowhere to feed our families."

The crow told Sammy his plan and when the farmer came to his field again he was surprised to see the crows fly off as Sammy danced on his pole in the wind.

"CAW! CAW!" cried the crows as if they were very frightened.

"Well, I never," chuckled the farmer. "Sammy does his job after all. Now I won't have to replace him."

Sammy was very pleased to hear this. To thank the crows he allowed them to eat a few seeds out of the field every day. Now everyone was happy again.

Tom's Ball

Tom was given a new ball for his birthday. "Can I play with it?" asked his best friend, Andrew.

"No, it's mine!" snapped Tom. "You'll only burst it."

"I'm going home then," said Andrew.

"Let's have a game of football," suggested a group of boys. "We can use Tom's ball."

"No, you can't," sulked Tom, keeping a tight hold of the ball. "It's mine! I'm not letting anyone play with it."

"Be like that!" grumbled the boys. "We'll find another ball and you can't play in our game."

"Don't care!" said Tom, but he did really. Tom played at heading the ball, and then he kicked it against the wall of his house until his Dad came out and told him off. He tried keeping the ball in the air by bouncing it on his knee and then practised balancing the ball on the end of his nose. But for some reason he didn't feel very happy.

"It's no fun playing by myself," he thought. Tom went to find Andrew. "Will you play with me?" he asked, holding up the ball. "And with the ball, of course."

"All right," agreed Andrew.

"How about a game of football?" Tom asked the group of boys who were still searching for a ball. "We can use my ball."

"Okay," said the boys.

Tom had a lot of fun playing with his friends. "Toys are nice," he thought. "But they're more fun when you share them with your friends."

Dimple and the Ogre

Dimple is a dragonet, which is a name for a young dragon, and he lives high in the mountains with his family and friends. "Who lives in that castle?" he asked his father one day, pointing with one of his small scaly wings towards a huge castle that stood on another mountaintop.

"That is the Ogre's castle and you must never, ever go near there or he'll eat you up!" said his father sternly.

Dimple listened to his father but he was a very inquisitive dragonet and soon forgot the warning.

"Surely there won't be any harm in taking a look?" he thought and with that he flew off towards the castle.

Spying an open window Dimple flew inside. "Gosh! There's the Ogre now!" Dimple gasped as he landed on the floor for a rest. The flight to the castle had worn him out and he couldn't fly any further.

The Ogre, a giant of a man with a bald head, was sitting at a large table eating a bowl of porridge. Suddenly he turned round and when he saw Dimple he bellowed, "HO! HO! WHAT DO WE HAVE HERE?"

Dimple squealed in fright as the Ogre lumbered towards him. "Oh, no! He's going to eat me!" Dimple cried.

The Ogre picked Dimple up and patted him on the head. "Nice Dragon," he said, smiling happily. "Thank you for visiting me. I don't have any friends because I'm so big. Everybody's scared of me." The Ogre started to cry.

"Poor Ogre," said Dimple, feeling very sorry for him. "I'll be your friend. And I'll come and visit you every day."

Dimple kept his word and soon the two became the best of friends. So if you should ever see an Ogre pass by your home with a dragonet on his shoulder you'll know who they are. Remember to give them a wave!

The Letter

Every morning Sally watched the postman as he delivered the letters to the houses in her street.

"Is there a letter for me?" she would ask eagerly as the postman passed by her garden gate.

"Not today, Sally," the postman would smile cheerfully. "Perhaps tomorrow." But there never was. There were letters for mummy from Auntie Rose, there were business letters for her daddy, and letters that smelt of perfume for her eldest brother, Simon. "No one sends me a letter," she said sadly as she watched the postman pass by one morning.

"Who would want to send you a letter?" laughed Alec, the nasty boy from next door. The postman overheard this and decided to do something to help Sally.

"POST!" he shouted next morning.

"I don't care," sulked Sally. "There won't be a letter for me."

"One for Mr Brown, two for Mrs Brown from Auntie Rose, and one for Simon Brown," smiled the postman. Then his smile turned into a grin. "Oh, yes, and one for Miss Sally Brown!"

"FOR ME!" Sally couldn't believe her ears. The postman handed Sally a blue envelope. Sally quickly opened it and took out the letter. It read, "DEAR SALLY, I KNOW HOW MUCH YOU WANT A LETTER SO I THOUGHT I WOULD SEND YOU ONE. I HOPE YOU LIKE IT. LOVE, BOB THE POSTMAN. xxx

"It's lovely," Sally said happily. "I'll treasure it always!"

climbed on top of the crate and unlocked the cage with the key. Soon all the elephants were free. They crept quietly back into the safari park. All, that is, except for Tiny, who stood in one of the opened cages.

When the poachers awoke and discovered the elephants were free they were very angry. "He must have let them out!" snarled one, pointing to Tiny. They all ran into the cage to catch Tiny but as they did so he slipped through the bars of the cage, ran round to the cage door and slammed it shut, locking the poachers inside.

"Now the park warden can arrest them," Tiny thought happily.

The other elephants made a big fuss of Tiny and never again did they joke about his size.

"I think I like being small after all," Tiny said to his mother.

Tiny Saves the Day

There was once an elephant who was very small. In fact he was so small he was positively TINY! So that is what his mother named him.

All the other elephants laughed at Tiny's size but his mother said, "Ignore them. They'll learn it's not size but *who* you are that counts."

One day poachers arrived in the safari park where Tiny lived. They were looking for elephants to capture and sell to circuses where the animals would be forced to do tricks and be kept in cages. The poachers quickly rounded up all the elephants, including Tiny's mother. Luckily Tiny was so small the poachers could not see him.

When the poachers were asleep Tiny crept out of hiding and lifted the key to the cages from one of the poachers pockets with his trunk. Only then did he realise he was too small to reach the lock in the cage door. But Tiny had an idea. He pushed a large crate that the poachers had used to carry their supplies , over to the cage his mother was being held in. This was hard work because he was small and wasn't very strong. Tiny

The Treasure

Scrappy was in trouble again.

"That dog has got to go!" stormed Mr Higglebottom. "He's dug up all my roses to bury his bone!"

Scrappy didn't like the sound of this. If Mr Higglebottom threw him out he would end up in a dog's home and if he sold him Scrappy might go and live with someone who was cruel to dogs.

"I'll dig up my bone and put it somewhere else," he thought.

Scrappy worked all morning digging up his bone. Then he started digging a hole at the

other end of the garden, right where Mr Higglebottom's cabbages were growing. Mr Higglebottom was outraged.

"That does it!" he bellowed. "That dog goes — NOW!" Reaching into the hole Mr Higglebottom lifted Scrappy out roughly . . . and then stopped. Inside the hole were lots and lots of gold coins. "Goodness! Scrappy's dug up a set of ancient coins! They must be worth a lot of money!"

They were too. With the reward money Mr Higglebottom treated himself to a new car and Scrappy to a new kennel. He never complained if Scrappy dug up his flowers to bury his bones and never again did he threaten to get rid of Scrappy.

The New Dress

Sarah's mum had bought her a new red dress. "It's lovely!" said Sarah. "I'll wear it all the time."

Sarah wore her dress when she went shopping with her mum and when she visited Grandma. She wore the dress to school and on trips to the countryside with her uncle. In fact she wore it everywhere!

One day a terrible thing happened. Sarah was playing in the garden when her pretty dress caught on a nail and when she tried to pull it free she tore a large hole in it.

"My dress is ruined!" she cried.

"Oh, well. You've got lots of other nice dresses to wear," said her mum. But Sarah wasn't interested. "I like this one best!" she said.

The next day Sarah went to the shops with her mum and dad. Sarah was wearing a lovely blue dress but she was still feeling miserable. While her mum did the shopping Sarah and her dad went to look at the toys. "I don't want a silly toy," Sarah sulked. "I want my pretty red dress!"

"If you hadn't worn it all the time it wouldn't have got ruined so quickly," said her dad.

Back home Sarah's mum handed her a large package. "This is for you," she said. Sarah quickly unwrapped the package.

"My red dress!" she squealed happily as she held it up.

"Well, a new dress," smiled her mum. "But you must look after this one."

"I will!" Sarah promised. "I'll only wear it on very special occasions."

The Rainy Day

Thomas looked out of the window and watched the rain as it fell splish-splash in the puddles.

"I want to play outside," said Thomas. "But it's too wet."

"Why not play an indoor game?" suggested his dad.

Thomas watched as his dad turned the small coffee table upside-down on the carpet. "What are you doing?" Thomas asked, puzzled.

"Wait and see," said his dad with a smile.

Thomas' dad took a broom from the cupboard. To the broom handle he tied two ends of a towel.

"This is a mast," said his dad, pointing to the broom. He placed the broom in the upturned table. And this table is your boat."

"Now I can play at pirates!" Thomas said happily.

While Thomas fetched his teddy bears his dad made him a pirate's hat from a sheet of newspaper. "All pirates wear hats," he laughed.

Thomas sat in his boat and set sail.

Thomas sailed to an island where he met a tribe of Indians who invited him into their wig-wam for tea. Afterwards Thomas set sail again. The weather turned very windy and Thomas' little boat was tossed up and down by the waves. "Hold tight, teddy!" Thomas shouted. "I don't want you to fall overboard!"

Thomas' dad came into the room. "It's stopped raining," he said. "You can go out to play now."

"No, thank you." said Thomas politely. "I want to play indoors after all." And with that he set sail for Australia!

The Witch's Problem

"Oh, bother! My spells never work!" Treacle Tart was a Witch but she was not very good with her spells. They never turned out the way she wanted them to. She had tried to magic a new tile on her roof to stop the rain from leaking in. Her spell made the roof disappear altogether! Then she wanted to magic a bunch of flowers to brighten her house. Her spell brought a lion instead who chased her all around the house until she managed to make him vanish again. And now by mistake she had turned her favourite chair into a mushroom.

"I'm a hopeless Witch," she sighed.

A fairy was passing by and felt sorry for Treacle Tart. "Here, use my magic wand. Then all your spells will work," she said.

Treacle Tart did this and found the fairy's words came true. All her spells turned out perfectly from that day on.

The fairy smiled to herself. She knew the wand wasn't really magic at all. Treacle Tart's spells only failed because she lacked confidence. When she thought the wand was doing the magic for her all her confidence returned and so her magic worked. The fairy would never tell Treacle Tart this — will you promise not to?

The Wish

A fairy offered a gnome one wish.

"Hmm, what shall I wish for?" thought the gnome. "Pots of gold? A new house? Fine clothes?"

"Hurry up!" said the fairy, who was getting impatient.

"Oh, hold on!" snapped the gnome. "I wish I knew what to wish for!"

PING!

The gnome's wish came true. "I know what to wish for now!" he cried happily.

"Too late," said the fairy. "You've had your one wish." And she vanished in a puff of smoke, leaving the gnome to think nasty thoughts about fairies!

The Proverbs

Susan was reading from a book of proverbs. A proverb is a short saying that has some truth in it.

"Look before you leap!" she laughed as Derek jumped over a small hedge and landed in a dirty puddle. Derek wasn't very pleased.

Hurrying home to change out of his dirty clothes Derek accidently knocked over a bottle of milk on the doorstep. "Oh, no! Mum will be cross!" he said worriedly.

"More haste, less speed," said Susan, reading from her book. "It's no use crying over spilt milk."

Derek was getting fed up with Susan's proverbs. Just then she saw a pin their mother had dropped on the floor. "See a pin and pick it up and all the day you'll have good luck!" she read from her book.

Susan bent down to pick up the pin. "YEEEOOW! It pricked me!" she cried.

"Ha! Ha! So much for proverbs," laughed Derek. "Now I've got one for you. He who laughs last, laughs longest!"

The Sleepy Troll

Slumber, the troll, enjoyed sleeping best of all.

"Don't forget the shops will be closed for the holidays after tonight," reminded his friend Skippy. "So remember to stock up your cupboard with food."

"I will," said Slumber. "After I've had a little nap."

It wasn't long before Slumber was fast asleep. He slept through breakfast, and through dinner. He slept through the afternoon and half way through the evening. When he did wake he said, "Why is it so dark?" Then he realised what he had done. "Oh, no! All the shops will be shut and I have no food in the house!" Poor Slumber. He had to go hungry until the shops opened again three days later.

"That's the last time I oversleep!" he said crossly. Do you think that will be so. No, nor do I!

Freddy and the Shopping

Freddy the fox wanted to go swimming with his friends.

"Later," said his mother. "After you've done my shopping."

Freddy grumbled and groaned, he sulked and he scowled, but his mother took no notice. "Come back here straight after you've done the shopping," his mother said.

Freddy quickly did the shopping and was heading for home when he met his friends, Clive Crocodile and Albert Alligator.

"Aren't you coming swimming?" they asked.

"Well . . .," said Freddy, thinking about his mother's shopping. "Only for a short while."

Freddy put the shopping down behind a tree. "It'll be safe here until I get back," he thought.

Freddy did enjoy splashing about in the pool. He showed off his diving skills to Clive and Albert and the three friends had swimming races. It was much later when Freddy remembered the shopping.

"I had better hurry home," he told Clive and Albert. "Mum will be wondering what has happened to me."

Freddy went to the tree to fetch the shopping . . . but it was no longer there!

"Oh, no! It's been stolen!" Freddy cried.

Freddy went home and told his mother what had happened. She was very cross. "No tea for you tonight. Off to bed with you!"

Freddy sat up in bed feeling sorry for himself. "Next time I'm asked to do a job I'll do it straight away," he thought.

The Bird-Watcher

Mr Tweet the troll was very fond of bird-watching. He set off one morning and soon reached the countryside. "I'll find lots of different birds to watch here," he thought.

But Mr Tweet was too busy looking for birds and didn't watch where he was stepping. Suddenly he found himself falling into a fast-flowing stream. "Goodness! If I don't get out I'll drown!" he gasped.

Catching hold of the overhanging branch of a tree Mr Tweet pulled himself out of the water. But as he let go of the branch it sprang back and struck a bee hive hanging on the tree. The bees were very angry and chased Mr Tweet all over the countryside. Luckily he found an overturned box to hide in until the bees had flown away.

"This is hopeless," he said. "I haven't seen one bird. I'm going home."

Back home Mr Tweet had an idea. Sitting comfortably in his armchair he turned on the television. "This is my idea of bird-watching," he laughed as a nature programme about birds came on.

"I don't get wet or stung by bees this way!"

Patch Gets Lost

Patch was Andrew's teddy bear. He was called Patch because he only had one good eye and had a black patch over the other.

"I'm bored waiting for Andrew to come home from school," said Patch one day. "I think I'll go and meet him."

Patch climbed down from Andrew's bed and hurried out of the bedroom. Downstairs he crawled through the gap in the door. Once outside Patch wriggled through the hole in the garden fence and found himself on the pavement.

"Hmmm, I don't know the way to Andrew's school, "he frowned. "I'll try this way." With that he set off down the street.

"WOOF! WOOF!" Patch looked round and saw a big dog chasing after him. "He'll shake the stuffing out of me!" wailed Patch, running as fast as his little legs would carry him.

Patch ran across the road to escape the dog. He was in such a hurry he didn't stop to see if any traffic was approaching.

VROOOOM! "EEEEK!" Patch squealed. He only just escaped being knocked down by a big lorry. Patch managed to reach the other side of the road safely but he was very scared and shaken. "I wish I'd stayed on Andrew's comfortable bed," he sighed. "Now I'm lost."

Just then an old lady passed by. She stopped as she saw Patch and then she picked him up. "I wonder who this bear belongs to?" she said. "I'll take it home for my grandson."

Patch was shocked. If he went to a different house he might never see Andrew again! He tried to wriggle free but the old lady pushed him inside her shopping basket. He was trapped!

Patch was so upset he fell asleep in the basket. When he awoke he was surprised to find himself back on Andrew's bed. Andrew was sitting next to him, smiling.

"Gran found you in the street and brought you home," Andrew was saying. "I wonder how you got out of the house?"

Patch just smiled. He would never tell. He was glad to be home at last!

The Foggy Day

The fog was feeling very mischievous. "I think I'll make this such a foggy day that no one will be able to see where they are going!"

The fog descended and soon the country was thickly covered in it. Cars bumped into each other because the drivers could not see where they were going. Schools had to be closed because the children were unable to find their way along the foggy streets. People walked into each other or tripped over dogs they couldn't see. The fog was enjoying itself!

"This is fun. I think I'll stay here all day."

The wind heard this and was very cross. "The fog is upsetting everyone. I'll have to do something about it." The wind began to blow, gently at first, and then harder and harder.

"STOP! You'll blow me away!" cried the fog. But it was too late. With one mighty puff the wind broke up the fog and it drifted away. "GURRR! I'll be back soon!" grumbled the fog.

"And I'll be waiting!" laughed the wind.

A Surprise for Mum

Steven's mum had a bad cold and had to stay in bed.

"Let's give mum a surprise," Steven's dad suggested.

In the kitchen Steven and his dad put on long aprons and set to work to bake mum a cake.

They put all the mixture into a bowl and Steven stirred this with a wooden spoon until his arms felt quite tired. "This is hard work," he smiled. After Steven had finished, his dad poured the mixture into a cake tin and put it in the oven to bake.

When the cake was ready dad put it on a wire tray to cool. Then he cried out in dismay. "Oh, no! We haven't any decorations to finish off the cake and the shops will be closed now."

Steven ran upstairs to his room. He came back carrying a box of toy farm animals. "Why don't we use these instead?" he asked. His dad thought this was a clever idea.

Steven carefully placed his farm animals on top of the cake. There was a horse, a cow, two pigs, three sheep and a collie dog who looked as if he was laughing.

Steven carried the finished cake upstairs to his mum, dad following behind. "SURPRISE!" they shouted as they burst into the room, and mum couldn't help smiling. They each had a slice of the cake and mum said it was the best GET-WELL-SOON cake she had ever tasted. Steven did feel proud!

Barry has a Fright

Barry Bluetit was a cheeky bird. Instead of feeding with the other birds in the country fields he would fly into town and swoop down to the people's gardens. He would gobble up the scraps of food that had been shaken onto the grass. Or he would peck the tops off milk bottles so that he could drink the milk.

"You'll be for it one day," warned his friend, Samantha Sparrow. Barry just laughed. "I'm too quick. No one can catch me."

The next morning Barry was feeding in a garden, pecking at the crumbs of bread that lay scattered around, when . . . POUNCE! Tom, the alley cat, had sneaked into the garden and upon seeing Barry he leapt, pinning the poor bluetit beneath his paws.

"SHOO!" shouted a woman running out of her house. "Leave that poor bird alone!"

Tom ran off and Barry quickly flew back to the trees in the country. "That was close," he gasped. "I almost became a cat's dinner."

"Aren't you going into town?" Samantha asked the next day.

"Er, no, I think I'll stay in the country from now on," Barry said.

The Trickster

There was once an elf who loved to play tricks.

"Smell this beautiful flower in my button hole," he told Mr Clogs the shoemaker. Mr Clogs sniffed at the flower and jumped back in surprise as a jet of water sprayed from the flower into his face. "Ha! Ha! Caught you with my trick flower!" laughed the elf and ran off.

Later he invited his friend Cherryblossom to have tea with him.

"Sit on this chair," he said, pointing to a chair near the table of food.

CRASSH!

As Cherryblossom sat down the chair collapsed under her weight and she landed on the floor with a BUMP!

"Only kidding!" laughed the elf. "Here, have a cream bun."

Cherryblossom took a large bite of the bun and black ink squirted into her face. "Hoo! Hoo!" chortled the elf. "I've tricked you again!"

Cherryblossom was very cross and left the elf who was still laughing.

Now the other elves were fed up with these silly tricks. "It's time that elf was taught a lesson," Mr Clogs said. "And I know just how to do it."

The naughty elf walked along a woodland path thinking up new jokes to play. He spotted three gold coins on the ground close by. "Someone must have dropped them," he grinned. "I can use the coins to buy more tricks."

The elf ran over to where the coins lay but as he reached them the ground gave way beneath him and he fell into a deep hole which was full of muddy water.

"SPLUTTER!" I've been tricked!" he cried angrily.

"Now you know how we feel," said Mr Clogs as he helped the elf out of the hole. "It's not so funny when you're on the receiving end of a trick." The elf stormed off, very angry indeed, but never again did he play tricks on his friends.

Squirrel Looks Again (2)

The next morning Squirrel got up very early to hunt for Mrs Fox's necklace. He searched in the cupboard but everything had been thrown higgledy-piggledy onto the shelves. As he opened the cupboard door everything inside fell out on top of him, making his tree-house even messier than yesterday. "Oh, well, I'll tidy up later," Squirrel said, but not really planning to.

Badger knocked on the door. "I say, Squirrel. Mrs Fox tells me you're looking after her necklace. May I see it, please?"

Squirrel thought fast. Putting on a friendly smile he said, "I'm afraid not, Badger. I've, er, hidden it in a secret place so no robbers can steal it." Squirrel hoped his friend believed him.

Badger laughed. "Ho! Ho! Your house is so untidy no one could find anything to steal!" With that he went on his way, still chuckling to himself.

Squirrel spent the whole day searching for the necklace, without success. "I'll look again tomorrow," he said. "I'm sure I'll find it then."

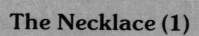

The Necklace (1)

"You should keep your home tidy," said Badger to Squirrel one day. "There are leaves and litter and acorn cups all over the place."

"I'm happy the way I am," said Squirrel, who was really too lazy to clean up.

"Hello, Squirrel," said Mrs Fox later. "Will you look after my necklace while I go and visit my sister for a few days?"

"Of course," said Squirrel. "You can trust me to keep it safe."

That evening, after Badger had visited for tea and crumpets, Squirrel looked worried. "Oh, my! Where did I put Mrs Fox's necklace? I can't find it anywhere."

Squirrel hunted all over his tree house but there was so much litter it was impossible to find anything.

"Not to worry," decided Squirrel as he tucked himself in bed for the night. "I'm sure it will turn up tomorrow."

Squirrel Tidies Up (3)

"It's no use," Squirrel sighed after he had spent all the following morning hunting for the necklace. "I can't find it in all this mess." He kicked angrily at the rubbish on the floor.

Squirrel knew that Winter was drawing in and that he should be collecting acorns and hazelnuts to store away in his tree-house before the snows came. "But Mrs Fox comes home tomorrow. I must find her necklace before then or she'll be very cross with me."

Squirrel scampered over to Badger's house. "May I borrow your broom, Badger?" he asked his friend. "I want to tidy up my tree house."

"Goodness, this is a surprise," chuckled Badger, his eyes sparkling with mischief. "You haven't lost anything in the mess, have you? A necklace, perhaps?"

"No! No! Nothing like that!" Squirrel said quickly and scampered away with the broom before Badger could ask him any more awkward questions.

Squirrel spent the rest of the day sweeping up all the litter and leaves that were scattered over the floor of his house into a big pile. Then he picked up all the acorn cups he had dropped and put these in another pile. When he had finished his house was sparkling clean, but Squirrel did not look happy.

"I've tidied up everywhere but I still can't find the necklace. "What will Mrs Fox say when she comes home tomorrow?"

Squirrel has a Surprise (4)

"Good morning, Squirrel," said Badger early the next day. "You don't look very happy. Is anything the matter?"

Squirrel told Badger the whole story of how he had lost the necklace.

"Poor Squirrel," said Badger after Squirrel had finished. He held something up in his paw. It was Mrs Fox's necklace. "Surprise!" chuckled Badger. "You dropped the necklace in your rubbish when I came to tea three nights ago. I thought it was a good chance to teach you a lesson about tidiness so I took the necklace home with me."

Before Squirrel could feel angry at Badger's trick, Badger went on, "If you had kept a tidy house you wouldn't have dropped it in the rubbish in the first place. Just think if you had really lost it."

Squirrel agreed this would have been terrible. "From now on I'll tidy up every day," he said.

"Glad to hear it," said Badger. "Now come to my house and I'll treat you to a special breakfast."

There was another surprise for Squirrel at Badger's house. A box full of acorn and hazel nuts. "Since I played a trick on you I thought it only fair I should collect your Winter store of food before the snows come," explained Badger. Squirrel was delighted. It was nice to have such an especially good friend.

The Little House

The little house in Crabapple Lane did feel sad. "I haven't been properly looked after for years. My windows are all broken, my gutter leaks, I have damp patches in the bedroom and woodworm in my floorboards. My plaster has cracked in lots of places, the tiles on my roof have been blown off by the wind, my chimney is blocked with soot and the front door is coming off its hinges. No wonder no one wants to buy me." The little house had been put up for sale four times in the last year. "My last owners were just awful. They were too busy, having loud parties and jumping up and down on my floor dancing, to care for me properly. And my owners before that were no better. They kept taking me to pieces but never got around to putting me back together again."

Just then a man from the council arrived and looked all over the little house. You're in a shocking state," he said. "I'm afraid we'll have to pull you down and build flats on your ground instead."

The poor little house was horrified by this. "Pull me down? You can't!" The little house didn't know what to do.

As the man from the council was leaving he was stopped by a man wearing very fine clothes and driving a very smart car. "I say," he said, in a loud voice. "I'm Lord Moneybags and I'm terribly, terribly rich. I want to buy this little house for my butler to live in. I'll fix the guttering, replace the windows and doors, plaster over the cracks, re-tile the roof, give it a new coat of paint and make it look as good as new."

Lord Moneybags wrote out a cheque for a lot of money and the man from the council went away very happy. The little house could hardly believe its luck. Lord Moneybags kept his word and soon the little house was the best-looking house in Crabapple Lane.

The Jester

The King's jester was very worried. "I can't think of any funny jokes to tell the King. He'll be ever so angry if he finds out."

The jester thought hard all day but still he couldn't come up with a good joke. "It's no use," he sighed. "The King will throw me in the royal dungeons if I don't make him laugh."

The King called the jester to the palace. "Jester, make me laugh!" demanded the King, who hadn't laughed for a long time and was feeling very miserable.

The jester became so worried about upsetting the King that he tripped over his own feet, tumbled into the guards knocking them flying, and crashed into the royal throne, tipping the King out of his seat.

"Oh, no!" cried the jester as he picked himself up. "Now the King will lock me up and throw away the key!"

"HO! HO! HO!" The jester was surprised to hear a roar of laughter echoing around the palace. "That's the funniest thing I've seen!" the King cried, tears of happiness running down his face. "You're the best jester I've ever had!" The King gave the jester a chest of gold coins to reward him.

From that day on the jester did his tumbling act every evening and the King was never sad again.

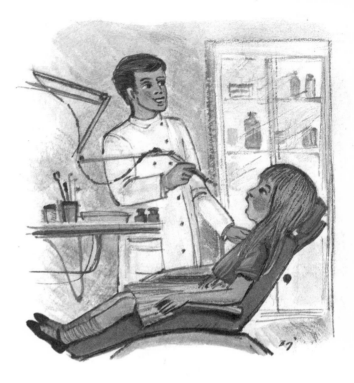

Too Many Sweets

Tracy's mum frowned as she saw her daughter on the sofa tucking into a large bag of sweets.

"Where did you get those sweets?" her mum demanded. "You know I don't like you eating too many."

"I like sweets," said Tracy. "And I got them from Grandpa for helping to clean out his shed."

"Sweets are full of sugar and this ruins your teeth," her mother warned her.

"Oh, rubbish," scoffed Tracy as she ate another toffee. "my teeth are really strong."

A little while later Tracy's mum found Tracy crying. She looked very sad. "What's the matter?" she asked Tracy, even though she suspected what the problem was.

"I've got toothache!" Tracy groaned, holding the side of her face which was throbbing with pain.

The dentist frowned as he looked into Tracy's mouth. "You'll have to have a filling in that tooth," he said. "You've been eating too many sweets."

Tracy's mum looked at Tracy as if to say, "I told you so!"

A Giant Sneeze

One day the giant who lived near a pretty town sneezed very hard. "A-A-A-A-A-TISCHOOOOOOOOO!" The giant sneezed so hard all the houses in the pretty town were blown down and the townspeople were very cross.

"Let's run the giant out of town!" they cried, and with their pitchforks and their clubs hurried to where the giant lived in his huge castle. The giant was very scared when he saw the angry mob.

"Oh, please don't hurt me!" he pleaded. "I didn't mean to do it."

"Don't cry!" shouted the townspeople. "Your tears are so big they'll wash us away." But they did feel just a bit sorry for the giant.

"All right," they said after discussing the matter. "You can stay. But where are we going to live? All our homes are ruined."

"Stay here with me," said the giant. "There's more than enough room in such a big castle and while you're here I'll rebuild the town for you."

The townspeople were very pleased and all agreed their giant was the best giant of them all.

"Sam Can't Whistle!"

More than anything else in the world Sam wanted to learn to whistle. But no matter how hard he tried he just could not do it.

"Ha! Ha! Sam can't whistle!" teased his friends at school, and they all started whistling very loudly to show Sam how it was done.

"I could hear you all whistling," said the teacher as she came into the classroom. "So I've decided to hold a whistling contest. There will be prizes for the children who can whistle the best."

The other children looked at Sam and laughed. "Ho! Ho! Sam won't win. He can't whistle at all!"

Sam practised whistling as he walked home from school but however hard he tried he still could not whistle.

"If you want to whistle, copy me," said Mr Print, the newspaper seller and he began to whistle a cheerful happy tune that made Sam laugh.

"Your turn," said Mr Print when he had finished.

Sam blew . . . and blew . . . and blew . . . but it was no use. "I'll never learn to whistle," said Sam, feeling very miserable.

Just then Sam met Mrs Bloom the lady at the flower stall who was always smiling. "Can you whistle?" Sam asked her.

"Whistle? I'll say I can whistle!" chuckled Mrs Bloom. She began to whistle a very jolly tune that made Sam want to dance.

"You have a go," Mrs Bloom told Sam.

Sam tried to whistle once . . . twice . . . three times, but all that happened was that his cheeks turned bright red with all his blowing.

"I'll never win the whistling contest," Sam thought as he got into bed that night. "I just can't whistle!"

Sam Tries Again

The next morning Sam told his mother about the whistling contest and how he could not whistle.

His mother smiled and said, "Keep practising and one day you'll find you can whistle when you need to most."

Sam practised whistling as he had his breakfast and as he dressed for school. He practised when he walked to school and again as he put his coat in the cloakroom and as he sat down at his desk. But he couldn't make a noise that even sounded like a whistle. "I'll never be able to whistle," he sighed glumly.

"Right, class," said the teacher. "We're going to have our whistling contest now." Sam groaned as she looked at him. "Let's start with you, Sam."

All the children laughed at this. "Ha! Ha! Sam can't whistle!"

Sam ignored the laughter. He stood up, took a deep breath, and blew. Gently at first, and then a little harder. Suddenly a beautiful whistling sound came from his lips.

"I CAN WHISTLE!" cried Sam, proudly.

"SAM CAN WHISTLE!" cheered his friends.

"And a lovely whistle it is too," smiled the teacher.

Sam won a prize for his whistling. He whistled all through playtime and after school he whistled all the way home.

"I told you a whistle would come when you needed it most," smiled his mother. "You have the most beautiful whistle I've ever heard."

The Balloon

"I want to fly the balloon!" shouted Graham.

"No! It's mine!" cried Lisa.

Like all brothers and sisters Lisa and Graham sometimes quarrelled. This time it was about their new balloon.

Graham pulled on the balloon string to snatch it from Lisa. "I should have first go! I'm the youngest!" he sulked.

Lisa pulled on the string the other way. "I'm the oldest! I want to fly it first!"

SNAP!

The string broke in the struggle and a gust of wind blew the balloon high into the air. Soon it was lost from sight.

"That will teach you to argue," said their mother. "Now neither of you can fly the balloon."

Just then the children's uncle visited them. "Here's a toy for you to play with," he said, and handed the children a pretty kite.

"I want first go!" grumbled Graham.

"Not likely! Girls first!" argued Lisa.

"Oh, dear," sighed their mother. "Here we go again!"

Pirate Treasure

Cap'n Greeneye was a very rough, tough pirate who worked his men very hard. He was not a kind man and all his crew hated him but they were too scared to run away in case he caught them and made them walk the plank.

One day the pirate's ship anchored near a desert island. Cap'n Greeneye made his men row him to the island in a small boat. "Dig up the treasure while I have a doze," he ordered.

The men worked very hard digging away the soil and brought up the treasure chest full of gold coins.

The Cap'n was still asleep and the pirates didn't like to wake him in case he awoke in one of his terrible tempers. They rowed back to the ship and put the treasure safely away.

"I suppose we'd better go and fetch the Cap'n," said the first mate later.

"Or we could sail away and leave him behind," suggested one of the crew. "Then he could never shout at us again."

Everybody agreed this was a fine idea, and so that's what they did.

When the Cap'n woke up and discovered both the treasure and his ship were gone he flew into a terrible rage, but there was nothing he could do. He was stranded on the island forever.

Crazy Car

A thief decided to rob the jewellers shop while everybody was watching the carnival. He entered the shop carrying a bag and a club. He threatened to use the club on the assistant if he didn't fill the bag with jewels. When this was done the thief ran out of the shop and jumped into the first car he saw. It was a funny-looking car but the thief didn't mind. "It will help me escape!" he crowed.

The thief started the engine and the car began to rattle. Then it began to shake. The doors fell off and the windscreen wiper squirted water into the surprised thief's face. The exhaust pipe suddenly went BANG! and the seat sprang up on a giant spring and the thief was sent flying into the air to land with a bump on the street.

"Stupid car!" he growled as he was arrested by a policeman. "It's falling to pieces!"

"Of course it is," said a clown, running up. "It's part of the carnival. It's a clown's car!"

Treacle Tart Straps In

Treacle Tart the Witch was not very good at flying. Every time she tried riding her broomstick she would fall off.

"This is silly!" she thought crossly. "I can't be a real Witch if I can't ride a broomstick!"

Later that day she saw a human getting into a car. The man made sure he fastened his seat belt before he drove off, in case he was involved in an accident.

"That's it!" cried Treacle Tart happily. That night she cast a magic spell and made a belt on her broomstick and strapped herself on. "Now I can't fall off!" she laughed as she flew high into the sky.

The Old Boots

The old boots stood on top of the dustbin feeling very unhappy. "Our owner has bought a new pair of boots and he doesn't want us anymore."

A tramp passed by, also feeling unhappy. "Oooh! My poor feet. These shoes I'm wearing have worn away to nothing but I can't afford a new pair."

Teddy's Train Ride

One day Rob's mum took him to see a display of trains at the nearby railway station.

"Can I have a ride on one?" he asked eagerly.

Rob's mum paid for two tickets at the ticket office and they climbed aboard the train as the guard waved his flag and shouted, "ALL ABOARD!"

Rob enjoyed his train journey very much. When he got back home he ran upstairs to his room. Later his mum heard him shouting loudly. Peering into his room she smiled as she saw Rob's toy train set laid out on the floor and Rob's teddy bear riding on one of the tiny carriages. "I'm a guard," Rob said, waving a toy flag. "ALL ABOARD!"

"How marvellous," laughed his mum. "It's just like a real railway station!"

He stopped as he saw the old boots on the dustbin. "They're just what I'm after," he thought and asked the owner if he could have the boots.

The boots were very excited when the owner said the tramp could take them. "Tramps walk all the time," thought the boots. "So we will be working all the time. It's nice to feel useful again."

"Has everyone gone mad?" demanded the King. "What is so funny about me?"

"S-S-Sorry, Sire," giggled one guard. "But look at what you're wearing!"

The King looked down and then he too began to laugh as he saw he was still wearing his yellow-and-green striped pyjamas.

"That's what I tried to tell you," said the sergeant. "But you wouldn't listen."

"My, my! What a forgetful fellow I am," chuckled the King. "I completely forgot to change out of my pyjamas when I got up this morning!"

The Dolphin

Lucy was a very nasty girl. She enjoyed being cruel to animals and went out of her way to upset them.

"Stupid creatures," she would say as she shot at them with her pea shooter.

One day Lucy's father took his spoilt daughter for a ride on his yacht. Lucy played too near the side of the yacht and fell into the sea.

"Help! I can't swim!" she cried.

To Lucy's horror a dolphin who had been playing nearby swam towards her. "EEEK! It's going to eat me! she wailed.

But the dolphin swam underneath Lucy and carried her on its back towards the yacht.

"The dolphin saved me!" Lucy said once she was back on board safely. "I'll never be cruel to animals again."

King Muddletop's Walk

King Muddletop, the very forgetful King, woke up one day and decided to walk around his kingdom to show his people what a kind and happy king he was.

"I must look my best," he thought, and put on his very best crown.

The royal guards were astounded when they saw the King. "Sire, surely you're not going out like . . . like that?" asked the sergeant.

The King looked cross. "Of course! Now come on, and I don't want to hear another word from you!"

All the people lined the street as the King and the royal guard approached. Flags were flying and pretty coloured balloons were let free into the sky. Everybody was feeling very excited. It was not often they met royalty.

"My people love me," beamed the King happily. But then his smile turned into a frown as he heard the people tittering. Then they began to chuckle. Finally they all burst out laughing very hard and loud.

"HA! HA! HA! Doesn't the King look funny?"

"FUNNY?" roared the King. "What a cheek! Guards, arrest them all for laughing at me!"

But to the King's amazement the royal guards were also laughing at him.

Jill's Busy Day

Jill was helping her mother clean the house.

"I'll polish the table," said Jill.

"And I'll sort out the cupboard," said her mother.

Jill set busily to work. She polished very fast and soon the table shone so brightly Jill could see her reflection in it.

"You have done well," said her mother. "Now you can do the dusting." Jill took the feather duster and gently swept the dust from the shelves and from the top of the cupboards. Her mum disappeared into the kitchen and came back with two glasses of lemonade.

Jill sat down to enjoy her drink. Then her mum cried out, "I've lost my ring!" she held up her hand. "It must have fallen off while we were cleaning."

"I'll help you find it," said Jill.

Jill looked on top of the cupboards and behind the settee. She looked under the table. But the ring was nowhere to be found.

"Oh, dear," said her mum, looking at the clock. "We had better go to the shops. Fetch the umbrella from the store cupboard, Jill. It's raining outside."

Jill took the umbrella and opened it. "Don't do that," shouted her mother. "It's bad luck to open an umbrella indoors."

But suddenly to Jill's surprise her mum's ring fell out of the umbrella.

"Clever Jill!" smiled her mum. "It must have fallen in there while I was cleaning."

"So opening umbrellas indoors isn't such bad luck after all!" laughed Jill.

The Beautiful Mermaid

Pippi the mermaid was very beautiful and all the other mermaids were very jealous of her. Whenever it was time to feed they would push Pippi to the end of the queue and that meant Pippi usually went hungry.

One day a hunter came to the mermaids lagoon and captured the mermaids to sell. All except for Pippi, who was bathing elsewhere at the time.

When Pippi saw what had happened she quickly thought up a plan. Waving to the hunter who had returned to the ship with the mermaids, she began to sing one of her lovely songs.

"That's the most beautiful mermaid I've ever seen," thought the hunter, and he chased after Pippi in his ship.

Pippi led the hunter a merry chase towards some rocks that were submerged under the water. The ship struck the rocks and began to sink. This gave the mermaids the chance to escape. The poor hunter had to swim all the way back home and because Pippi's beauty saved them, the mermaids were never jealous of her again.

Bee Goes Swimming

The bee buzzed over a stream as it searched for flowers to get the pollen.

"I wonder what it's like to be a fish," she thought. "Swimming in that nice clean water must be refreshing on such a hot day."

The bee flew down to the stream and landed on a lily pad. "I think I would like to try to swim."

The bee jumped into the water and found to her horror that she could not swim at all and she could not fly into the air again. "The water is stopping me from using my wings! I'm going to drown!"

Just then a fish swam past. When he saw the bee struggling in the water he lifted her onto his back and put her on the lily pad to dry off. "Silly bee," he said. "Fish live in the water, bees live in the air."

"I'll remember that from now on," said the bee. Thanking the fish again, the bee flew off to find a flower to feed on.

Adam's Apple

Adam was feeling hungry so when he saw an orchard of apples he decided to help himself to some. A notice on the fence read: PRIVATE! KEEP OUT!

"No one will mind if I just take a few," Adam thought as he climbed over the fence. Once in the orchard Adam scrambled up into the branches of a tree and started feeding on the rosy red apples. "Delicious!" he slurped as he ate five apples all at once. "Scrumptious!" he smiled as he gobbled up another six. "Nice!" he said, not quite so sure, as he slowly ate another four. "Er, maybe I won't have any more," he decided as he finished off another three. After eating all those apples Adam was feeling rather sick.

"Hey, you!" shouted the owner of the orchard as he saw Adam. Adam almost fell out of the tree in fright. He leapt out of the tree and ran off, chased by the owner. Adam was feeling very scared. "He's going to catch me!" he wailed, and then he saw a hole in the fence.

Adam struggled to push himself through the hole but it was a tight squeeze. "I shouldn't have eaten so many apples!" he thought. "I'm too fat!"

Adam pushed and pushed, and suddenly he fell through the hole. He ran home as fast as he could.

"All that running's made me hungry again," Adam thought as he entered his house. "What's for tea, mum?" he asked as he saw his mother in the kitchen.

"Your favourite," smiled his mother. "APPLE PIE!"

Adam's face turned bright green. "Oh, no!" he groaned, holding his stomach and feeling sick again. "I've gone right off apples!"

Albert and Leonora

Albert the hippopotamus loved to roll in the muddy jungle river.

"How disgusting!" snorted Leonora the lioness as she watched from the bank. "You wouldn't catch me doing that. I like to keep clean and beautiful."

"The mud keeps me cool when the sun is very hot and the mud is a good disguise when I want to hide from my enemies," Albert told her, and he rolled in the mud again.

Leonora moved back quickly as the mud splashed up from the river and almost landed on her sleek shiny coat. "I have better things to do than watch you getting dirty," she snapped, and padded off into the jungle.

Leonora was feeling hungry and when she saw a dead antelope near the tree which belonged to Thomas the leopard, she quickly feasted herself upon it.

When Thomas returned home and found his dinner had been eaten he was very angry. "This is the work of Leonora," he roared smelling her scent. "I will make her pay for stealing my food."

Leonora overhead this and was very frightened. Usually she could hold her own against Thomas but recently she had injured her paw and could not defend herself properly.

Leonora ran to Albert and asked what she should do.

"Get into the river and cover yourself all over with mud," Albert told her. Leonora did not like this idea but she did as Albert said. Soon she was as muddy as he was. "Now stay low," Albert warned her.

Soon Thomas came past. He called to Albert from the bank. "Have you seen Leonora?" he asked sternly.

"No," said Albert. "I have been in the mud all day with my cousin." Albert looked towards Leonora who was so muddy she didn't look like a lioness at all.

"If you see her tell her I want a word," growled Thomas. "Several words in fact."

"Thank you, Albert," said Leonora as she struggled free of the mud and climbed onto the bank. "You saved my life. I'll never complain about the mud again."

Jack gets a Scare

Jack enjoyed living in the toyshop. He liked to jump out of his box on his spring and frighten people as they passed. Best of all he liked to wait until the toyshop was closed and then leap out at the other toys and pull ugly faces at them. The toys had come to life because it was night time.

"BAAALOOOOGAA!" Jack would shout as the lid of his box opened and he bounced upwards.

"EEEEEK!" screamed Frances, the pretty china doll, who was so scared she fell off the shelf and landed on the floor with a bump.

"That Jack-in-a-box is a pest," frowned John, the clown. "It was lucky she didn't break when she fell."

Jack didn't care. "You can't stop me," he sneered. "I can jump out and frighten whoever I like."

As Jack popped back into his box and pulled the lid shut John had an idea. With Frances' help he moved the toyshop mirror over to where Jack's box stood.

"Ha! Jack doesn't scare me!" boasted John in a loud voice.

Jack heard this in his box and became very angry. "Oh, don't I? We'll see about that!"

Jack leapt out of the box and pulled his ugliest face. "BAAAALOOOOOOGAAAA!" he roared. Then he saw his ugly reflection in the mirror and it frightened him so much he sprang back into the box and slammed the lid shut.

"Ha! Ha! Jack will be more careful who he frightens from now on," laughed Frances. "It just might be himself!"

Toby Loses Himself

Toby liked to go exploring but his mother warned him, "Stay close to me or you'll get lost."

One day while he was out walking with his mother Toby ran into a nearby forest. "Come back, Toby!" called his mother but Toby didn't listen. He ran deeper and deeper into the forest to see where it would lead.

As Toby went further into the forest the trees blocked out the sun and everywhere became dark and frightening. Suddenly Toby realised he couldn't find his way back. "I'm lost!" he said, and he began to cry.

Toby heard footsteps coming towards him. Closer and closer they approached and Toby's imagination began to think up all sorts of terrible ideas. "Perhaps it's a monster coming to eat me!" he thought.

"Toby, there you are!" It wasn't a monster at all, it was Toby's mother. "You shouldn't run off like that. I almost lost you for ever this time."

"I'll never do it again," promised Toby as he hugged his mother. And he never did.

The Fairy

"I will grant you one wish," the fairy said to a cross-looking elf.

"I wish you would go away!" snapped the elf who had just set fire to his dinner and wasn't feeling very happy.

PING!

The fairy did as the elf wished and was never seen again. So if you meet a fairy who offers you a wish be very careful what you wish for!

Patch Feels Sad

Patch, Andrew's favourite teddy bear, was frowning. Andrew was being very secretive. He hadn't said "Good morning, Patch," as he usually did, and now he had taken all his other toys downstairs to play with and had left Patch all alone in the bedroom.

"Andrew's gone off me, that's what it is," Patch decided. "He doesn't like me any more. Soon he'll put me in the cupboard and forget all about me."

Just then Andrew came in. He lifted Patch off the bed and hurried downstairs with him. "What's going on?" Patch wondered.

In the living room all the toys were sitting at a table laid out with food. A cake in the centre of the table had the words HAPPY BIRTHDAY PATCH! written in icing on it. "You forgot today is your birthday," smiled Andrew. "So I thought I'd hold a surprise party for you!"

Treacle Tart Shows Off

Treacle Tart the Witch was showing off her flying skills on her broomstick at the annual Witches Convention. The other witches laughed as she drove her broomstick into a wall. "That will teach you to try flying with your eyes shut!" they said.

Treacle Tart was more worried about her broomstick, which was now broken in two.

"How am I going to get home?" she said. "I left my "mending" spell at home."

"Here, use this," said one of the witches, and handed Treacle Tart a tea saucer. With a wave of her wand Treacle Tart made the saucer grow and grow until it was big enough for her to sit on comfortably. But she wasn't very happy. As the saucer flew into the air the other witches could hear Treacle Tart grumbling, "Whoever heard of a witch riding a flying saucer?"

Mr Colliwobble's Sneeze

Mr Colliwobble couldn't stop sneezing. He sneezed through breakfast and all through lunch. He sneezed extra hard at dinner and again during supper. In fact the poor man sneezed all day.

"You must have a cold," said his wife.

"You must have the flu," said his brother.

"You might have pneumonia," said his best friend.

Mr Colliwobble went to see his doctor who gave him a complete check-up and said, "There's nothing the matter with you, Mr Colliwobble. You're in fine health."

"But why do I keep sneezing?" asked Mr Colliwobble.

The doctor took Mr Colliwobble to a restaurant and bought him a fine meal. Mr Colliwobble liked pepper on his food so he sprinkled some on his meal. Then he sprinkled some more . . . and some more . . . and then some more.

"A-A-TISCHOOO!" he sneezed.

"That's the problem," laughed the doctor. "You cover your food in so much pepper it goes up your nose and makes you sneeze!" Mr Colliwobble did feel silly!

The Grumpy Troll

Crosspatch was a troll who was very grumpy and always miserable.

"My dinner's too hot!" he would grumble.

Or, "The baby troll's are too noisy!" he would complain.

All the other trolls of the village tried to have as little to do with Crosspatch as possible.

"Crosspatch is never happy unless he's grumpy," they would say. "He makes everyone's life a misery."

One day Crosspatch awoke in a terrible mood. He fell out of the wrong side of bed, bumped his head, tripped over Drizzle, his cat, and tumbled bumpity-bumpity-bump down the stairs.

"OOOOH! I'M SO CROSS!" he bellowed as he quickly dressed and hurried to the train station.

"Bah! My cousin is paying me a visit," he grumbled as he pushed past a queue of trolls waiting on the station platform. Apart from being grumpy Crosspatch was also very rude! "Now I'll have to feed him my food and offer him my bed!"

The train pulled in to the station and off stepped a finely dressed troll.

"I'm your cousin, Ever-So-Angry!" snapped the cross-looking troll. "This train station is the wrong colour!" he complained. "Why isn't it sunny? I don't suppose you've brought me a present? Huh! I thought not! I don't like your clothes! I know your cooking will taste awful!"

"Dear me," thought Crosspatch. "He's even more miserable than I am!"

Poor Crosspatch. All week long Ever-So-Angry grumbled and complained. He complained about his bed and about Crosspatch's pretty toadstool house. He complained about Crosspatch's vegetable garden and the way he made custard. He complained and complained and complained. . . .

"Hurray!" Crosspatch gave a sigh of relief and then did a little dance as his cousin waved crossly when the train pulled out of the station. "He's going home at last."

Crosspatch was so relieved he started to smile. Then he started to grin. Finally he came out with a giant bellow of laughter.

"Ho! Ho! What a miserable troll I've been! My cousin has taught me that. From now on I shall greet each day with a smile!" And that's what he did!

A Trip to the Stars (1)

Neil and Jane were having trouble sleeping. "I keep having nightmares," said Jane, feeling very upset.

"So do I," said Neil.

"Not to worry," said the Sandman, who looks after everyone's dreams. "I'll give you the nicest dream ever." And he sprinkled sleepidust over the children's eyelids. Soon they were fast asleep.

Neil and Jane found themselves in a rocket flying to an unknown planet. "This is exciting," they both agreed as the rocket landed.

Once on the planet the children were delighted to find the thinner atmosphere meant they could leap very high and run very fast.

Suddenly they found themselves surrounded by little green spacemen who had four arms, two legs, three eyes, long snouts and two antennae sticking up from their heads.

"Hello," said one of the spacemen. "I'm Blooper, chief of the Ping-Pongs." The children were surprised they could understand what he was saying but as Blooper explained in dreams anything can happen.

"Come home with us and stay a while, friends," Blooper offered the children.

Neil and Jane followed the spacemen to a town where the houses were set in a high cliff face. Blooper treated them to a meal of Zipplepods, tiny seeds that tasted of whatever you wanted them to. "Now you can sleep and tomorrow you can explore our planet," Blooper said. The children felt very excited at this.

In the Jungle (2)

The next day Blooper took the children to visit the planet's jungle in a flying car. Strange-looking animals, and birds that flew backwards filled the jungle with such a chattering, roaring and singing it made Jane's head shake.

All at once the flying car gave a loud BANG! and black smoke appeared under the bonnet. Blooper looked worried. "We're going to have to crash-land!" he told the children.

Blooper was an excellent flyer and managed to land the flying car safely. "But how are we going to get back home?" Neil wanted to know. "We could be stranded here forever!"

A large pink-spotted hairy creature with a long trunk and six legs appeared, and moved towards Jane. It reached out for her with its trunk and Neil cried out, "Run, Jane! It could be dangerous!"

But the creature's trunk snuffled inside Jane's coat pocket instead. "I know what it wants," laughed Jane, and pulled out a handful of Zipplepod seeds which the creature gratefully ate. Before they could move the creature lifted the three friends onto its back and started off through the jungle. Soon they were back at Blooper's cliff-house. "It's brought us home!" cheered Blooper.

The creature winked at Jane as if to say, "One good turn deserves another."

The Challenge (3)

Jane and Neil awoke in Blooper's cliff-house at the sound of shouting outside. "The giants are coming! The giants are coming!" cried Blooper as he rushed into the children's room, looking very frightened.

"Who are the giants?" asked Jane.

"They live on the other side of the planet and they're always coming here and wrecking our town with their silly games."

"Can't you stop them?" Neil wanted to know.

"They'll only go away if we beat them in their games but we never do because we are so small," Blooper explained.

The children ran outside to meet the giants. "They ARE big!" Neil gasped as he looked up and up and up to the top of the giants' heads.

"Who challenges us in the games?" demanded the chief giant, not expecting a reply.

"WE DO!" the children shouted together.

"HO! HO! YOU? I can hardly see you!" The giant looked down at the children and laughed. "You will have no chance of winning!"

But the children were determined. "Come back tomorrow and we'll see!" said Jane. The giants agreed and went away. The children spent the rest of the day training to get fit.

The First Game (4)

"If we win the games do you promise never to come around here and pester our friends again?" Jane asked the chief giant the next day.

"I promise!" chuckled the giant, believing that his people had no chance of losing.

The first game was to see who could leap the furthest. The chief giant went first and took a mighty leap which sent him high over the top of the tallest mountain.

"Your turn!" he bellowed loudly when he returned. "Or do you want to admit defeat?"

"NEVER!" said Jane and she took a long run before leaping high into the air. Jane leapt over the mountains, and over the jungle where she had befriended the pink-spotted creature. Her leap carried her to the night side of the planet and back again. In fact Jane leapt so far she travelled all the way around the planet and landed back where she started!

"We win! We win!" cheered Neil. The giants went away, very angry. "Wait until tomorrow," they said.

"How did you manage such an amazing leap?" Blooper asked Jane.

"If you wish hard enough your dreams come true," said Jane. "And remember, our adventures on this planet are all a dream!"

Neil Wins Through (5)

"You won't win this game!" snapped the chief giant to Neil the next morning. "It's a race to the jungle to fetch a rock and back again."

Neil didn't trust the giants. He was sure they were up to something.

"On your marks, get set, GO!" shouted Blooper. The giants' runner took off like a streak of lightning, leaving Neill behind in a cloud of dust.

"Why aren't you running?" Jane cried frantically when she saw Neil still at the starting line.

"Someone's tied the laces of my running shoes together," Neil frowned. He looked over to where the chief giant was laughing. "And I can guess who!"

Neil pulled off his running shoes. "I don't need them anyway. I can run faster in my bare feet."

The giant had reached the jungle and had sat down to rest. "The Earth boy has no chance of winning," he chuckled. The giant looked up in surprise as Neil suddenly sped past him, snatched up the rock, and ran off towards the finishing line. The giant started after him but it was too late. Neill passed the winning line first.

"Hurray for Neil!" cheered Jane and Blooper.

"We still have one more game to go," growled the chief giant as he stormed off. "We'll see who wins that tomorrow."

Test of Strength (6)

The giants, Neil and Jane stood facing one another near the Ping-Pongs cliff-houses.

"This is the hardest game of all," chuckled the chief giant. "A test of strength. Even you won't beat us this time!"

"You first," said Neil. The giant who was chosen for this game took hold of a huge boulder. Struggling hard he eventually succeeded in lifting the boulder over his head. "Urrfh! Gasp! Beat this!" he challenged Neil and Jane.

"We will lift that mountain," said Jane, pointing to a mountain range close by. The giants laughed at this. "Impossible! No one is that strong!"

Jane and Neil went over to the mountain and slowly but surely they lifted it high over their heads. "Easy!" smiled Neil.

"We win!" cried Jane.

The giants were terribly afraid. "They must be the strongest beings in the Universe!" they thought.

"You must keep your promise never to bother our friends again," Jane warned the chief giant sternly. "Or we will deal with you!"

The giants promised to be good and quickly hurried away.

When the giants were gone the Ping-Pongs, Neil and Jane burst out laughing. "The giants never suspected the mountain was made out of papier maché!" chuckled Blooper. "We spent all last night building it for the game today."

"Yes, we could never lift a real mountain," grinned Neil. "But this one is as light as a feather!"

Farewell Ping-Pongs (7)

The day came for Neil and Jane to leave their spacemen friends. The Ping-Pongs held a farewell party for them and everyone was invited. There was lots of dancing and singing, the cliff-houses were decorated in beautiful moonbeams and wishing stars and Jane and Neil were the special guests of honour.

The pink-spotted creature Jane had befriended in the jungle arrived with its friends and presented the children with a going-away present of a necklace each of beautifully perfumed flowers.

"Come and see us again soon," called Blooper as the children's rocket was ready to leave.

"We will!" they promised. Soon the rocket was speeding on its way back to Earth. "What a marvellous adventure this has been," Neil said to Jane.

His sister nodded. "Yes, it's been out of this world!" she laughed.

Jane and Neil Wake Up (8)

Jane and Neil woke up the next morning to find themselves tucked up safely in their beds.

"Wasn't that a lovely dream we shared," said Jane. "Even though we spent days on the planet with the Ping-Pongs in our dream it really only lasted one night."

"The Sandman kept his word," agreed Neil. "We didn't have a nasty nightmare this time. If we think hard of nice things before we go to bed perhaps we never will again." The Sandman, who was still watching over the children, nodded wisely at this.

"I do wish our dream had been real," Jane said sadly. "It would have been nice to know that Blooper and his friends did exist and were not just something we had imagined."

Neil didn't answer. He was too busy staring at the necklace of flowers around Jane's neck. "The necklaces which the pink-spotted creature gave us, we're still wearing them!" he gasped.

Jane looked at her brother in astonishment. "But that means . . . no, that's impossible. Isn't it?" Jane and Neil spent the rest of the day wondering whether their dream had really happend or not. What do you think?

The Conceited Princess

There was once a Princess who was very conceited. This means that she thought highly of herself and was always boasting. "I am the prettiest Princess in all the world!" she would say. She was also very bossy and liked to order all the townspeople to do as she told them. "Clean the palace windows, take my dogs for a walk, tidy up the royal garden, bake me a special cake for being such a wonderful Princess," she would say, and she did this all day long. Naturally the townspeople soon became very fed up with her.

One day the Princess went to see her only friend, a Princess who lived in the next town. She rode there on her bicycle because she liked to stay fit and trim to show the people what a beautiful Princess she was. On her way home the Princess rode over a sharp stone and the front tyre went POP! "Oh, dear, my bike has a puncture," frowned the Princess. "I'll have to walk home." This was easier said than done for the Princess still had a long way to go.

A man passed by in his car. The Princess called out to him in a very haughty voice. "I say, you there! I demand you give me a lift to the castle!" But when the man saw it was the conceited Princess he drove straight past her.

A while later a postman rode past on his motorbike. The Princess waved to him and shouted, "Postman! I am the Princess! You will take me to the castle immediately." But the postman was already late delivering his letters, and when he saw it was the boastful and bossy Princess he hurried on his way.

The Princess walked on but before she was half way home it began to rain heavily. "My nice clothes will be ruined!" she thought angrily. She was so cross she didn't look where she was walking and landed SPLASH! in a muddy puddle.

When the Princess finally reached the castle she told the Queen how no one would stop and give her a lift. "Nobody likes me!" she cried.

"I'm not surprised," said the Queen. "If you stopped being so conceited I'm sure people would like you."

The Princess decided the Queen was right, and from then on she tried hard not to be conceited, or boastful, or bossy and soon all the townspeople began to make friends with her.

The Chestnut Tree

There was once a naughty chestnut tree. Whenever people passed by it would swipe out at them with its long branches.

Its favourite game was trying to knock the hats off people's heads as they hurried to work each morning. The chestnut tree also enjoyed snatching away children's kites and balls, and trapping them in its branches. The tree did not give them back until they were torn or had burst. He really was a bad sort of tree.

"Something must be done," complained a very cross man after his best bowler hat had been speared on one of the chestnut tree's branches.

"Ho! Ho! No one can stop me! I'm too clever!" laughed the chestnut tree.

The next day a workman from the council drove up to the tree. He set a ladder against the tree and climbed up, carrying a large saw.

"What's he up to?" scowled the chestnut tree. "I think I'll give him a jab in the tummy for disturbing me." But before the tree could move the workman had sawn through one of its branches. Then another, and then another!

Soon all the branches on the tree had been pruned right back and the tree could no longer play any more tricks . . . at least until its branches grew back again!

The Race

Two flies were having an argument about who was the best.

"I can fly circles around you any time," said the first fly.

"You're not as fast as me," said the second.

They decided to have a flying race. "GO!" they shouted and took off, buzzing loudly.

"I'm the best!" said the first.

"I'm the best!" said the second.

They were arguing so much they didn't notice where they were going and flew straight into a hungry spider's web.

"I think they were both the best . . . the best meal I've ever tasted," said the spider soon after, and she went off to sleep feeling very contented.

Nigel the Gnome

Nigel the garden gnome was just about as fed up as he could be having to stand in the family's garden in all weathers. "I get wet when it rains and my paint peels when the sun gets too hot," he moaned.

Little Judy was playing tea parties with her dollies in the garden. Each doll was dressed in a pretty pink dress and they each held a parasol to protect them from the warm sunshine.

Suddenly the weather changed and it began to rain very hard indeed. Judy went running indoors with her dolls.

"Oh, bother!" complained Nigel the garden gnome. "Now I'm going to get wet again."

Then he saw one of the doll's parasols lying on the grass. "Judy must have dropped it in her hurry," Nigel thought. He picked it up and held it over his head. "That's much better," he said, listening to the pitter-patter of the rain as it bounced off the roof of the parasol. "The parasol is keeping me from getting wet."

The rain soon ended and Nigel shut up the parasol. When the sun came out again it shone brightly.

"Phew!" gasped Nigel uncomfortably. "My paint will crack and peel even more."

Then he remembered the parasol and opened it high over his head. The parasol shaded Nigel from the rays of the sun and he felt much happier.

When Judy saw Nigel holding up the parasol she thought he looked so smart she decided to let him keep it all the time. This pleased Nigel and he never complained again.

The New Horse

Big Chief Itchy Nose came out of his wig-wam dressed in his grand feathered headdress. "Uggh!" he grunted crossly, looking at his beautiful black stallion. "Big Chief Itchy Nose's horse too slow. Couldn't catch a cold. Itchy Nose want something faster."

So Big Chief Itchy Nose rode into town on the beautiful black stallion he no longer wanted. In the town he saw some cowboys riding a big noisy motorbike which roared up and down the street very fast indeed.

"Heap fast horse!" beamed Big Chief Itchy Nose. "Me swop um for my horse."

The cowboys tried to explain that the motorbike wasn't a horse at all, but Itchy Nose wouldn't listen. He sat on the motorbike and the cowboys started it up for him.

VROOOOOOM! VROOOOOOM! roared the motorbike loudly.

"This heap good dragon-horse," grinned Itchy Nose, and letting out the clutch, he took off along the dusty road.

VROOOOOOM! roared the motorbike as it raced away.

"HELPUM!" squealed Big Chief Itchy Nose who was having a lot of trouble steering the motorbike.

CRAAASSH! The motorbike smashed through the side of a hay barn and CRAAASSH! out at the other side again. Big Chief Itchy Nose was so busy shaking the hay off himself he didn't notice where he was going, and SMAA-AAASSH! crashed through the window of a women's clothes shop.

"EEEEEEEK! Get out, you horrible brute!"

screamed the lady who owned the store, hitting Itchy Nose over the head with her broom. The motorbike smashed through the door of the clothes store and KER-RUUMMMP! collided with a horse trough outside.

SPLAASSSH! Big Chief Itchy Nose tumbled head-over-heels over the handlebars of the motorbike and landed in the horse trough full of water.

Shortly afterwards Big Chief Itchy Nose rode out of town . . . on his beautiful black stallion. "Horse maybe heapum slow but heapum safer!" thought Itchy Nose happily.

Fillmytummy's Long Night

All the trolls in Crabapple Lane were getting very excited about the street party that was taking place tomorrow. There would be party games, dancing and lots and lots to eat.

"We must stop Fillmytummy the troll from coming," said one troll to his friend. "He eats so fast and so much there won't be any food left for the rest of us. He's such a greedy troll."

"But what can we do?" asked the other

troll. "He'll wake up in the morning like the rest of us."

"Not if we play a trick on him, he won't," chuckled the first troll. "Come on, we have work to do."

It was very dark when Fillmytummy went to bed. "I can't wait for the party tomorrow," he smiled excitedly. "There'll be ever so much to eat!"

Fillmytummy soon fell into a deep sleep. When he eventually woke up again he said, "Ahh! It must be morning." But when he looked out of his bedroom window it was still pitch black so he went back to sleep.

When Fillmytummy woke up the second time he leapt out of bed full of excitement. "It must be morning now," he thought. "All that sleeping has made me very hungry." But when he looked out of his window it was still as black as night. "Oh, dear," he sighed, and got back into bed. "Morning seems to be taking such a long time to come." And he fell asleep again.

Fillmytummy woke up once . . . twice . . . three times, but whenever he looked outside it was still night so he went back to sleep.

The next time he woke up and saw it was still dark outside, Fillmytummy began to get worried. "Perhaps morning will never come," he thought. "Perhaps it will always be night!" He didn't like that idea at all!

Just then he heard voices and laughing from outside his bedroom window. Very puzzled and thinking it might be a burglar he crept over to the window and pulled it open to see if he could see anyone in the dark.

To his surprise bright sunshine streamed into his bedroom. It was daytime after all! "Ha! Ha! Sorry we tricked you," said the troll outside Fillmytummy's house. "We covered your window with black paint so you would think it was still night. Then we were able to have our party in peace without you scoffing all the food."

"But we kept you some food anyway," said the second troll, handing Fillmytummy a large tray of cakes, jelly and ice cream. When Fillmytummy saw all the delicious food he forgave his friends for playing such a rotten trick on him. "I'm going to eat all day to make up for what I've missed," he said. And that's exactly what he did!

The Counting Horse

"I wish I could count," sighed Henrietta the horse as she stood in her grassy field one sunny day.

"Of course you can count," said the grasshopper. "It's easy."

"It's not easy at all!" snapped Henrietta, a little sharply. "It's jolly difficult!"

"Look," said the grasshopper. "Every time you lift up a leg and put it down again count that as one. Now how many legs have you got?"

"Er, three?" asked Henrietta hopefully.

"No, no! You have four legs, otherwise you'd topple over. You have one, two, three, four legs." And the grasshopper counted Henrietta's legs one by one.

"Oh, yes," neighed Henrietta happily. "So I have. How marvellous!"

"So as you walk all you have to do is count one, two, three, four, each time you lift up a leg and put it down again."

"One, two, three, four. One, two, three, four." Henrietta sang as she trotted round her field. "Yippee! I can count! I can count!"

The grasshopper didn't have the heart to tell Henrietta that four wasn't a very high number to count up to, but she was happy so it didn't really matter. How many can you count up to? A lot more than four, I'm sure!

The Lost Mittens

"I've lost my mittens," Tiddlewinks the kitten cried, searching through her coat pockets without success. "I'm sure I had them when I came home from playing yesterday."

"You naughty kitten," scolded her mother. "It's too cold to go out without them."

Tiddlewinks didn't like the idea of staying in but she did as her mother told her. The birds singing loudly in their nest only made her want to go out more.

"I wonder if they saw where I dropped my mittens?" Tiddlewinks thought. When her mother was busy in the kitchen Tiddlewinks sneaked outside into the garden and quickly scampered up the tree.

"Meeoow!" she called to the birds, hoping they wouldn't fly away. She knew birds didn't trust cats very much. "Can you help me? I've lost my mittens."

It was then Tiddlewinks reached the nest and looked inside. There were the birds, sitting comfortably on her mittens.

"Don't eat us!" sang the birds in fright. "We only took your mittens to keep us warm. It gets so cold in our nest in winter."

Tiddlewinks felt sorry for the birds and left her mittens in their nest. She didn't have to worry. Her mother soon knitted her another pair.

Dreamy Daniel

Dreamy Daniel was looking very miserable one day.

"What's the matter?" asked his mother, who couldn't understand why he should be so sad.

"Do I have to grow up?" Dreamy Daniel asked

"Of course you do," laughed his mother. "You'll grow taller and taller as you get older."

"I don't want to grow up!" Dreamy Daniel snapped crossly.

"Why ever not?" asked his mother, somewhat puzzled.

"Well, he said quickly. "I'm scared of heights!" He is silly, isn't he?

The Argument

Two ants were arguing over a scrap of bread.

"Let's have a fight," said one. "Winner takes all."

"Agreed," said the other.

The two ants fought and fought with neither gaining an advantage over the other. While they were fighting a large bird swooped down and snatched up the scrap of bread in its beak. When the ants saw this they stopped fighting.

"Now we will go hungry because we were too busy fighting to watch the bread," said one. "Next time we find food let's share it."

"Agreed," said the other.

The Untidy Town

The people of the town were surprised to wake up and find their once spotlessly clean streets covered in litter. There were broken bottles, old tin cans, empty cigarette packets, worn tyres, sticky chewing gum, and paper of all sizes and colours scattered along the streets as far as the eye could see.

"What a horrible sight," complained the people. "Someone could cut themselves on the glass, the children could become trapped while playing in the tyres, and old people could fall over the rubbish and badly injure themselves. Who could have done such a bad thing?"

"We did," said the animals of the forest. "All this rubbish is what people have carelessly dropped or dumped in our forest, instead of putting it in the litter bins or taking it to the rubbish dump. Squirrels and badgers have been cut by the broken bottles, birds have choked to death after swallowing discarded chewing gum, and the fish in the lake have perished from all the rubbish dropped in the water."

The people of the town were very ashamed when hearing this. "If we are to live with nature we must care for it properly," they said.

Flapper and Delilah

Flapper the dragonet was very good friends with Delilah Dolphin who lived in the sea. The two chums would splash about in the water and sometimes Delilah would allow Flapper to ride on her back.

One day a fisherman saw Delilah splashing about in the sea and decided to capture her to sell to a zoo. He chased after her in his ship and when he came close to her he threw out a large net. Poor Delilah was caught!

Just then Flapper flew overhead looking for his friend. When he saw what the fisherman had done he became very angry.

Swooping down on his strong wings Flapper snatched up the fisherman in his mouth and flew him high into the air.

"WAAAAAAAAAAAAAAAAAAAAAHH!" screamed the fisherman as Flapper let him go and he fell down, down towards the water.

Meanwhile Delilah had struggled free of the netting and swam towards where the fisherman had landed PLOP! in the sea. Before the fisherman could catch his breath Delilah had lifted him onto her nose and was juggling him around and around. The fisherman became so dizzy he couldn't see straight. Then Delilah tossed him back aboard his ship. When the fisherman could stand up straight again he was so frightened to see a dragonet with the dolphin that he set sail never to return, leaving Flapper and Delilah to play happily together.

Benny's Bad Mood

Benny woke up and decided there and then to have a Bad Mood day.

"I'm going to stay in a bad mood all day," he grumbled. He started by getting out on the wrong side of the bed. "That has really made me in a bad mood," he moaned.

Benny went downstairs for his breakfast but he was in such a bad mood he didn't want any.

"My, you are in a bad mood," said his mother.

"I am, aren't I?" agreed Benny proudly in a Bad Mood sort of way.

Benny's mother dressed him in his warm winter coat and took him to the shops.

"My coat's too warm," he complained moodily. "And my legs ache from walking."

Benny's friend Joanna waved to Benny but he ignored her and went on walking.

"Benny must be in a bad mood," said Joanna's mother.

"THAT'S RIGHT! I AM!" Benny shouted crossly to them.

Benny's mood lasted all day. He grumbled and complained and moaned and groaned.

"I don't want to go to bed!" Benny snapped that evening.

"Maybe you'll be in a better mood in the morning," said his mother.

The next morning Benny woke up, and guess what? He WAS in a better mood.

"I feel much happier today," he told his mother as he tucked into his breakfast. "My bad mood has gone away again."

"That's wonderful," said his mother. "You're much nicer when you're in a good mood."

The Poisoned Blueberries

A wicked Witch gave a beautiful Princess a bunch of poisoned blueberries to eat. "When she swallows them she will die and I will rule the land," cackled the Witch.

One day passed, and then another, and another one after that, and each day the Witch passed by the Castle and saw the Princess in the best of health.

"Bah! My poisoned blueberries didn't work," cursed the Witch angrily.

Then one day the Witch was called to the Castle to have tea with the Princess. The Witch decided she had better go in case the Princess became suspicious and sent her soldiers to fetch her. Anyway, there might be an opportunity to poison the Princess while they were eating.

The tea was delicious and the greedy Witch ate almost all the food on the table.

"Wine?" asked the Princess sweetly, pouring some wine into a goblet for the Witch to drink.

The Witch swallowed the wine in one gulp. Then she frowned. "What a funny taste this wine has? What is it made from?"

"Why, blueberries, of course," smiled the Princess. "The blueberries you so kindly gave me many days ago. They only made a little wine so I gave it all to you." But the Witch no longer heard the Princess for she was already dead.

Tug-O'-War

Tiny the elephant was having a game of tug-o'-war with his friends the monkeys. However, Tiny was so small and not very strong that the monkeys always managed to pull him off his feet.

"It's not fair," Tiny grumbled. "I'll never win this game." He swished his tail crossly to show how annoyed he was. It was then he had an idea.

The next day Tiny and the monkeys were having another game of tug-o'-war. The monkeys pulled and pulled on the vine they were using as rope to try to pull Tiny over but this time he stayed on his feet. Then Tiny gave one big tug and the monkeys tumbled head over heels.

"Tiny's the winner!" they cheered, laughing merrily. "But how did you manage to stay on your feet when we've always been able to pull you over?"

Tiny smiled and showed the monkeys how he had tied his tail to the branch of a tree. "You could have pulled all day and I wouldn't have fallen over," he chuckled.

Doozleflumph Must Go!

Doozleflumph the Glumf was a strange creature. Well, with a name like that you would expect him to be strange, wouldn't you? He was a striking bright green colour and very furry, with a big fat tummy, two bright yellow eyes, a pair of long floppy ears and two enormous big feet. He didn't really resemble much of anything but this didn't matter to Timothy O'Reilly.

Timothy had found Doozleflumph the Glumf at the seaside, inside a cave where Doozleflumph was living. Timothy took him home to have some tea and Doozleflumph had stayed with him ever since.

Doozleflumph was not what you would call small. In fact he was very very big! He was much bigger than Timothy, bigger than Timothy's Mum and even bigger than Timothy's very tall Dad, who was a policeman. Doozleflumph was so big he had a problem getting in and out of the small rooms of Timothy's house.

"It's no good," said Timothy's Dad one day after Doozleflumph had become stuck in the doorway of the living room for the sixth time that morning. "Doozleflumph's too big to stay here. He'll have to go."

Timothy thought this was a terrible idea and so did Doozleflumph. He had grown very fond of Timothy and his parents since he had come to live with them. A big wet tear ran down his furry bright green face. "GLUMF!" he cried sadly. And then "DOOZLEFLUMPH! GLUMF!" he added. I suspect now you can guess why Timothy named him Doozleflumph the Glumf for "DOOZLEFLUMPH!" and "GLUMF!" was all Doozleflumph the Glumf ever said.

"Don't worry, Doozleflumph. I'll think of something," said Timothy. But Doozleflumph wasn't so sure and he went to bed feeling very sad indeed.

Timothy has an Idea

"It's not fair," sulked Timothy as he sat with Doozleflumph the Glumf on the garden seat the next day. Well, actually Doozleflumph sat on the grass because he was so big and heavy if he had sat on the garden seat he would have squashed it flat.

"We have a home to live in," Timothy went on. "Pongo my dog has a kennel to live in. Even the birds have a bird-box to nest in. You should have somewhere too."

"GLUMF!" cried Doozleflumph, nodding his furry head in agreement.

Timothy sprang up suddenly. "I've got an idea!" he said and rushed off down the street, followed somewhat slower by Doozleflumph whose feet went FLIP-FLOP! FLIP-FLOP! as he ran, or, to be more precise, lumbered.

Timothy's uncle was a carpenter and he always had lots of wood left over from his work. When Timothy arrived and asked if he could have some wood, his uncle was only too pleased to help his nephew, and Doozleflumph, who was the nicest Glumf he had ever met. Actually Doozleflumph was the the only Glumf Timothy's uncle had met but he didn't tell Timothy that.

Doozleflumph helped Timothy carry the wood home but he was very puzzled. What was Timothy's plan? Timothy wouldn't say and Doozleflumph went to sleep feeling very confused.

Doozleflumph's New Home

The next day Timothy and Doozleflumph set to work. They worked all morning sawing and hammering and hammering and sawing at the pieces of wood. They did the same in the afternoon, even missing lunch to get the job done.

When Dad returned home from work that evening he couldn't believe his eyes. There in the back garden was the most enormous dog's kennel he had ever seen. It towered over the house like a giant with its mouth open.

"B-B-B-But. . . .!" stammered Timothy's Dad, not knowing quite what to say.

"It's Doozleflumph's new home," Timothy explained. "I got the idea from seeing Pongo's kennel. Now Doozleflumph doesn't have to live inside the house and keep getting stuck in the doorways. He can live here in his own home instead. Please say he can, Dad? Please?"

"DOOZLEFLUMPH!" pleaded Doozleflumph hopefully.

Timothy's Dad grinned. "After all this work you two have put in, of course he can stay. And we'll hold a special house-warming party for him too."

Doozleflumph was so happy he gave Timothy's Dad a big "thank-you" hug which squashed all the breath out of him. "GLUMF!" cried Doozleflumph happily. "DOOZLEFLUMPH! GLUMF!"

The Tramp

Shirley was a poor orphan girl who had very little money and could only afford one loaf of bread to eat every other day.

One day she was leaving the baker's when she saw an old, bearded tramp sitting in the street looking very miserable. Everyone passed by on the other side of the road and pretended he wasn't there.

"Poor man," said Shirley to the tramp. "Here, take my loaf of bread and fill your stomach with food." And she handed the tramp her loaf of bread.

At this the tramp stood up, took off his dirty old coat and pulled off his dirty grey beard, which was false. To Shirley's surprise there stood before her a handsome young man in the finest of clothes.

"I am Prince Brion," he said, kissing Shirley's hand tenderly. "And I have dressed like a tramp to see who in this town would show kindness to an old man down on his luck." The Prince smiled warmly at Shirley. "No one did until you came along and offered me your last crust. You are the kindest soul I have ever met and I would very much like to marry you."

Shirley and the Prince were soon married and Shirley went to live in his very grand palace and had lots of fine food to eat. But she never forgot her humble beginnings and always left a table of food outside the palace each day for any tramps who might pass by.

Frances Fib-a-Lot

Frances Fib-a-Lot is a funny name for a little girl, don't you think? She was just named Frances really, but everyone put Fib-a-Lot on the end because that's what she did. She fibbed . . . a lot. A fib is when you don't tell the complete truth, and Frances never did that.

"Who pinched the cakes?" asked her mother, looking at Frances.

"Not me," said Frances, hiding the cake she was holding behind her back. "It must have been mice, I think."

"Who broke the window?" asked her father, looking at Frances.

"Not me," fibbed Frances, knowing full well she did break the window with her ball. "It must have been the dinosaur who passed this way, I think."

Now you can see why she was called Frances Fib-a-Lot . . . she was always telling fibs.

One morning Frances awoke to find her fairy godmother sitting on the end of her bed.

"Every time you tell a fib you shall shrink a little bit," her fairy godmother told her. "But if you tell the truth you shall start to grow again." The fairy godmother vanished leaving Frances feeling very scared. But it wasn't long before she forgot her fairy godmother's warning.

"Who tore a hole in my best tablecloth?" asked her mother, looking at Frances.

"Not me," fibbed Frances, who had cut a hole in the tablecloth with her scissors only moments before. "It must have been a mole, I think."

Frances felt a cold shiver down her back and suddenly she began to shrink until she was no taller than the kitchen table.

"Who has used all the hot water?" asked her father, looking at Frances.

"Not me," fibbed Frances, who had filled the bath with water to sail her toy boats. "It must have been a thirsty ogre looking for a hot drink, I think."

A second shiver ran down Frances' back and she began to shrink until she was no taller than Pom-Poms, her cat.

"Who has crayoned on the walls?" asked her parents together, looking at Frances.

"N-Not m-me," fibbed Frances nervously, but she had really when she couldn't find any paper to crayon on. "It m-must have been a b-burglar w-who likes to c-crayon on w-walls, I th-think."

Frances felt herself shrinking smaller and smaller until she was no bigger than a mouse. Pom-Poms looked at her hungrily.

"I DID! I did tear the tablecloth and use all the hot water and crayon on the walls!" Frances squealed in fright as Pom-Poms leapt at her with his mouth wide open to swallow her whole.

To Frances' relief she felt a shiver down her back and she began to grow, and grow, and grow, until she was back to her normal size.

"Thank goodness!" Frances gasped happily. "I'll never tell another fib in my life." And from that day forward no one ever had cause to call her Frances Fib-a-Lot again.

Ernie and the Fence

Ernie the fox had been told by his mother to paint the garden fence.

"This will take ages," he groaned as he splashed yellow paint on the fence with a large brush. Just then Billy Badger came wandering up.

"Cor! I like painting," he said. "Can I have a go?"

Ernie was only too happy to let his friend do some painting. As he watched Billy at work Ernie had an idea. He hurried home and wrote a large sign which read: HAVE FUN! PAINT THE FENCE! BRING YOUR OWN PAINTS! and he placed the sign beside the fence.

Very soon a long queue of animals stood in line along the fence waiting to have a go. They all carried their own paint tins and brushes.

"Now I can have a snooze," Ernie chuckled happily. "When I come back my friends will have painted the fence for me."

Ernie had a lovely sleep in the warm sunshine and when he awoke he hurried back to the fence. "I'll tell Mum I painted the fence on my own."

But oh, dear! When he saw the fence Ernie's face dropped in dismay. His friends had painted it all right . . . but in different colours! "Oh, no! When I told my friends to bring their own paints I forgot to tell them it had to be yellow!" Ernie groaned.

When his mother saw the fence she was very cross. She made Ernie paint the fence properly before he could have any supper. "I'll never be lazy again" Ernie sighed.

Vinnie the Vampire

Vinnie was a vampire with a problem. He fainted at the sight of blood.

"I'm useless," sighed Vinnie when he had recovered from fainting, after he had cut himself shaving. "How can I be a vampire if I can't drink blood?"

Vinnie went to see Dr Eccles-Cakes to see if she could help.

"My, you do look pale," said Dr Eccles-Cakes when she saw Vinnie's pale complexion. "You're not getting enough sunshine."

Vinnie explained how he couldn't stand the thought of drinking blood. "I don't blame you," said the doctor. "Disgusting habit. Here, try this instead." She handed Vinnie a glass of red liquid. At first Vinnie thought it was blood and that the doctor was playing a trick on him. His tummy went topsy-turvey but he tried to be brave and took a sip. Then he took another, and then he drank it all up.

"It's delicious," he said happily. "What is it?"

"Tomato juice," said Dr Eccles-Cakes. "Full of vitamins and much nicer than blood, too."

Vinnie agreed and from that day on he had a glass of tomato juice after every meal and never fainted again.

The Dripping Tap

DRIP! DRIP! DRIP! DRIP went the tap over the kitchen sink.

"It must need a new washer," said Mr Fix-It to his wife. He fetched his toolbox and set to work.

BANG! BANG! BANG! went his hammer. It wasn't long before he had replaced the washer on the tap.

"There. That's fixed it," said Mr Fix-It.

DRIP! DRIP! DRIP! went the tap, much to Mr Fix-It's annoyance.

"Perhaps it needs a smaller washer," Mr Fix-It said, and so he set to work again.

BANG! BANG! BANG! went his hammer again.

"I've fixed it for sure this time," said Mr Fix-It when he had finished.

DRIP! DRIP! DRIP! went the tap.

Mr Fix-It's face turned beetroot red as he became more and more angry.

BANG! BANG! BANG! went his hammer quickly as he changed the washer for a third time.

DRIP! DRIP! DRIP! went the tap when he had finished.

BANG! BANG! BANG!
DRIP! DRIP! DRIP!
BANG! BANG! BANG!
DRIP! DRIP! DRIP!

Mr Fix-It kept on changing the washer and the tap carried on DRIP! DRIP! DRIPPING, merrily away.

"I give up," sighed Mr Fix-It much later. "I can't stop the dripping. We'll have to call out a plumber." "Nonsense," said his wife. "I'll stop the dripping tap."

"You?" laughed Mr Fix-It rudely. "Why, if I can't fix it you certainly won't be able to."

DRIP! DRIP! DRIP! went the tap as Mr Fix-It and his wife argued.

"Tap," said Mrs Fix-It crossly. "If you don't stop dripping − now! − I'll turn the water off at the mains and you'll never work again."

DRIP! D-R-I-P! D−R−I−P! The tap began to drip slower and slower until finally it stopped altogether.

"Amazing!" gasped Mr Fix-It. "How did you do it?"

"It was easy," smiled his wife. "You just have to say the right things, that's all."

Bath Night

Esmeralda was a tomboy, which meant she liked playing rough games and getting dirty.

"You need a bath tonight," said her mother when she saw Esmeralda caked in mud and grime.

"Not likely!" said Esmeralda, running out of the house.

Esmeralda's mother chased her down the road and into the park. Esmeralda wasn't watching where she was going and accidently stepped on a roller skate that had been left in the park by another child.

"WURRGLE!" squealed Esmeralda as she slipped on the roller skate and landed KER-SPLASSH! in the pond.

"Ha! Ha! I thought you didn't like having a bath," laughed her mother. "But now you're wet you might as well do the job properly." She threw Esmeralda a bar of soap and a flannel, and Esmeralda had to get washed in front of all the people in the park. Next time I think she'll have a bath without any fuss, don't you?

The Friendless Skunk

Sammy the skunk had rather an embarrasing problem. He smelt awful!

"Poooh! You pong!" grimaced Ribbet Frog and he leapt into his pond.

"Pongy Sammy! Pongy Sammy!" sang the other animals as they danced around the poor skunk, holding their noses.

Sammy was very upset and ran home crying to his mother. "I have no friends because I smell funny," he sobbed.

"There, there, dear," said his mother kindly. All skunks have a strong smell. You'll find it will come in very useful one day."

That afternoon while Sammy was out walking, alone as usual, he saw Ribbet Frog and Hoppy Rabbit hurrying towards him.

"Run, Sammy, run!" they called. "Mr Fox is coming".

He saw Mr Fox chasing after Hoppy Rabbit. Hoppy tripped, and Mr Fox pounced on him!

"Oh, no! Mr Fox will eat Hoppy!" cried Sammy, and even though Hoppy had been one of the animals who was always teasing him, Sammy raced to save him.

Mr Fox looked up when he saw Sammy coming and pulled a face. "Oh, poooh! A skunk!" he snorted as the smell from Sammy drifted across to him, and he raced away.

"You saved me!" Hoppy cried gratefully." And after all the nasty things I've said about you."

From that day on all the animals were much kinder to Sammy and they even played with him . . . after they had put clothes pegs on their noses to keep away the smell, that is!

Jock's Revenge (2)

That day came sooner than Jock had expected. The ENORMOUS fat black cat had just raided Mrs McMurphy's dinner again. He had overturned her full dustbin just for fun, and was now running past Jock, out of reach as usual, laughing its "MEE-HEE!-HEE!-OOOW!" laugh. Jock was barking louder than ever. "ARF! ARF! ARF! You nasty cat! If I could catch you I would teach you a lesson!" Jock pulled and pulled on his rope trying to reach the ENORMOUS fat black cat, when TWANG! the rope snapped away from the tree and Jock was free!

"HISSSSS! MEEEEOOOOWW! Leave me alone!" wailed the ENORMOUS fat black cat as Jock chased him around and around the garden until they were both quite dizzy.

"ARF! ARF! ARF!" barked Jock happily, snapping at the ENORMOUS fat black cat's tail.

"MEEE-YEEEOOOOOWW!" screamed the ENORMOUS fat black cat when Jock took a nip of his tail. The ENORMOUS fat black cat ran through Mrs McMurphy's flower beds, leapt over the garden fence and raced down the road.

"That'll teach him!" snuffled Jock proudly as he went back to sit under the shady tree. "And if he comes back I'll give his tail an even harder nip!" But the ENORMOUS fat black cat was never seen again. I wonder why?

The Challenge (1)

There was once an ENORMOUS fat black cat who thought he was the toughest cat in all the land. He enjoyed overturning dustbins and watching them go CLATTER! CLATTER! down the street, emptying their contents all over the place as they go. He enjoyed entering Mrs McMurphy's house and eating up all her dinner. She would leave it on the kitchen table for when she returned home from work. But most of all he enjoyed teasing Mrs McMurphy's small brown dog, Jock.

"MEE-HEE!-HEE!-OOOW!" chuckled the ENORMOUS fat black cat as he ran into Mrs McMurphy's garden.

"ARF! ARF! ARF! ARF!" barked Jock frantically trying to chase after the ENORMOUS fat black cat and give his tail a good nip. But Jock was tied up to a shady tree and he could only run as far as the rope would let him. The ENORMOUS fat black cat always kept just out of reach.

"MEE-HEE!-HEE!-OOOW! You can't catch me!" hissed the ENORMOUS fat black cat as it spat and ruffled its fur at Jock.

"ARF! ARF! ARF! I'll catch you one day, you nasty cat!" barked Jock loudly. "Just see if I don't!"

Tackingstitch the Pixie

Tackingstitch the pixie was out late one night tacking stitches in the leaves of the wood that had become torn in a terrible gale.

All at once a cruel old man caught Tackingstitch in his hands and carried her to his home. "Starting tomorrow you can stitch me a new suit of clothes every day," he said.

Every morning she would start work stitching and tacking cloth together.

This went on for many weeks and Tackingstitch soon became ill from working so hard.

"I must escape," she thought. "Or I shall surely die." So that night, as the old man was about to put Tackingstitch in the box he kept her in she said, "Old man, why don't I stay up tonight and stitch together a new suit to present you with in the morning?"

The old man agreed but he made Tackingstitch promise she wouldn't try to escape during the night.

"I promise," said Tackingstitch.

The old man knew that pixies never broke a promise so he went to bed satisfied. When he was asleep Tackingstitch set to work, but not on a new suit as she had said. Instead she began to stitch the pyjamas the old man was wearing to his bed.

The old man was furious when he awoke and found he could not move. "You promised not to try to escape!" he roared angrily.

"And I have kept that promise," said Tackingstitch. "But now it is morning and so my promise is fullfilled." Tackingstitch flew out of the house and back to the wood.

The Artist

Once upon a time there was a very famous artist who was well known for his wonderful paintings. He was also very boastful and rather rude.

One day an old lady came to his studio and said, "Please could you paint my ceiling? I don't have much money but I will pay you for your work."

The artist became very angry at this. "PAINT YOUR CEILING?!" he roared, frightening the old lady very much. "I am an artist! I paint portraits of the richest Kings and Queens in all the world! I do not paint ceilings!" And he threw the old lady out of his shop and into the gutter.

Now when the townfolk heard how cruel the artist had been to the old lady they refused to have anything to do with him. With no work coming in he soon ran out of money and became very poor.

One day there was a knock at the old lady's door. It was the artist, unshaven and very thin. He was dressed in white overalls and carried a large pot of paint. "May I paint your ceiling, please?" he said. "No one wants to buy my paintings anymore and if I don't make some money soon I shall starve."

The old woman took pity on the artist and agreed to have him paint her ceiling. He worked very hard and made a very good job of the ceiling. When he had finished, the old lady paid him and then invited him to have tea with her.

Life

A white cloud and a black cloud floated high in the sky. The white cloud was happy and cheerful while the black cloud was sad and miserable.

"Isn't life wonderful?" said the white cloud merrily.

"Is it?" moaned the black cloud gloomily. "I think it's rather awful. All those humans down below arguing and fighting and polluting this beautiful planet with their poisons."

"You shouldn't look on the black side," said the white cloud. "Think of all the beautiful animals, the pretty flowers and trees, and the humans who are kind and thoughtful towards one another."

"You shouldn't be blinkered by the good side of life," grumbled the black cloud. "The humans are hunting the animals to extinction, tearing down the forests, choking the flowers with their chemicals and are always doing nasty things to one another."

"Well, perhaps we are both right and wrong," said the white cloud amicably. "There is both good and bad in this world. Nothing is just black or white. I suppose life is really what you make it."

The black cloud agreed that this was so and the two friends floated peacefully away.

At the Seaside

The Ogre went to the seaside one sunny day.

"There's not enough sand on this beach for me to build a sandcastle," said the Ogre sadly. Actually there was lots of sand but the Ogre was so big it was no more than a thimbleful.

"I'll have a splash in the sea instead," he decided after he had changed into his yellow and pink striped swimming shorts. He ran down to the sea and leapt in. KER-SPLOOOSH! But he was so big he splashed all the sea away.

"You great lump!" roared the people on the beach. "You've turned the sea into a desert!" The bottom of the sea was sand, just like the beach.

The Ogre didn't mind. Now he had lots more sand to play with.

53

A Tin of Peas

"Oh, bother! My can opener is broken and I can't open this tin of peas for our dinner," said Mrs Shortnose glumly.

"Let me try," said Mr Shortnose who wasn't very bright, and he put the tin on the floor and jumped on it.

"WAAAAH!" he cried as he slipped on the tin and fell WHUMP! on the floor.

"I'll open it," said Johnny Shortnose. "My big strong hammer will break it open."

WHAM! The hammer struck the top of the tin.

"OOOOYAAH!" Johnny Shortnose squealed as the hammer bounced back and hit him on the nose.

Sally Shortnose came in with a saw. "This will do the trick," she said.

"R-R-R-R-R-R-R-R-R-R-R-R! went the saw across the top of the tin of peas.

TWANG! TWANG! TWANG! went the saw's teeth as they snapped off one by one.

Just then a steamroller trundled along the road outside their house. Running outside they threw the tin of peas into the road and the heavy steamroller rolled right over it. "This is bound to break open the tin," chuckled Mr Shortnose.

But when the steamroller had passed by, the tin of peas was squashed flatter than a pancake.

"Er, anyone for soup?" asked Mrs Shortnose.

The Elephant and Mouse

There was once an elephant who was very strong and boasted to everyone how powerful he was.

One day the elephant was walking along, pushing the other animals out of his way, when he accidently trod on the tail of a tiny mouse.

"You great oaf!" squeaked the mouse angrily. "Why don't you watch where you're going?"

Now the elephant did not like to be shouted at, especially by an animal no bigger than the nail on his foot, and so he bellowed, "I AM THE MIGHTIEST ANIMAL IN ALL THE WORLD! NO ONE IS MORE POWERFUL THAN I! IF YOU DO NOT BEG FOR FORGIVENESS I WILL SQUASH YOU FLAT!"

The mouse laughed at this and said, "You are not so strong. I know an animal who is even stronger than you."

"Stronger than me?" trumpeted the elephant merrily. "Impossible. If you can show me such a creature I will gladly leave, never to return."

"Come with me then," said the mouse. The elephant followed and when they came to a clearing he saw the mouse standing beside a very old tortoise.

"What?" chortled the elephant. "This tortoise is stronger than I? You must be mad!"

"Can you carry a house on your back!" the mouse demanded to know.

"No," agreed the elephant. "No one is that strong."

"The tortoise is," said the mouse, pointing to the shell on the tortoise's back. "He carries his house on his back wherever he goes."

The elephant realised he had been tricked but he kept his word and the animals were never bothered by him again.

The Lonely Flower

Once upon a time there grew a lovely flower outside the royal palace. The flower was quite happy with her lot in life but there were times when she would think how nice it would be to have some flower friends to rustle in the breeze with.

One day the Princess of the palace saw the lonely flower and felt very sad. "Poor flower, all alone. Perhaps I shall pick you and put you in a vase in the royal palace."

The flower shrank back upon hearing this. "Please don't!" she begged, trembling with fear. "I'm here to make the world look beautiful. If everyone keeps picking the wild flowers soon there will be none left and the world will look sad and grey."

The Princess nodded and gave the flower an understanding smile. "Don't worry, little one. I promise I won't pick you."

The Princess went back to the palace and when she returned she brought with her a tray of seeds which she planted around the flower. The Princess watered the seeds every day and in a few short months the lonely flower was surrounded by lots of flower friends.

"Now you have friends to talk with," said the Princess. "And they help to make the royal palace look even more beautiful than before. And you are the prettiest flower of them all."

The Missing Star

The Man In The Moon was busy counting the stars in the night sky. "One million and one, one million and two, one million and. . . ." He stopped, looked all around, and frowned in a puzzled way. "That's strange. There seems to be one missing."

"There is," said a sweet voice behind him. "Me!"

The Man In The Moon was surprised to see a tiny star floating over his head. "B-But you should be up there," he said, pointing up to the rest of the stars.

"I'm bored," said the star. "How would fancy being stuck in the sky, night after night, with nothing to do!"

The Man In The Moon had to agree this didn't sound much fun.

"So I've decided to travel the Universe instead," said the star, showing The Man In The Moon her packed suitcase. "I'll shoot past the planets, loop-the-loop around the Milky Way, and tumble higgledy-piggledy through a black hole or two."

"B-But what if someone notices you're missing?" said The Man In The Moon. "There'll be a terrible fuss!"

"Well, I won't tell if you don't," laughed the star. With that she took off, leaving a sparkling trail of dust behind her.

The Panto

Jack and Judith were putting on a pantomime in their garden.

They worked very hard and everything was soon ready for their production of "JACK AND THE BEANSTALK".

"Where's my other boot?" Jack asked Judith as they were dressing up in their costumes backstage.

"I don't know," said Judith. "You'll have to go on without it. The audience are waiting."

So Jack hobbled on stage wearing only one boot. He blushed when he heard the audience laughing. "They're laughing at me!" he groaned.

"No, they're laughing at Tiddles," grinned Judith, pointing over to the corner of the stage. "There's your boot!" To Jack's surprise the children's cat was fast asleep in the old black boot.

"We should have staged PUSS IN BOOTS instead!" laughed Judith.

Eric the Sea Monster

Eric the Sea Monster enjoyed chasing passing ships and giving the seamen on board a fright.

"Why can't you behave yourself," scolded an old Sea Monster after Eric had leapt out of the water at a sailing ship and caused all crew to faint in shock. "You're giving the rest of us sea monsters a bad name." Eric ignored the old Sea Monster and carried on enjoying himself, splashing about in the water.

Now one day a large trawler came by and began dropping huge metal drums into the sea. It wasn't long before the Sea Monsters began to feel very sick. "These humans are wicked," cursed the old Sea Monster. "They get rid of the poisons they make by dumping them into our sea."

Eric knew he had to do something or all the Sea Monsters would soon die. He swam down to the bottom of the sea bed and picked up the drums in his large mouth. The drums burned his mouth, but he was very brave and ignored the pain, and swam back to the surface again. He saw the trawler sailing away and even though by this time he was feeling very sick he chased after it.

When Eric caught up with the trawler he threw the drums of poison on board the ship's deck. The seamen were very frightened of the drums and were about to push them back into the sea when Eric rose high in the air on his long neck and gave a tremendous RRRRROOOOOOO-AAAAAAARRR!! which shook the trawler from stem to stern. This was enough for the terrified seamen and they quickly sailed away, never to return.

"Well done, Eric," praised the old Sea Monster. "You've saved us!" Eric felt very pleased and no one ever told him off for scaring humans again.

Tony's Umbrella

"It looks like rain so take my umbrella," said Tony's Dad, handing Tony a smart black umbrella. "It'll save you getting wet. But mind you take care of it."

"Aww, Dad. Umbrellas are soppy. I don't mind the rain," Tony whined, not wanting his school chums to see him with an umbrella.

But his Dad insisted and so Tony set off for school with the umbrella tucked underneath his arm.

It wasn't long before Gnasher Groggins, the school bully, saw him, and shouted out, "HAW! Tony's gone soft!" This made Tony very annoyed and he charged at Gnasher waving the umbrella in the air like a flag of battle.

"Soft, am I!" he cried, hitting Gnasher over the head with the umbrella.

"Ouch! Gerroff!" shouted Gnasher and he ran off crying, threatening to tell his Mum on Tony, but Tony didn't care.

"That was fun," he smiled, feeling proud of beating Gnasher in a fight.

A little further on he met a little girl who was crying as she stood beside a tall tree. "My ball's stuck in the branches of the tree," she told Tony.

Tony lifted up the umbrella which he still kept closed, and began to poke and jab at the ball to knock it out of the tree. JAB! JAB!

POKE! POKE! went the umbrella. It kept getting caught between the branches and Tony had to pull it free but eventually the umbrella knocked the ball out of the tree and into the hands of the girl.

"My umbrella's coming in useful after all," Tony thought happily.

At school Tony met his best friend, Simon. "Let's have a sword fight," Simon suggested, holding up a wooden sword.

"Ha! Have at 'ee, me hearty!" cried Tony in his best pirate's voice. He swiped at Simon, using the umbrella as his sword. He parried and thrust and hacked away until the umbrella was quite battered and torn.

When school was over Tony took his coat and umbrella from the cloakroom and headed down the street for home. Then all of a sudden it began to rain, very heavily. "I'd better put up my umbrella after all," thought Tony as the rain ran down his neck. But when he opened up the umbrella he found it was full of huge holes.

"Crikey! I must have torn it fighting Gnasher . . . or rescuing the ball . . . or playing pirates with Simon . . . or perhaps all three!" Tony groaned. The rain poured in through the holes in the umbrella and by the time he reached home Tony was soaking wet.

Tony's Dad was not amused and gave him a spanking, and instead of using a slipper he used the umbrella. "Huh! I don't think I like umbrellas after all!" Tony grumbled.

Breakfast in Bed

Timothy Turtle was a lazy fellow. He always slept until late in the morning while his poor wife did all the housework. When he finally did get up he just sat in his favourite armchair until it was time for bed.

"Breakfast is ready," his wife would call each morning but Timothy would just snuggle down deeper under the blankets. This meant Mrs Turtle had to bring the breakfast up to him to stop it from going cold.

"You are lazy," she complained as she watched him tuck into his favourite meal, boiled seaweed.

"Well, I like my breakfast in bed," is all he said.

Timothy was so lazy he didn't bother to do any jobs around the house. One day Mrs Turtle was in such a hurry to bring him his breakfast before it went cold, she tripped over a loose floorboard which Timothy hadn't bothered to mend. The breakfast dish flew out of her hands and SPLODGE! landed on Timothy's head.

Timothy looked so funny with boiled seaweed running down his face Mrs Turtle just laughed and laughed. "Well, you did say you liked your breakfast in bed," she chuckled.

From that day forward Timothy was always up bright and early to have his breakfast at the table . . . just in case!

The Disagreement

Two cries of pain were having a terrible disagreement.

"Someone who hits their thumb with a hammer would cry YEEEOOOW! rather than OOOOOOAAAH!" said the YEEEOOOW!

"Rubbish!" said the OOOOOOAAAH! "Of course he would cry OOOOOOAAAH! rather than YEEEOOOW!"

"Prove it!" they both challenged the other.

And so the two cries of pain waited for someone to hit their thumb with a hammer. They waited . . . and they waited . . . and they waited. They had to wait a jolly long time because everyone was being extremely careful when they were hammering and no one was hitting their thumb.

But one day a man, who wasn't really concentrating on what he was doing, accidently struck his thumb with his hammer instead of the nail he was banging into the wall.

"This is it!" said the YEEEOOOW! excitedly. "He's going to shout YEEEOOOW!"

"Twit! snapped the OOOOOOAAAH! "It's going to be an OOOOOOAAH! for sure!"

"AAAAAAAAAAAAAAAAARRRRR-GGGHHH!" screamed the man, sucking his sore thumb.

"AAAAAAAAAAAAAAAAARRRRR-GGGHHH!?" said the YEEEOOOW! disappointedly.

"AAAAAAAAAAAAAAAAARRRRR-GGGHHH!?" said the OOOOOOAAAH! unhappily.

"AAAAAAAAAAAAAAAAARRRRR-GGGHHH!" said the AAAAAAAAAAAAAAAAARRRRR-GGGHHH! proudly.

The two cries of pain felt so ashamed at being beaten by an AAAAAAAAAAAAAAAAARRRRR-GGGHHH! they never argued again.

Dewdrop Goes Missing

Pickles the rabbit was not very happy. His mother had made him stay in the burrow to look after his little sister, Drewdrop, while she went shopping.

"This is boring," Pickles complained, watching Dewdrop playing on the burrow floor. "I want to go and play."

Pickles scampered out of the burrow pushing an acorn ball along the ground with his feet. "Dewdrop will be safe in the burrow while I have a quick game," he thought.

Pickles soon found an empty field where he could play a game of "chase-the-tail". He ran around and around in circles chasing his bushy white tail. He never caught it but it was great fun anyway.

Pickles frowned as he saw the sun up overhead. "Oh, dear. Is that the time? Mother will be home soon. I must get there before her."

Pickles bounded over the fields and was soon inside the burrow again. But what do you think?

"Great daisies! Dewdrop has gone!" Pickles looked frightened as he saw the empty burrow. "She must have wandered off!"

Poor Pickles! He searched in the fields and behind the trees, hunting high and low, but there was no sign of his sister anywhere.

"Mother will be so angry," thought Pickles miserably as he returned to the burrow. "Dewdrop could be hurt or maybe the humans have caught her to make stew!" Pickles trembled at this thought. He had lost a number of his friends the same way.

Just then Pickles heard a noise behind a bundle of straw in the corner of the burrow.

"M-Maybe it's a fox!" thought Pickles. "Perhaps he's eaten Dewdrop and now he's waiting to pounce on me!"

Plucking up courage Pickles shuffled slowly over to the straw.

"DEWDROP!" he cheered when he peered around the straw. It was his little sister, fast asleep. "She must have grown tired and snuggled down behind the straw to sleep," thought Pickles happily. "What a shock I've had, but I've learnt my lesson. I'll never leave Dewdrop alone again."

The Boy Who Wasn't

"I don't want to be a boy," said Kelly to his mother one morning. "I think I'll be a cow instead. Then I wouldn't have to go to school and do homework. MOOOO! MOOOO!" he went, practising his cow impersonation.

"Don't be silly, dear," said his mother. But Kelly spent all morning walking on all fours and going "MOOOO! MOOOO!"

"What's this?" Kelly asked his mother at lunch time as he looked at a plate of grass on the floor.

"It's your lunch," said his mother. "If you're a cow you have to eat grass all the time."

"Er, I'm not a cow anymore," said Kelly quickly. "I'm a dog. WOOOF! WOOOF!" He ran around the floor on all fours, playfully biting at his mother's ankles.

"Kelly, stop messing about," said his mother, but Kelly kept on biting and snapping at her heels.

His mother picked him up and carried him outside to the dog's kennel. "What are you doing?" he asked.

"If you're a dog, you can live here with Rover, our other dog," his mother said.

"Oooh! No! I'm not a dog!" said Kelly, standing up quickly. "I'm a . . . a bird! TWEET! TWEET! TWEET!"

"Act your age, Kelly," said his mother, but Kelly just flapped his arms like wings and sang his bird song. "TWEET! TWEET! TWEET!"

"That's a nice bird," said Kelly's father as he came home from work and saw Kelly acting like a bird. "We must get a cage to keep it in and then it can sing to us all day."

Kelly didn't like this idea at all! "I've decided," he said, standing up properly. "To be a boy, after all."

"Good," said his mother as she and his father set the table for tea! "Because this is your favourite. Strawberries and peaches."

"YUM!" said Kelly happily. "Being a boy's not so bad . . . in fact, I think I like it!"

The Vacuum Cleaner

"I am much better than you," sneered the vacuum cleaner to the old broom as they stood in the shop window waiting to be sold. "I can clean up twice as quickly as you can."

The old broom felt very sad for it knew the vacuum cleaner was right. "No one will want to buy me when they can buy him instead."

An old man came into the shop and pointed to the vacuum cleaner and the old broom in the window.

"He's come to buy me," said the vacuum cleaner proudly. "You'll be here until your head drops off and they throw you away, you will old broom!"

The old man walked over to the window . . . and took hold of the broom. "This is what I need," he said to the shop keeper. "It's just right for cleaning up the leaves in my garden."

The old broom was so happy. "Vacuum cleaners may be faster and more powerful but they can only clean indoors," it laughed, waving goodbye to the vacuum cleaner who was still stuck in the shop window, feeling very miserable.

Olivia Owl Moves Out

"Bother!" hooted Olivia Owl as she opened her eyes for the eighth time that morning. "I just can't get to sleep."

Olivia looked outside her treehouse and blinked as the bright sunlight hurt her eyes. "It's too quiet in the country," she said. "I'll go and live in the town instead."

It wasn't long before Olivia had found a nice hole in a tree in a nearby town. "This is much better," she said, closing her eyes. "I'll soon be asleep now."

D-R-R-R-R-I-I-I-I-I-I-N-N-N-G!

Olivia tumbled off her perch in fright at the terrifying ringing noise which made the tree shake and quiver.

"Ghooo-ooodness!" she hooted. "What is that awful noise?" She looked out of the tree and watched as two fire engines raced past, ringing their alarm bells loudly to warn drivers to clear the road. "I can't live here," Olivia cried. "I wouldn't get any sleep."

A little later Olivia came to rest in a dark loft of a large building.

"This looks better," she said. "Now I shall get some sleep."

Olivia had just fallen asleep when she was woken up by loud shouts and laughter. "Whoo-ooooh! What now?" she groaned.

She looked down from the loft. Below was a school playground full of happy, laughing children enjoying their morning break. "I can't sleep with all this noise!" Olivia hooted with annoyance, and flew away again.

It took awhile longer to find another empty tree to nest in but when she was settled Olivia bedded down to sleep. "My gooooooooodeness! I am tired now!" she thought.

B-R-R-R-R-R-R-R-R-R-R-R-R-R! A dreadful noise shook Olivia rudely awake. "Wh-What is i-it?" she gasped, clasping her wings over her ears to keep out the noise.

Workmen had begun to dig up the pavement beside the tree and were using a pneumatic drill to cut through the paving slabs. The noise was so bad Olivia thought her head would burst.

"I've h-had enough!" she cried as the tree vibrated from the noise of the drill. "I'm g-going h-home!"

Back in the country Olivia nestled down in her comfortable treehouse. There was a hushed silence, not even the birds were singing. "Ah! Peace at last!" Olivia sighed, and was soon fast asleep.

A Photograph for Mum (1)

Leroy the Lion wanted to have a photograph taken of himself to send to his mother in Africa.

"I must look my best," he thought, and so he had three baths, one after the other. Then he covered himself in a pleasant smelling deodorant, and then covered himself some more, and some more after that, until the pleasant smell deodorant began to smell very unpleasant indeed.

"My hair is a mess," Leroy frowned, looking at his reflection in the bathroom mirror. Leroy combed and combed and combed his mane until it sparkled in the sun. Finally he dressed in his freshly pressed trousers, his new cream shirt, a smart grey jacket and a top hat.

"This will be the best photograph my Mum will ever have," he thought happily. Unfortunately, Leroy had spent so long getting ready that the sun had gone down over the hills and all the photographers' shops had closed for the night.

"Oh, well," sighed Leroy disappointedly. "I'll just have to go first thing tomorrow instead."

An Apple for Colliwobble

"An apple a day keeps the doctor away," Mr Colliwobble was always saying.

One day he passed an apple seller on the street. "An apple a day keeps the doctor away," he said, and pulled a large apple from the bottom of the stack of apples on the street seller's barrow. This made the rest of the apples tumble off the barrow all over the pavement. As Mr Colliwobble hurried to pick them up again, his foot slipped on an apple and he toppled backwards, banging his head on the ground. The apple seller sent for a doctor and Mr Colliwobble was put to bed.

"An apple a day keeps the doctor away," said the doctor after he had bandaged Mr Colliwobble's head.

"Not always!" groaned Mr Colliwobble, rubbing his sore head.

The Quiet Day (2)

The next day Leroy woke up very early indeed, and even before the birds in the trees had begun their morning chorus. He quickly had another three baths, covered himself all over in more deodorant, combed his mane until it sparkled, and dressed in his freshly pressed trousers, new cream shirt, smart grey jacket and top hat.

Leroy set off down the street feeling very important. "I must say, I do look grand. When my Mum sees the photograph she will be ever so proud."

The street Leroy was walking down was very quiet. There were no cars, no buses and no people. Since this was a main road Leroy was very puzzled.

"Where is everyone?" he wondered. 'If they don't hurry they'll all be late for work."

Leroy reached the row of shops and when he came to the photographer's shop his face fell in disappointment. There on the door was a sign which read: CLOSED ON SUNDAYS.

"Oh, dear. That's why it's so quiet," Leroy groaned. "In my excitement to have my photograph taken I'd completely forgotten it's Sunday." There was nothing for it but to go back home.

"I'll have to have my photograph taken tomorrow," Leroy sighed, hoping that nothing else was going to go wrong.

The Photographer (3)

The following day Leroy woke up, not quite so early. He only had two baths, used a lot less deodorant, quickly combed his mane and dressed in his now rather scruffy trousers, creased cream shirt, grey jacket marked with dirt where a lorry had splashed him, and his top hat.

He slouched down the road very slowly towards the shops.

"Surely I'll have my photograph taken today," he sighed.

When he reached the photographer's shop and found it open he breathed a sigh of relief. "My Mum can have a photograph of me after all!" he beamed happily.

When the photographer saw a lion dressed in trousers, shirt, jacket and top hat enter his shop he squealed loudly. He leapt into the air in fright, and hung from the light fittings to stop himself from falling to the floor again.

"I've come to have my photograph taken," said Leroy, somewhat puzzled by the photographer's strange behaviour.

"G-Go a-away!" squealed the photographer, who was very scared. "I-I'm not t-taking a p-photograph of you. You'll m-most l-likely eat me a-afterwards! S-Shoo! B-Be o-off with y-you!"

Leroy felt very hurt by this. He was a very gentle, friendly lion who wouldn't say "BOOO!" to an insect. And anyway, he was a vegetarian. But he could see that the photographer had no intention of taking his photograph so Leroy bid him good day and went home feeling very miserable.

"Perhaps I'll try and have my photograph taken tomorrow," he thought sadly. To be honest he was going off the whole idea.

The Fourth Attempt (4)

Leroy is a Winner (5)

Leroy woke up late the next day. He only had one bath, gave himself a quick squirt of deodorant, pushed the comb once through his mane and pulled on his now extremely scruffy trousers, badly creased cream shirt, awfully dirty grey jacket and top hat.

He caught the bus to the shops. Eventually he reached another photographer's shop. With sinking heart he pushed open the door and went in.

When the photographer saw a lion dressed in trousers, shirt, jacket and top hat . . . he smiled pleasantly.

"Welcome, dear Sir," he said. "Would you like your photograph taken?"

"Y-Yes, please," said Leroy, somewhat taken aback by the photographer's warm manner. "It's for my mother. She lives in Africa, you know."

The photographer sat Leroy in front of a big camera. Leroy took off his top hat and held it in his lap. "At last, I'm going to have my photograph taken," he thought happily.

Just then a lady came in with her six children. When she saw a lion sitting in front of the camera, she let out a very loud "EEEEEEEEEEEEEEEEEEK!!" and she ran out of the shop with her six children.

"I'm sorry," said the photographer. "But I can't take your photograph. You're scaring all my customers away."

This upset Leroy very much, but he was a polite lion and just said, "thank you", and went back home.

Leroy didn't get up the next day. He didn't have a bath or comb his hair or cover himself in deodorant. He didn't put on his trousers (which were now in an awful state), his cream shirt (which now had a large hole in it), his grey jacket (which looked as though the dog had slept on it) or his top hat. He was feeling so sad he had decided to stay in bed ALL DAY.

"Sniff! Now my Mum will never get a photograph to see how grand I look," he cried uphappily and a warm wet tear ran down his face, along his nose, and dropped with a quiet "plop" to the bedcovers.

When the doorbell rang Leroy couldn't be bothered to answer it, but he got out of bed and went downstairs to see who was at the door.

"Hello," said a young man who was dressed in a smart business suit. "I'm from Bloggits and Bloggits, the clothes manufacturers. I saw you a few days ago when you were dressed in your freshly pressed trousers, new cream shirt, smart grey jacket and top hat."

Leroy just blinked and waited for the man to finish.

"Well, good Sir," continued the man from Bloggits and Bloggits. "You have won our Best Dressed Person of the Month Award. Congratulations! (Of course, you're not really a "person", but you dress so smartly who can tell?)"

Leroy blinked again and then he shook his

head in case his ears were blocked up and he wasn't hearing right.

"Your prize," said the man from Bloggits and Bloggits. "Is a set of photographs of your good self taken by our top photographer . . ." He paused a moment to let the excitement build up. "And. . . ." he went on, slowly. "A six week holiday in Africa!"

"Africa?" spluttered Leroy in disbelief. "That's where my Mum lives. I can deliver my photographs to her myself!" And that's just what he did!

The Matches

Rashmi found a box of matches on the living room table.

"Perhaps I can strike one and see what happens," thought Rashmi, feeling both excited and a little scared for she knew she shouldn't really.

Rashmi struck the match on the side of the box. The match flared up into a bright orange flame.

"Yow! It burnt me!" cried Rashmi, dropping the match quickly. The lighted match fell onto the fur rug. Moments later the rug was alight with flames and Rashmi was very scared. "What have I done?" she cried. "The house will burn down and I will be trapped inside!"

Luckily her mother came into the room. When she saw the flames on the carpet she emptied a flower vase of water over them to put them out.

"You must never play with matches," Rashmi's mother scolded her. "They can be very dangerous."

"I know that now," said Rashmi who was crying because she was still very frightened and her finger throbbed where the match had burnt it.

If you ever see a box of matches lying around I hope you will be sensible and leave them alone and then tell a grown up where you've seen them.

Hotty Bottle

There was once a hot water bottle whose name was Hotty. Now the hot water bottle thought "Hotty" was a stupid name but since everyone called her that she didn't have much choice in the matter.

"Fill Hotty up, please," Ann asked her mum. "My bed's cold."

"Huh! I'm only wanted when the weather's cold," sulked Hotty. "When its warm I'm thrown in a dark cupboard and forgotten about."

One day Hotty decided she didn't want to be filled up with boiling hot water each night and so when Ann's mum began to pour the hot water down her spout Hotty began to leak all over the floor.

"Hotty's leaking!" cried Ann sadly.

"Then we'll have to throw her out," said her mum. "We can't have a leaking hot water bottle in your bed."

Thrown out? Hotty didn't like this idea AT ALL! "This is another fine mess I've got myself into," she grumbled.

But then Mum had an idea. She filled the now empty Hotty with plastic beans and then made a furry coat which she wrapped around the hot water bottle.

"There," said Mum when she had finished. "Now you can use Hotty as a bean bag to sit on."

"We can't call her Hotty bottle anymore," said Ann. "We'll have to call her Bella Bean Bag instead."

Hotty, sorry, Bella, was very pleased with her new name and didn't mind Ann sitting on her at all.

The Hot Cakes

Fillmytummy the troll had been very naughty. Every day he would pass by Mrs Doughnut's cake shop and when she was busy serving a customer he would steal a plate of cakes from the shop window and eat them all up.

Now Mrs Doughnut's friend, Mr Spice from the corner shop, saw this and he told Mrs Doughnut how they could stop Fillmytummy from stealing her cakes ever again.

The next day as usual there was an enormous plate of cakes in the shop window. And as usual, when Mrs Doughnut was busy with a customer Fillmytummy sneaked into the shop and stole the cakes. Once outside he quickly ate them, but this time there was a surprise in store for the greedy troll.

"OOOO! AAAAAH! My mouth's on fire!" Fillmytummy squealed as his tongue burned hotly. He ran off to find a barrel of water to drink to cool him down again.

Mr Spice laughed as he watched Fillmytummy race off. "Those cakes were a special recipe filled with very hot curry powder. Fillmytummy is going to think twice before stealing Mrs Doughnut's cakes again!"

The Numbers Game

The numbers 6 and 9 were bored with being the numbers they were.

"I'd like to be the number 9," said the number 6.

"And I'd rather be the number 6," said the number 9.

So the number 6 stood on its tail and became the number 9, while the number 9 stood on its head and became the number 6. Now both the numbers were happy.

The Accident

Gary came in from school to find his father in the living room. But he looked different somehow. For a start he was upsidedown on his head with his eyes closed and his legs twisted in a knot above him.

"Daddy's had an accident!" Gary cried, running to find his Mum who was busy fixing the car. "He must have fallen over and now he can't stand up again!"

Gary's Mum came running indoors and when she saw her husband upsidedown she burst out laughing.

"Silly! Your Dad's doing yoga. It's a form of exercise to help keep him fit."

Gary felt foolish at making such a fuss but he soon forgot this when he joined his Mum and Dad and they all spent an enjoyable hour doing Yoga together.

Mr Moneybags

"I must lose some weight," sighed Mr Moneybags, weighing himself on the weighing machine in the High Street.

"I can help you lose weight," said a tramp who was standing beside the weighing machine. "You need to empty out your pockets. Then you'll weigh less."

Mr Moneybags thought this was a good idea. He started by emptying twelve wallets full of money from one coat pocket, ten wallets from the other coat pocket and another six wallets from his trouser pocket. He was, after all, a very rich man indeed.

"Hold these for me while I weigh myself again," said Mr Moneybags, handing the wallets to the tramp.

Mr Moneybags stepped back onto the weighing machine and sure enough he weighed much less then the first time he had weighed himself.

"It works!" he cheered, looking around to thank the tramp. But the tramp had already disappeared . . . with all of Mr Moneybags' wallets!

"This will teach me to be vain," sighed Mr Moneybags as he went in search of a policeman. "I lost some weight . . . and all my money too!"

Patch gets it Wrong

Patch, the one eyed, black patch teddy bear, had been taken into the country with Andrew and his parents.

Patch soon became bored with looking at flowers and slimy things in ponds and he wandered off from the others. In a field he saw a large brown animal with two horns on its head.

"Hello, Mrs Cow," said Patch, running into the field. "Mind if I ride on you?"

By pulling on the cow's tail Patch managed to climb onto its back. "Gee up!" Patch cried, but the cow shook its head and stayed where it was.

"Huh! You're not much fun!" grumbled Patch as he slid off the cow's back again. As he did so the cow, which was really a bull, turned quickly and tossed Patch into the air with its horns.

"YEEEEEEOOOOOOW!" squealed Patch as he sailed across the field to land with a BUMP next to Andrew's parents car.

"There you are, Patch," shouted Andrew, running up to him. "I've been looking all over for you. Where have you been?"

"You wouldn't believe me if I told you!" Patch thought with a little groan.

Mr Higglebottom's Path

Mr Higglebottom had spent all morning working hard cementing his new garden path.

"I have done well," he said proudly when he had finished.

"WOOF!" barked Scrappy, Mr Higglebottom's dog, as he chased the ENORMOUS fat black cat around the garden.

SPLISH! SPLASH! SPLOSH! went the ENORMOUS fat black cat's feet as he ran through the wet cement.

SPLISH! SPLASH! SPLOSH! went Scrappy's feet as he chased after him.

"MY NEW PATH!" roared Mr Higglebottom, looking at all the footprints in the cement. Scrappy knew he had done something wrong so he went and hid until Mr Higglebottom had calmed down.

With a grumble and a sigh Mr Higglebottom set to work re-cementing his path. It took a long time but finally he was finished. He stood up, feeling very pleased with is effort.

"WOOOF!" yapped Scrappy. He ran towards Mr Higglebottom and leapt up at him for a cuddle. Scrappy jumped so fast he knocked Mr Higglebottom off his feet and SQUEELLCH! the poor man fell flat on his back in the wet cement.

"SCRAPPY!" bellowed Mr Higglebottom angrily, but Scrappy had already run off again.

Mr Higglebottom had to change into a new set of clothes before starting work a third time cementing his path. When he had finished he looked all around for Scrappy but the dog was nowhere to be seen.

Just then Mr Higglebottom saw his wife coming along the road carrying a heavy bag of shopping.

"Let me help you, dear," called Mr Higglebottom and he ran along the garden path towards the gate, quite forgetting about the wet cement.

'SPLOT! SPLUDGE! SPLIDGE! went his feet in the cement.

"You are silly," scolded Mrs Higglebottom when she saw her husband's ruined path and his feet covered in cement. "You wouldn't catch Scrappy running through wet cement!"

Mr Higglebottom was too embarrassed to tell his wife how wrong she was!

The Forgotten Train

Ethelreda the old steam train was feeling blue. "No one rides on me any more," she sighed, tooting sadly on her whistle. "They all ride on the smart new electric train instead."

Ethelreda's driver Rob, cleaned and polished Ethelreda each day and made sure she was in working order. One day he came to Ethelreda looking very worried.

"The Mayor of Piffletown boarded the smart new electric train to go to a meeting with the Mayor of Nodtown, but the train hasn't arrived yet. It left ages ago . . . where can it be?"

Ethelreda tooted loudly and Rob laughed as he realised what Ethelreda was trying to say. "You want to go and look for the train, eh? Come on then!" Rob boarded Ethelreda, stoked her up with enough fuel for the journey, slipped off the brake and off they went.

CHUG-A-CHUG! CHUG-A-CHUG! CHUG-A-CHUG! Ethelreda sang as she rolled merrily along the rails. It wasn't long before she reached a sharp bend on the track and there was the smart new electric train, lying on its side, off the rails. "I was going too fast when I reached the sharp bend and I came off the rails," the smart new electric train told Ethelreda sadly.

"More haste, less speed," Ethelreda tooted wisely.

The Mayor of Piffletown was very cross. "I'm going to be late for my very important meeting with the Mayor of Nodtown now," he shouted.

"Not at all," laughed Rob. "Hop aboard Ethelreda. She'll take you instead."

The Mayor didn't like the idea of riding in an old-fashioned steam train but he didn't have any choice.

CHUG-A-CHUG! CHUG-A-CHUG! CHUG-A-CHUG! went Ethelreda as she took off again with the Mayor on board.

An hour later Ethelreda pulled into Nodtown Station. "Well done, Ethelreda," said the Mayor. You got me here in time, and what a lovely journey. I had time to enjoy the scenery too."

"I may be slower than the smart new electric train but I get there in the end," Ethelreda tooted proudly.

The Mayor was so pleased with Ethelreda he made her his Official Service train and she took him on trips around the country all year long.

Stubbleback the Dinosaur

Stubbleback was a dinosaur who lived millions and millions of years ago, long before people appeared in the world.

Stubbleback was the type of dinosaur known as Stegosaurus. He looked rather strange, to be honest. He had a small, narrow head and the back of his large body was topped by two rows of large, bony plates. Stubbleback wasn't very bright, and was always getting himself into trouble.

One day when Stubbleback was out walking, or, to be more precise, lumbering, for that is what he did, he came across an enormous boulder blocking his path.

"Dear me, what a nuisance," he grumbled crossly. "It's almost time for supper. If I go back to the other path I've just passed it will take twice as long to reach home."

Stubbleback was a very strong dinosaur and so he pushed at the boulder to see if he could move it, but the boulder didn't move even a little bit. Then Stubbleback tried climbing over the boulder but he was not meant for such strenuous tasks and gave up the effort.

"Drat!" he sighed with a huff and a puff. "I'll have to go back along the other path, after all."

Tina the Pterodactyl flew overhead. She called out to Stubbleback when she saw what the problem was. "Silly! All you have to do is walk AROUND the boulder. There's more than enough room for you to pass."

Stubbleback looked and sure enough there was. "I do feel daft!" he said, giving an embarrassed grin, and then he lumbered off home for his supper.

Dinny the Duck

"I'm not going into the lake," said Dinny nervously. "I can't swim!"

"Of course you can," said his mother. "All ducks can swim."

But Dinny refused to go near the water so his mother left him on the bank while she took her other children for a trip around the lake.

Dinny was quite happy sitting on the bank until he spotted the nasty ENORMOUS fat black cat creeping up on him.

"QUACK! QUACK! He wants me for his dinner!" squawked Dinny in fright and he waddled off as fast as he could go. Now ducks are not very good at running on land and the ENORMOUS fat black cat soon caught up with him.

"MEE-HEE!-HEE!-OOOW! You can't escape me!" cackled the ENORMOUS fat black cat and pounced at Dinny who leapt squawking into the lake and paddled away as fast as his flippers could take him.

"I can swim! I can swim!" he cried happily as he met his mother.

"Of course you can, dear," said his mother. "You just needed encouragement, that's all."

Treacle Tart Cleans Up

Treacle Tart the Witch was casting a spell to clean her house.

"INKY, PINKY, POO, HOUSE BECOME CLEAN, DO!" she chanted. "She wasn't very clever at making up rhymes.

KA-BOOM!

The Runaway Hat

Mrs Smith had a terrible memory. She knew she had to go somewhere important this Saturday but for the life of her she could not remember where it was.

"I'll go for a walk and blow the cobwebs out of my head," she decided. "That will help me to remember."

It was a very windy day and as Mrs Smith stepped outside her dainty cottage her best hat was blown off her head by a powerful gust of wind.

"Oh, my! I must get it back!" she cried and raced after it. Mrs Smith chased her hat down the road, past the row of shops, into the park and out the other end. Then the wind died down and she was able to catch her hat before it blew away again.

"Hello, Mrs Smith," said Mrs Turner, who was standing outside her house. "I'm glad you made it. I thought you might have forgotten you were having tea with me today."

"So that's where I was supposed to go," chuckled Mrs Smith as she followed Mrs Turner into the house. "If it wasn't for the wind blowing my hat here I might never have remembered at all!"

A large black cloud appeared over Treacle Tart's head and suddenly a heavy shower of rain began to fall indoors.

"Well, I suppose the rain will clean my house," Treacle Tart sighed as she sheltered under her umbrella. "Now all I have to do is think up a spell to dry everything out again!"

Benjamin's New Wallpaper

"Benjamin, you have far too many comics," said his mother after tripping over another pile that had been left on the floor. "I'm going to have to throw them out."

Benjamin was upset to hear this. He liked reading comics. He could escape into a magical world of cowboys, and dinosaurs, and little green spacemen whenever he was bored. And comics helped him with his reading too. Only last week he had received top marks from his teacher in the reading test.

Benjamin went to find his father who was redecorating Benjamin's bedroom. His father was frowning when Benjamin arrived. "I

can't decide what sort of wallpaper to put on your walls," his father said.

"I know!" said Benjamin quickly and he told his father exactly what he wanted.

When Benjamin's father had finished his mother came to see the new wallpaper. She burst out laughing when she saw all Benjamin's comics pasted to the wall.

"Now my comics won't make the house messy and I can read them whenever I want to," Benjamin chuckled happily.

The Smoke Signals

Big Chief Itchy Nose was sitting outside his wigwam when he saw clouds of black smoke rising up from beyond the nearby hills. This worried him very much for the Pongytoe tribe lived beyond the hills and they were the Chief's sworn enemies!

"Uggh! Pongytoe tribe must be on warpath!" grunted Itchy Nose as he watched the smoke become thicker and thicker. All Red Indians sent messages by smoke signals to one another, and this is what Big Chief Itchy Nose thought he was reading now.

The smoke signals became even blacker and Itchy Nose became more and more worried.

"Uggh! Perhaps Pongytoe tribe want to capture Big Chief Itchy Nose!" he thought. He had seen enough. Leaping up he raced away to look for a safe place to hide.

Beyond the hills Big Chief Dirty Ears frowned crossly at his chef who handed him a plate of blackened food from which came the thick black clouds of smoke.

"Uggh! Chef burnt-um dinner again!"

The Lost Balls (1)

"May we have our ball back, please?" Pam asked Mr Grumpy one afternoon after her brother George had accidently kicked it over the old man's fence.

"No, you can't!" snapped Mr Grumpy angrily. "I keep all balls that come over my garden. It teaches kids not to do it again."

"Ooh! What a rude, nasty man!" said George as the two children went sadly home.

The children's mother was sorting out a basket of costumes for a play she was producing at the local theatre. There were all sorts of different costumes. Pretty coloured dresses, a large old mackintosh, frilly ballgowns, and trousers, shoes, shirts and hats of all sizes and descriptions.

As Pam searched through the basket she smiled mischievously as an idea came to her. "May George and I borrow some of these costumes?" she asked her mother. "We'll take care of them."

"What are you up to?" George asked his sister after their mother had agreed.

"Mr Grumpy needs to be taught a lesson," said Pam. "And we're the ones to do it."

George went to bed wondering what Pam had in store for Mr Grumpy tomorrow.

The Inspector (2)

The next day Mr Grumpy answered a loud knocking on his door. On the doorstep was a very tall, strange looking man with a moustache, glasses and a bowler hat. He wore a long coat and on the lapel of the coat was a badge which read: INSPECTOR.

"I am the Inspector of Lost Balls," said the Inspector in a rather gruff voice. "I believe you may be hiding a lost ball in your house, Mr Grumpy."

Mr Grumpy went weak at the knees at this. "Gulp!" he swallowed hard. "W-Well, I m-might have one, or perhaps two, in my s-shed," he whispered, feeling very scared.

"Tut! It is a serious offence to be in possession of lost balls." said the Inspector of Lost Balls in a very official voice. "We will have to confiscate them, I'm afraid."

Mr Grumpy hurried to fetch the balls. In fact he had over twenty balls of different sizes and colours.

The Inspector of Lost Balls put the balls into a large sack and then said to Mr Grumpy, "If you are caught taking children's balls again we may have to take further action!"

"Oh, I won't! I promise!" said Mr Grumpy, who didn't want to see another ball in his life. "Any balls that come over my fence I'll throw back straight away."

The Inspector of Lost Balls left Mr Grumpy trembling at the knees and walked back to Pam and George's house. Of course, that is who the the Inspector really was. The children had dressed up in costumes from their mother's costume basket and to make their disguise look real George had sat on Pam's shoulders. This had made the Inspector seem very tall indeed.

"I don't think we'll have any more trouble with Mr Grumpy," chuckled George, pulling of his false moustache.

"And we'll share all these balls with our friends," said Pam.

The Genie

There was once a wicked, cruel King and all his people despised him. One day the people found an old green bottle washed up on the beach. "It's mine!" cried the King, and snatched it away from them before they could open it.

The King pulled the cork from the spout of the bottle and out floated a blue-skinned Genie wearing a large turban on his head.

"I will grant you one wish," said the Genie.

"Then I demand you make me stronger and more powerful than ever!" shouted the King.

There was a flash of smoke and when it cleared there stood before the people a statue of the King made of pure marble.

"Where is the King?" they asked the Genie.

"There is your King," said the Genie, pointing to the statue. "He is now much stronger and more powerful than when he was mere flesh and blood." With that the Genie disappeared back inside his bottle.

The people were overjoyed to see the end of the King and they danced and sang late into the night. As for the King, he was now loved for the first time ever by the birds who flew into the royal garden and perched on his marble head.

The Pretty Toadstool

"I'm much prettier than you," the toadstool said to the mushroom as they stood together in a wood. "I'm bright red with lovely yellow spots while you're just a boring plain white."

"That's true," agreed the mushroom who was used to the toadstool's boasting. "You're very pretty indeed."

A woman came into the wood looking for fresh food to eat. She saw the toadstool and the mushroom and said. "What a pretty coloured toadstool. What a pity toadstools are poisonous." And she stamped on the toadstool with her shoe, squashing it flat. "My children play in the wood and I don't want them tasting the toadstool by mistake." Then she picked the mushroom and took it home for her tea.

"The toadstool may be prettier but I'm tastier," laughed the mushroom.

Max's Arm

Adam enjoyed playing "pretend fighting" with his teddy bear, Max. He would punch Max, he would throw Max, he would jump up and down on Max, and then he would whirl Max around the room by his furry ear.

"If you don't care for Max he won't last long," Adam's mother told him but Adam didn't listen and kept on fighting the poor bear.

One day while Adam was being extra rough and was throwing Max about the room he heard a loud R-I-I-I-I-I-P! and Max's arm came off. This upset Adam very much because he loved Max really, he was just a boisterous little boy.

"I don't think I can mend him," said Adam's mother after she had looked at Max. "I'm afraid we'll have to throw him out." This upset Adam even more and he went to bed feeling very miserable without Max.

That night while Adam was asleep Tackingstitch the pixie visited his house. When she saw Max she was appalled at the state he was in. Pulling out her needle and thread she set to work stitching Max's arm back on.

When Adam awoke and found Max's arm repaired he was overjoyed and never had "pretend fights" with him again. Well, perhaps only now and again.

A Headache for Geoff

Geoff the Giraffe had a very long neck and so he was always banging his head when he entered his friends' houses.

"Buttercups!" he snorted crossly after he had bumped his head on the top of Horace Hedgehog's front door. "I have such a long neck I keep forgetting to duck. I must have lots of bruises on my head by now."

Horace wanted to help his friend. "I can't make my house any bigger. Perhaps we could saw a piece out of your neck to shorten it?"

Geoff didn't think this was a good idea at all! "I like my long neck," he said. "It gives me an air of importance." Horace had to agree with this. Geoff was rather arrogant and he was always looking down on his friend, but Horace didn't really mind. "I have a better idea," Horace said. He painted "MIND YOUR HEAD!" on a piece of wood and hung it over his door.

"How clever," said Geoff. "Now I'll always remember to duck low."

But the idea didn't work out as Horace had hoped. True, Geoff ducked as the sign said, but because the sign was hanging over the door he kept bumping his head on the sign instead.

"Oh, well," sighed Geoff after Horace had taken the sign down again. "I'll just have to remember to duck low, after all. Or else I shall have a terrible headache."

The Disguise

Wiggles the Worm met his friend Cuthbert Caterpiller in the garden.

"I'm fed up with being divebombed by the birds every time I go out," Wiggles grumbled.

"I don't have any trouble with most birds," said Cuthbert. "The bright colours on my back tell them I'm poisonous to eat."

Wiggles returned home and painted bright red stripes on his back. Then he went out in the garden. The birds swooped down when they saw him but then they noticed the red stripes and flew off again.

"You're a funny looking caterpillar," said Cuthbert when the two friends met under a shady leaf. "But if it stops you from being eaten I don't mind what you look like."

The Pen and the Sword

"The pen is mightier than the sword," said the King to his warrior.

"Rubbish!" cried the warrior. "My sword can chop down a forest of trees, kill an army of men, smash the hardest rock to pieces. Can your pen do that?"

"No," admitted the King. "My pen cannot do any of that."

"Then how do you claim it is mightier than my sword?" demanded the warrior.

"My pen is mightier because with a flourish of my hand I can sign a declaration proclaiming all swords to be banished from my kingdom. How mighty is your sword then, O Warrior?"

The warrior had to admit the King was right. In the proper hands the pen will always be mightier than the sword.

The Snowman

A kind fairy had brought a snowman to life but the snowman was far from happy.

"I'm melting under this hot sun," he complained.

So the kind fairy waved her wand and the snowman appeared in the Antarctic where it is very cold with lots of ice and snow.

"Now you won't melt," said the kind fairy, but the snowman was still far from happy.

"I have no friends to play with," he grumbled.

The fairy told the snowman to make lots more snowmen. This he did. When he had finished she waved her wand and all the

snowmen came to life.

"Now you have lots of friends," said the fairy. Then she disappeared to find someone else to help.

Jogging is Fun

Belinda enjoyed jogging with her mother. "Jogging is fun and it keeps you fit and healthy," her mother told her.

But Belinda's friends laughed when they saw her out running through the park.

"That's too much like hard work," they shouted. "You are silly, Belinda."

Belinda ignored them as best she could but she didn't like to be laughed at. "Perhaps I won't jog any more," she thought.

Old Mrs French was standing beside her gate looking very worried. She held a letter in her hand.

"I wanted to post this important letter to my sister but the post van collects the mail out of the post box soon and I'll never get there in time."

"Leave it to me," said Belinda taking the letter from Mrs French.

Belinda jogged down the road towards the post box, pretending not to hear the rude remarks from her friends as she passed them.

Belinda reached the post box just as the post van drove up. She handed the letter to the postman and then jogged back to Mrs French to let her know that her letter was safely on its way.

Mrs French was very grateful and she paid Belinda for her trouble. All Belinda's friends were watching.

The next day Belinda was surprised to see all her friends wearing track suits and out in the park jogging. "If we keep fit perhaps we will get paid for helping someone," they told her.

Belinda had to laugh. "Jogging is fun but it's even nicer when you do it with friends," she thought.

The Flower Garden

King Muddletop decided to turn the royal palace land into a flower garden. "I'll have pretty flowers covering everywhere," he told his wife.

King Muddletop worked very hard, digging and weeding and sowing the seeds. He watered the garden every day and looked forward to the time when the flowers would be out in bloom.

"Quickly, dear," called his wife one morning. "Come and see your garden.

The King hurried to the garden. "My flowers must have bloomed," he thought. "I can't wait to see how wonderful they look."

When the King reached the garden he looked at it in surprise. Then he began to laugh. For the garden was filled, not with flowers, but vegetables of all kinds. There were cabbages and carrots, tomatoes and beetroot and onions. Large potatoes, small potatoes, parsnips and brussel sprouts. There were cucumbers and marrows and chives and aubergines. But there was not a single flower to be seen.

The King laughed again when he realised what he had done. "I must have planted vegetable seeds instead of flower seeds!"

The garden looked very strange indeed but the King didn't mind because vegetables were his favourite food. "I can always grow flowers next year," he said as he tucked into a delicious bowl of vegetable soup.

"That's if you don't muddle things up again," laughed the Queen.

Doozleflumph at School

Doozleflumph the Glumf was feeling very miserable. His friend Timothy had gone to school leaving him alone with nothing to do.

"GLUMF!" he cried sadly, which was his way of saying, "I'm bored!" Then he had an idea. He knew where Timothy's school was. He had passed there one day when Timothy's father took him to the barber's to get his very long bright green fur cut. But that's another story.

Doozleflumph leapt up quickly from where he was sitting. Well, not very quickly because Glumfs are not known for their agility. Anyway, he lumbered down the road towards Timothy's school.

Timothy's teacher almost had a fit when she saw Doozleflumph entering the school playground. She didn't know Doozleflumph belonged to Timothy and she didn't want her class disrupted by this strange creature. She ran out into the playground waving her arms and shouting, "SHOO! GO AWAY! BE OFF WITH YOU!"

Now Doozleflumph, being a playful sort of Glumf, thought the teacher had come out to play with him. He took hold of Miss Behave's hands and began to dance in a circle, swinging her high in the air as he went.

"DOOZLEFLUMPH! DOOZLEFLUMPH! GLUMF! GLUMF! DOOZLEFLUMPH!" he sang loudly, which was his way of singing, "Ring-a-Ring-a-Roses". When it came to the part of the verse where you sing "We All Fall Down!" Doozleflumph sat down on the playground, letting go of Miss Behave who flew through the air to land with a KER-SPLASH! in the school swimming pool.

"Doozleflumph? What have you done?" Timothy cried, running out of his classroom. "You'll be in terrible trouble now!"

Poor Doozleflumph felt very sad. He knew Timothy was angry with him but he had only wanted to have some fun.

The Headmaster came out of his office and when he saw the state Miss Behave was in, he ordered her home and to have the rest of the week off.

"And since your teacher won't be here," he said to all the children in Timothy's class. "You will have to have the week off school too!"

"YIPPEE!" cheered the children as they ran out of the school. "Three cheers for Doozleflumph the Glumf!"

The children played with Doozleflumph all week long. He was the happiest Glumf in the world.

The Nightingale

One day a rich Princess heard a nightingale singing its beautiful song outside her window.

The Princess ordered her courtiers to capture the nightingale and bring it to her. This they did and the Princess locked the bird in a small wire cage.

"Sing to me," the Princess order the nightingale, but the nightingale remained silent.

Every day the Princess came to the cage and ordered the bird to sing but the nightingale remained as silent as the day it was brought to the palace.

The Princess soon became fed up with this. "Release the bird," she told her courtiers. "I don't think it can sing at all."

The courtiers opened the cage door and the nightingale flew out of the palace window. Once outside it began to sing and sing and sing.

The Princess nodded wisely as she understood. "Birds cannot live in cages when they have wings to fly. The nightingale can only sing when she has her freedom." The Princess ordered that from that day forth no one was allowed to keep a bird in a cage. The nightingale was so pleased when she heard this, she sang outside the palace every morning and so did all her friends.

The Picture

I chalked a picture
On the pavement
On a sunny day,
Black clouds appeared,
The sun went in
And the rain washed my picture away.

Shopping Day

"Would you like to come shopping with me?" Leroy Lion asked his neighbour, Bouncer the Kangeroo.

"Delighted," said Bouncer, who always enjoyed hopping up and down the supermarket aisles looking for bargains.

The two friends quickly did their shopping, but as Leroy was carrying home his goods a terrible calamity happened. The bottom of his shopping bag gave way and all the tins and packets fell into the road.

"Oh, Moggletops!" he roared loudly. "How will I carry my shopping home without a bag?"

"Don't worry," smiled Bouncer. "I'll help you."

Bouncer picked up all Leroy's shopping and put it inside his big Kangeroo pouch." "It's lucky I came with you!" he chuckled as he bounced along the street beside his friend.

"Yes," laughed Leroy. "You're better than a shopping bag any day!"

Blackberry Pie

"Hmmm! pie! My favourite!" Squirrel slurped rudely as he smelt a delicious aroma drifting out of Badger's set.

"Cooee! Badger! I'm here!" Squirrel called as he entered Badger's home.

"So I see," said Badger. "Here for what, may I ask?"

"Why, to share your delicious blackberry pie, of course," Squirrel said. "Old friend," he added quickly, because it seemed a polite thing to do.

Badger shook his head. "Whenever I invite you to supper I end up doing all the washing up while you go home, full and contented, to sleep off your feed."

"Please, Badger," Squirrel pleaded. His tummy was making a rumbling, grumbling noise and he knew this meant it was hungry. "I'll do all the washing up afterwards, I promise."

"I doubt that," said Badger. "But I have an idea. You wash all the dishes I've dirtied today and then you can have some of my delicious blackberry pie."

"All of them?" groaned Squirrel, looking at pile upon pile of dirty dishes in Badger's sink.

"All of them," said Badger firmly.

With a sigh and a mumble Squirrel set to work. He washed the plates and the spoons. He washed Badger's best jug, his saucers, cups, knives and forks. He washed the pie tin and then four more plates he found under another pile of dishes. Squirrel washed and washed until his arms felt as if they were about to drop off.

"Finished," he said at long last. "Now can I have some of your delicious blackberry pie?"

"You may," said Badger. "And I'm very grateful to you for washing all my dishes. I hope you've learnt a lesson too. You can never have something for nothing."

Badger cut Squirrel a giant piece of his delicious pie, but when he turned to give Squirrel the plate, he found his friend curled up beside the fireplace, fast asleep.

"Ho! Ho! Squirrel worked so hard he's worn himself out," Badger chuckled kindly. "Never mind. I'll keep his pie for when he wakes up."

The Grandfather Clock (1)

DING! DONG! DING! DONG! went the grandfather clock as it stood in the hallway chiming out the hour. "What a lovely sound I make," it thought proudly. "So beautiful and loud."

The grandfather clock looked forward to each hour so that it could chime again, but one day, when the hands of the clock reached twelve . . . nothing happened. Not a sound was heard.

"That's strange," thought the grandfather clock. "Where are my beautiful chimes? If I cannot ring out the hours how will people know what time it is?"

It was no use getting upset. The grandfather clock had to wait a whole sixty minutes before the hands on the clock face reached one o'clock.

"This time I'll ring for sure," thought the grandfather clock. It waited . . . and waited . . . and waited . . . but nothing happened.

"Oh, no!" cried the grandfather clock unhappily. "I've lost my beautiful chimes!"

The Clock Mender (2)

The next day the owner of the grandfather clock realised that he had not heard its beautiful chimes all that morning.

"This is no good," said the man, and lifting up the grandfather clock, carried it to his car.

"He must be going to throw me on the rubbish dump," thought the grandfather clock sadly. "After all my years of faithful service, too."

The man drove his car along the road and stopped outside a shop where the window was full of clocks of all different shapes and sizes.

"He must be going to sell me," the grandfather clock groaned. "After all the years of chiming out the hours, too."

Inside the shop the owner told the lady behind the counter how the grandfather clock no longer chimed.

"I'll soon fix that," said the lady, who was a clock-mender. She squirted the works of the grandfather clock with some oil. "Ooooh! That tickles!" it giggled.

Back home again the grandfather clock waited patiently for its hands to reach five o'clock.

DING! DONG! DING! DONG! echoed the grandfather clock's beautiful chimes around the house. This made it feel very happy.

"From now on I'll oil you once a week," said the owner. "Then you'll never stop chiming again!"

The Smiling Lion

Timothy Mouse didn't like going to school, so each day, after breakfast, he would say goodbye to his mother and father and pretend to walk to school like all the other children. But once out of sight of his house he would throw his satchel of school books into a bush and run off to play in the woods.

One day Timothy was playing in the woods when he met a lion, who was sitting in a clearing, smiling.

"Mr Lion, why are you smiling?" Timothy asked politely.

"I am the school truant officer," smiled the lion, showing its gleaming white, razor sharp fangs. "And it's my job to eat all little boys and girls who don't go to school when they should."

When Timothy heard this he became very frightened.

"You're not skipping lessons, are you?" The lion smiled at Timothy and licked its lips hungrily.

"N-No," squeaked Timothy, now very afraid. "A-Actually, I-I'm just on my way to s-school now, Mr Lion." And with that he collected his satchel and hurried as fast as he could to the safety of the school.

Timothy's father came out of hiding when Timothy had gone. He had known about Timothy missing school all the time.

"Thank you, Mr Lion. I don't think Timothy will stay away from school after today. Our plan worked a treat."

Of course, the smiling lion wasn't really a school truant officer, but one of Mr Mouse's friends. Poor Timothy. If only he knew!

Bedtime Lullaby

"Please sing me a lullaby," Karen asked her mother as she sat up in bed. "I don't feel at all sleepy."

So Karen's mother sang Karen a beautiful soft lullaby.

"That was nice," said Karen, who was still wide awake. "Please sing me another."

So Karen's mother sang Karen another lullaby. And another. And another!

Downstairs Karen's father was puzzled why his wife had not come down again to get his tea ready. He sneaked quietly upstairs and looked inside Karen's bedroom. And what do you think? There was Karen's mother, fast asleep on Karen's bed!

"Sssssssh!" Karen hushed her father. "Mummy sang me so many lullabys they sent her to sleep."

I Wish

I wish I was a squirrel
Scampering through the trees,
I wish I was a grizzly bear
Taking honey from the bees.
I wish I was a great big dog
Barking clear and loud,
I wish I was an eagle
Soaring high up with the clouds.
I wish I was a huge grey elephant
Going trumpety-trumpety trump,
I wish I was a kangeroo
Jumping high, then landing with a bump.
I wish I was a little kitten
Crying for its tea,
I wish I was a lot of things
But really, I'm glad I'm me!

Rabbit's Long Ears

"Rabbits did not always have long ears," Grandpa Rabbit told little Billy one day. "They were mighty short ears, in fact. But one day, old Whiskers Rabbit was out hopping in the fields looking for carrots to munch when he was bagged by a human! Well, old Whiskers, he thought his time had come. He didn't know how he could escape. He wriggled and wraggled inside the bag and then he had an idea. Using his big sharp teeth he gnawed a hole in the bag and slipped free."

"But how does that explain how rabbits have big ears?" Billy asked impatiently.

"Hold on, boy," said Grandpa. "I'm just coming to that. As Whiskers slipped out of the bag he was spotted by the human who grabbed him by his short ears. But Whiskers' rabbit friends saw this and caught hold of Whiskers' legs. The more the human pulled him one way to keep him, the more the rabbits pulled him the other way to save him. Then the human lost his footing in the soft ground and fell, letting go of Whiskers as he did so. Whiskers bounded away with his friends, but when they reached home he found that where the human had pulled on his ears so much they had stretched and stretched. And so from Whiskers' generation onwards all rabbits were born with long ears!"

Billy looked up at his Grandpa's mischievous face. He wasn't sure the tale was the whole truth, but it was fun to listen to anyway.

The Wishing Well

There was once a magical wishing well. It would grant a wish to anyone who threw a gold coin into its water. However, because it was rather a mischievous well its wishes never turned out the way people expected.

"I wish I was taller," said a young girl, throwing a gold penny into the well.

FIIIIZZZIIIIP!

The next moment a ladder stood next to the puzzled girl. "This won't make me taller!" shouted the girl into the wishing well.

"Yes, it will," replied the wishing well, giving a chuckle. "Stand on the top rung and you'll be taller."

The Wizard sat down feeling very miserable. "Perhaps a bite of an apple will cheer me up," he thought. The Wizard took a large bite of his apple . . . and out popped his singing tooth!

"My goodness!" chuckled the Wizard. "My tooth was singing to let me know it was ready to come out!" The Wizard had never had a singing tooth before so he placed it on his mantlepiece as a souvenir. The tooth was happy to be out of the Wizard's mouth. Now it could sing to its heart's content.

The Singing Tooth

The Wizard awoke one morning to find his front tooth singing merrily.

"TRA-LA-TRA-LA-LA!" sang the tooth loudly.

"How embarrassing," thought the Wizard. "I do hope it stops soon."

The Wizard went for a walk and met Mrs Bumblebee. He opened his mouth to say hello when his tooth sang out "TRA-LA-TRA-LA-LA!"

"How rude!" thought Mrs Bumblebee and hurried away.

"Oh, my," sighed the Wizard. "This tooth is a nuisance."

The Wizard went into the grocers shop for a bag of apples for his tea. "May I have a bag of apples?" he asked the shopkeeper. He was about to say "thank-you" when his tooth sang out "TRA-LA-TRA-LA-LA!" The shopkeeper gave the Wizard a funny look and he quickly left the shop.

"What am I going to do?" frowned the Wizard as he walked home. "If my tooth doesn't stop singing I'll never be able to open my mouth again."

Back home the Wizard tried all kinds of spells to stop his singing tooth. He tried the "HOCUS POCUS!" spell. Then he tried the "ZING BING BONG!" spell. He tried the "ALLAKAZOOM!" and the "TIPPY TAPPY TOE!" spells, quickly followed by the spells of "BOOP BOOP DE DOOP!" and "INGY WINGY WANGY WHOOO!" But when he opened his mouth after each spell he could hear his tooth singing "TRA-LA-TRA-LA-LA!" at the top of its voice.

The Bored Yo-Yo

"What a life!" sighed the pretty red yo-yo in the children's play room as it ran up and down its string for the umpteenth time that day. "Up and down, up and down, that's all I ever do. It makes me dizzy and it's so boring!"

As it began to run down the string for the umpteenth-and-one time the yo-yo came to a decision. Instead of travelling back up when it had reached the end of the string it pulled very hard and SNAP! it broke away from the string and fell to the floor.

"Free at last!" said the yo-yo as it rolled along on it's way. "I shall travel the world and see all the sights. Oh, what a happy life I shall lead!"

Just then the childrens' father came into the room in his big, heavy gardening boots.

KRRUUNNCH! He accidently stepped on the yo-yo and broke it into tiny pieces.

"What a shame," he said, throwing the broken yo-yo into the bin. "Such a nice yo-yo too."

If you have a yo-yo that is feeling bored perhaps you should warn it that there are worse things in life than running up and down a piece of string all day!

The Penguin (1)

"Excuse me," said the penguin as she stepped on the bus and handed the bus conductor a coin. "One half fare to Antarctica, please."

"Antarctica?" frowned the bus conductor, scratching his bald head. "We don't go there. Our last stop's the pier."

"It had better be," shouted a passenger from his seat. "Or we'll all get our feet wet! HAW! HAW!"

The penguin didn't understand this joke and since the bus wasn't going where she wanted, she got off again.

A taxi was driving past and the penguin stuck out a wing to wave it to stop.

"Excuse me," said the penguin as she entered the taxi and sat down. "I would like to go to Antarctica, please."

"Er, that be anywhere near Mrs Murphy's pizza shop?" asked the taxi driver, consulting his maps. "I can take you there, no problem."

The penguin wasn't sure if Antarctica was anywhere near Mrs Murphy's pizza shop but she asked the taxi driver to take her there anyway.

"No," said the penguin as she stepped out of the taxi outside Mrs Murphy's pizza shop. "This isn't Antarctica. Antarctica is cold and icy with lots of snow."

"If you want to be cold go and stand on a train station platform," suggested the taxi driver, grinning. "You'll be freezing by the time your train arrives. They're always late!" Laughing merrily he drove off.

"Hmmm, it's getting late," thought the penguin. "I'll go to the train station tomorrow."

At The Train Station (2)

"Excuse me," said the penguin the next day, as she waited on the cold station platform for the very late train to arrive. "Does the next train go near Antarctica?"

"Next train stops at Muddletown, Puddletown, Middletown and Diddletown," said the short-sighted guard who thought the penguin was a very short person in a dinner jacket. "I don't think it goes as far an Antarctica though."

The penguin was disappointed. Just then a little boy came up to her.

"Lost?" he asked. "You should try the Lost Property Office. They'll soon find you again."

The penguin thought this was a good idea and decided to go there the very next day.

Home At Last! (3)

"Excuse me," said the penguin to the woman behind the counter of the Lost Property Office the following morning. "I'm lost. I'm trying to reach Antarctica."

"Oh, that's easy," said the woman. "Stick a stamp on your head and post yourself in the nearest letterbox. That always works . . . unless the Post Office loses you. They're always doing that!"

"If they lose me I might end up in a jungle and get eaten by a lion!" thought the penguin, who didn't like the idea very much.

"Why don't you fly to Antarctica?" suggested a friendly-faced woman behind the penguin. "It so happens I'm a pilot and own my own aeroplane. I'll take you there if you like."

The penguin was overjoyed to hear this. It wasn't long before the aeroplane was flying over the icy wastes of Antarctica. When the penguin saw a group of her friends below, she leapt out of the aeroplane and sailed gently down on a large parachute.

"Where have you been these past three days?" asked the penguin's mother. "Your dinner's gone cold!"

"I got lost," said the penguin, cuddling up to her mother. "But now I've found myself again."

Bernie Bookworm

CHOMP! CHOMP! CHOMP! went Bernie Bookworm as he gnawed through the pages of a thick book.

"Ooh! Lovely grub!" he chuckled, patting his fat tummy. "Finding my way into this library was lucky. I can eat and eat and never run out of food."

Bernie was very happy, but not so the librarian when she saw her beautiful display of books with nibbled corners and pages with holes in them.

"That bookworm will ruin all my books unless I get rid of him," she sighed.

Later that day the librarian had an idea. She removed all the books from the shelves and replaced them with "ghost" novels.

When Bernie returned that evening and began gnawing through the books, which he enjoyed reading at the same time, his happy, smiling face quickly turned white with fear.

"Ooooh! A g-g-ghostie book!" he quivered. "I don't like those. They give me indigestion!"

Bernie tried the next book. And the next. And the one after that. Each time he had to stop because he was too nervous to eat any more.

"I can't stay here if there's only ghost books to chew on," he grumbled as he wriggled away. "I'm off!"

Where Bernie went is a mystery but the librarian was never bothered by him again. Perhaps you should look inside your books to make sure he hasn't come to visit you?

SSSSlither the Snake

Susie owned a very large, very long boa constrictor snake called SSSSlither. SSSSlither was always escaping from the house and scaring people.

"That snake should be in a zoo!" everyone complained.

SSSSlither felt very sad when he heard this. "SSSSusie's my friend," he hissed as he snaked along the street. "Life will be ssss-ssssad if I'm taken from her."

SSSSlither was so busy thinking he didn't notice where he was going and. . . .

"WAAAAAAH!" cried two rough-looking men as they ran out of the bank and fell over SSSSlither.

"Dear me, thissss issss terrible!" groaned SSSSlither. "I'll be locked up for ssssure now!"

But to SSSSlither's surprise the bank manager patted him on the head. "These two villians were robbing the bank and you stopped them! Well done!"

Everyone was proud of SSSSlither and no one ever mentioned putting him in a zoo again.

Heidi Helps

Heidi's big brother was busy in the garden fixing his motorbike.

"Can I help?" Heidi asked, but Tony just laughed. "This is a difficult job, even for me. You won't be much help, I'm afraid."

Heidi was upset to hear this. Then she saw that Tony's motorbike was covered in oil. Fetching a cloth she began to polish the motorbike while Tony was busy talking on the telephone to his girlfriend.

When Tony came outside again and saw his motorbike sparkling clean he was impressed. "You've helped me after all," he laughed.

Stubbleback Feels Ill

Stubbleback the Stegosaurus wasn't feeling very well.

"CROAK! CROAK!" is all he could say when he tried to speak. "What's the matter with me?" he thought. "I wish I could discover why I'm croaking like this."

What Stubbleback didn't know was that he was sitting beside the Wishing Well. At Stubbleback's wish, FZZZZIIIP! a large frog jumped out of his mouth. It had accidently hopped into his opened mouth in the dark.

"CROAK! CROAK!" it cried before bounding away.

"So that's why I was croaking," smiled Stubbleback. "I had a frog in my throat!"

The Comfy Armchair

Matilda's old aunt left her a great big armchair when she died. Matilda loved sitting in the armchair reading her books or watching television and she took care to keep it clean.

Richard, Matilda's cousin, came to visit. He was a bully and was always pulling Matilda's hair or pushing her over.

"STOP THAT!" Matilda cried as Richard jumped up and down on the cushions. You'll tear a hole in the material."

"Who cares?" snorted Richard, and jumped up and down again just to upset Matilda.

TWANG!

An extra-large spring shot out of the armchair's seat underneath Richard and catapulted him into the air like a stone from a catapult.

"WHURRFLE!" gasped Richard as he crashed into the wall. "That armchair's alive!"

"It's my friend," said Matilda. "So you had better not pick on me again!"

Matilda fixed the spring back into the seat of the armchair and then sat down to read a book. Richard didn't really believe in ghostly armchairs but then he never bullied Matilda again!

The Brave Knight

Sir Bottletop, a brave knight, rode out to kill a dragon and win the hand of a beautiful Princess.

"RRROOOAAAR!" growled the dragon when she saw the knight approaching. "Be off or I shall breathe fire over you and melt you!"

But Sir Bottletop had been crafty. He wore a necklace of strong-smelling onions around his neck. When the dragon smelt the onions her eyes began to water terribly and her tears put out the flames.

"Now I can cut off your head safely," said Sir Bottletop. But when he saw the dragon crying sadly his heart went out to her. "I'm not sure I want to marry a beautiful Princess anyway," he said. "She would only nag me to chop the firewood, clean the castle and wash the dirty clothes. That is no life for a brave knight."

The dragon was pleased to hear this. "I will come with you on your search for adventure. I'm very good at flying." And she flapped her mighty wings to prove this.

That evening Sir Bottletop and the dragon had muffins for tea, toasted by the dragon's flames. They were looking forward to having lots of fun together.

Henrietta's Job (1)

Henrietta the horse was standing in her field when a rough-looking man approached her.

"Good day, Henrietta," said the man, whose name was Cut-throat Jake. "How would you like to earn yourself a box of rosy red apples?"

Henrietta nodded excitedly. She was getting tired of eating grass all day and rosy red apples were her favourite dessert.

"Meet me outside the town bank at midnight and give me a lift out of town," Cut-throat Jake said. "I'll give you your reward then. Don't be late."

Henrietta felt very excited. She usually went to bed early but that night she would stay up late and meet Cut-throat Jake outside the bank. What an adventure this would be!

A Disappointing Night (2)

At midnight Henrietta trotted down the High Street towards the bank. Everything was quiet and dark and Henrietta felt nervous, but she had made a promise. "It's not good manners to break your word," she thought as she waited outside the bank. Then it began to rain and Henrietta shivered.

Suddenly there was a loud explosion inside the bank. This frightened Henrietta and she was about to gallop off when Cut-throat Jake ran out of the bank carrying a large sack. He leapt onto Henrietta's back and shouted, "GEE UP! MOVE, YOU NAG! YAAAH!"

Henrietta thought Cut-throat Jake was very rude and she was feeling very frightened of him. She did as he said only because she was afraid he might hurt her if she refused.

Outside the town Cut-throat Jake jumped off Henrietta. Before running off he snarled. "Forget you ever saw me . . . OR ELSE!"

Henrietta was glad when Cut-throat Jake had gone. She trotted back to her field feeling very miserable.

"What a nasty man," she thought. "I helped him and he didn't even give me my apples. This has been a bad day all round."

Henrietta the Brave (3)

"MIDNIGHT RAID AT BANK! HORSE INVOLVED!" said the headlines in the newspaper the next day.

"Oh, dear. It must have been Cut-throat Jake," groaned Henrietta. "That's what the explosion was. And I was his accomplice. What am I going to do?"

Henrietta went back to where she had dropped Cut-throat Jake off the night before. The ground was still wet from the rain and she could see his footprints in the mud. She followed the footprints until they lead her to an old barn.

Inside the barn Cut-throat Jake was sleeping soundly.

"NEIGH!" Henrietta called loudly.

Thinking it was the police Cut-throat Jake leapt up suddenly and ran outside. When he saw it was just Henrietta he shouted angrily. "What do you want? I warned you not to mess with me!" He pulled out a long knife from his pocket.

Henrietta was very scared as Cut-throat Jake approached her with the knife in his hand. Then she saw a bucket of water close by. Turning quickly she kicked out with her back legs, hitting the bucket into the air. The bucket struck Cut-throat Jake on the head, knocking him out!

The bank manager was very pleased to get his money back and the police were pleased to have Cut-throat Jake under lock and key.

"I'll make sure you're supplied with a box of rosy red apples every day as a reward," the bank manager told Henrietta. This made Henrietta feel very happy indeed!

The Tightrope Walker

Lanky was a tightrope walker at the circus. He enjoyed his job and practiced hard every day.

"Oh, disaster," Lanky wailed one morning as he entered the Big Top to practice on the High Wire and saw that it had snapped from its moorings. "This is a nuisance."

"I can get it fixed for tonight," said the Ringmaster. "But you won't be able to practice today."

"Come and help me bring in the washing instead," said the Ringmaster's wife, trying to take Lanky's mind off his troubles.

Lanky went to the washing line and collected all the dry clothes. Then he had an idea. He climbed onto the washing line and started walking backwards and forwards along it.

"This can be my High Wire," he smiled happily. "I can have my practice today after all."

Magic Food

The ENORMOUS fat black cat sneaked into the Wizard's house in search of food.

"MEE-HEE!-HEE!-OOOW!" he chuckled when he saw the table laid out with delicious food. "I'll have a wonderful feast today!"

But as the ENORMOUS fat black cat went to take a bite out of a large cream cake, the cake floated into the air and then fell SPLATT! on his head!

"MEE-YEEEOOOW!" screeched the ENORMOUS fat black cat and fled out of the house.

The Wizard laughed as he came out from hiding. "My magic 'floating' spell gave him a fright. In fact, I did two spells at once," he thought proudly. "I made my cake float and made the ENORMOUS fat black cat disappear!"

The New Invention

Professor Noodle was a bungling inventor. His inventions never turned out the way he expected.

"My new floor polish will make me rich!" he thought proudly, and held a demonstration at the Town Hall to prove it.

Professor Noodle rubbed the polish on the floor for the Mayor to see.

"Marvellous!" beamed the Mayor, looking at the gleaming floor. "I'll buy a dozen tins . . .WHOOOOOOOOPS!" CRRAA-AASSH!

As the Mayor stepped onto the polished floor he slipped from one end of the room to the other and crashed into a wall.

Of course, Professor Noodle was kicked out of the Town Hall without a sale. "Oh, gosh! My polish is too slippery. No one will want to buy it now," he moaned.

"I'll buy all the tins of polish you have," said the manager of the ice skating rink.

Professor Noodle was very puzzled but he gladly sold the polish. As he rubbed the polish on the cement path behind the ice skating rink the manager explained. "The ice rink is closed for repairs and no one can go ice skating. But now they can skate on the path instead . . .thanks to your polish!" And that's exactly what they did!

Glasses for Roger

Roger the rhinoceros was rather short-sighted. He was always bumping into things.

BUMP!

"Sorry," Roger apologised as he bumped into a tree, knocking it to the ground. Being so short-sighted he thought it was an old man. "I didn't see you there."

CRAAASSH!

"Sorry," Roger apologised as he crashed through a brick wall which he thought was a team of football players standing in a row.

KER-SMASSH!

"Yipes! My front door!" cried Leroy Lion as Roger walked through the door of Leroy's house without opening it first.

"Sorry," Roger apologised. "I thought the door was open."

"Roger, you need glasses," said Leroy, and so he took Roger to the opticians.

"My, he will need a big pair of glasses," said the optician after he had checked Roger's eyes. "They'll be ready in a week."

The following week Roger and Leroy went back to the opticians to collect the glasses. When Roger put them on he did look funny! Well, have you ever seen a rhinoceros wearing glasses? But Roger was happy because now he could go for walks without bumping into trees thinking they were people, and without crashing through walls thinking they were rows of football players. And Leroy, well, Leroy was happiest of all. Now he wouldn't have to keep repairing his front door every time Roger came to visit him.

The Dirty Mark

Val's ball had accidently bounced off the window of the living room, leaving a dirty mark.

"I'll remove it with some polish," her Dad said. As he wiped the window clean with a cloth he was sure he heard a tiny voice cry out, "I'll be back!"

A few days later Val's ball bounced off the window again. And there again was a dirty mark.

"There! I told you I'd be back!" the dirty mark laughed.

The Flying Dwarf

A lazy dwarf made himself a pair of wings out of bird feathers so he could fly everywhere instead of walking and wearing out his feet.

He climbed a high tree, strapped the wings to his back, and leapt off the branch into the air.

"Look at me!" he called to his friends below as he flapped his wings. "I can fly!"

The dwarf suddenly dropped out of the sky and SPLAAAAT! landed on the ground.

"I'll carry on walking, after all," he groaned as he sat up in a hospital bed, his feet encased in plaster. "Once my broken legs mend, that is!"

The Three Little Wolves

Once upon a time there were three little wolves who lived together in a wooden hut deep in the heart of a big forest.

In the forest lived a great big pig who had already eaten the little wolves mother and father and grandma and grandpa, and was now coming to eat the three little wolves themselves!

"Come out, come out, little wolves, so I may gobble you up!" roared the great big pig.

The little wolves were very frightened when they heard this. They came out of their hut and stood before the great big pig.

"You are indeed a great big pig," said the first little wolf. "But I don't suppose even you could eat that boulder over there." And the little wolf pointed to a large boulder next to the great big pig.

"That's easy," said the great big pig and swallowed the boulder in one gulp!

"You are indeed a great big pig," said the second little wolf. "But I don't suppose even you could drink the river dry."

"That's easy," said the great big pig, and he drank and drank until his tummy was swollen and the river was dry.

"You are indeed a great big pig," said the third little wolf. "But I don't suppose even you could eat the mighty oak tree."

"That's easy," said the great big pig, and pulling the mighty oak tree up by its roots, he swallowed it all in two gulps!

Having eaten and drunk so much the great big pig's tummy had swollen up like a huge hot-air balloon. The first little wolf took a long sharp thorn from a gorse bush. He stabbed the great big pig in the stomach with the thorn and POP! the great big pig exploded!

"That will teach the great big pig to be so greedy," laughed the three little wolves, and they went back indoors to play.

Hop To It!

The Ogre was hopping up and down. This made the houses in the town quiver and shake.

"The Ogre must be hopping mad," thought the townspeople. "If he doesn't stop hopping, all our houses will fall down again!" They still remembered when the Ogre had accidently sneezed their houses flat.

The Ogre hopped into town and the people were frightened in case he was so angry he squashed them beneath his big feet. But the Ogre sat down and began to cry. "Boo hoo! My foot hurts!" he howled.

The town doctor looked at the Ogre's foot and found a giant splinter of wood stuck in his toe. "That's why the Ogre is hopping," he explained as he pulled the splinter out. "It serves you right for not wearing shoes to protect your feet," he told the Ogre.

The Ogre was very grateful and promised to wear shoes from that day on. This pleased the townspeople very much.

Ernie's Swing

Ernie the fox was playing on the swing in his garden.

"You could help me flatten these bumps in our grass instead," complained his dad, hitting the bumps with a big spade.

Ernie pretended not to hear. He began swinging higher and higher, and then SNAP! the rope broke away and Ernie tumbled through the air to land with a WHUMP! on the grass, flattening a bump beneath him.

Ernie's dad laughed. "I see you're helping me flatten the bumps after all. But why don't you use a spade? It's a lot less painful!" Ernie scowled. His dad had a silly sense of humour at times.

The Fruit Stall (1)

Fillmytummy the troll passed a fruit stall in the market.

"Hmmm, I think I'll try a pear," he said, and he did. Then he ate a pumpkin in one swallow! Fillmytummy ate and ate until there was no fruit left.

"My fruit!" yelled the stall owner, who had returned from his dinner. "Greedy! You've eaten the lot!"

Fillmytummy hurried away. He didn't have enough money to pay for the fruit. The stall owner was very cross.

"We'll teach Fillmytummy a lesson," said the stall owner's friend. "I've been learning to throw my voice so it seems that someone else is speaking when really it's me. When Fillmytummy returns tomorrow he'll have a surprise!"

Talking Fruit (2)

Sure enough, the next day Fillmytummy went back to the fruit stall. The stall owner wasn't there. He was hiding nearby with his friend.

"I'll make it seem like the fruit is talking," his friend said.

Fillmytummy picked up a banana. "Yum! This looks delicious!"

"Don't eat me!" snapped the banana crossly. "You don't know where I've been!" Of course it was really the fruit stall owner's friend throwing his voice but Fillmytummy didn't know this!

"I must be hearing things!" Fillmytummy said nervously, and picked up a grapefruit instead.

"EEEEEEK! HELP! FILLMYTUMMY IS GOING TO EAT ME!" screamed the grapefruit at the top of its voice.

Fillmytummy jumped back quickly, dropping the grapefruit back on the stall. "I-I m-must be going crazy," he gasped. "Fancy thinking fruit can talk!"

Fillmytummy picked up an orange. Then he put it down quickly in case it started talking. When he saw the orange hadn't made a sound he felt very relieved. He picked it up again and was about to take a big bite when the orange let out a tremendous "GRRRRRROOOOWWWL!! Why should you eat me?" snapped the orange. "I think I'll eat YOU instead!"

This was too much for Fillmytummy. He dropped the orange and ran off to his house where he hid under his bed for the rest of the day.

"Ha! Ha! Fillmytummy will think twice about eating my fruit now," laughed the stall owner and he ate a lovely red apple — which didn't say a word!

New Baby

Sam's mum was expecting a baby.

"Will you make sure it's a boy?" asked Sam. "Then I can play pretend fighting games with him."

Mum laughed and explained that she wouldn't know what the baby would be until it was born.

Some weeks later the new baby arrived . . . and it was a girl, Sam was disappointed.

"Girls are soppy. They can't fight!" grumbled Sam as he looked down at his sister in her cot. Suddenly the baby grabbed hold of Sam's nose and pulled hard.

"Yeeeooow!" he squealed, and then laughed. "I was wrong. My sister's going to be good at pretend fights after all!"

The Magic Flute (1)

Miserytown was a place where no one smiled and all the people went around with sad faces.

A little girl named Esmeralda passed through Miserytown on her way to her grandmother's house. She was very upset to see the people so unhappy and tried singing a song to cheer them up. The people only grunted crossly and said, "If you don't shut up we'll lock you away in our jail!"

"I wish I could turn Miserytown into a happy place," Esmeralda told her grandmother when she reached the old lady's house.

"You can," said her grandmother and handed Esmeralda a golden flute. "This magic flute will banish all sadness and grumpiness away. Play it in the town square tomorrow."

Esmeralda promised that she would.

Happy Days (2)

Esmeralda did as her grandmother told her. The next day she stood in the town square and began to play the magical golden flute.

To her surprise Esmeralda could see the musical notes she was playing float out of the flute and dance into the air. They danced around the square and over the people's heads.

As the notes danced above them the people's feet began to tap on the ground in time to the music. Then their feet shuffled to and fro, and before long the people found themselves holding hands and dancing in a circle.

"How wonderful!" laughed a man as tears of delight ran down his face and he beamed a happy smile for the first time in his life. "What a lovely feeling it is to smile and dance."

Esmeralda played the magic flute all day and the people laughed and cheered and clapped.

"This isn't Miserytown any longer," thought Esmeralda as she led the procession of dancing people around the town. "We'll have to call it Cheerytown instead!"

A Boy and his Dinosaur

I found a dinosaur in the bath
It looked so funny I had to laugh.
It was big and green with scaly skin
And when it spoke it made such a din!
"Get it out!" my mother said.
So I hid it inside my bed.
It tossed and turned all through the night
And keeping my covers was such a fight.
In the end I could take no more
And, with my covers, slept on the floor.
When morning came I ached all over
Wondering what to do with "Rover",
This the name I gave my dinosaur
Not "Freda", nor "Bertram" nor "Elinore".
Down to breakfast I did go
Only to find I was too slow.
Rover, in a hungry mood
Had gobbled up my breakfast food.
Mum's breakfast too, and Dad's as well.
Dad roared loudly and then he fell
Over Rover's sticking-out tail
As he hurried to fetch the mail.
"That dinosaur has got to go!"
Shouted Dad, and Mum just nodded, "Quite so!"

Have you ever tried losing something so big?
I wish I'd found an earwig!
"DINOSAUR! FREE! TO GOOD HOME!"
   the notice ran,
But no one was interested, not one man.
"Pooh! What a whiff!" my Mum cried.
"It smells like a great big elephant's died!"
"I-It's R-Rover," I stammered, hating to
   admit
That my dinosaur ponged, well, just a bit.
Rover needed a wash, that's true
His scaly green skin was turning blue.
Into the garden we both did wander
To think out this problem, to pause and
   ponder.
Then it rained and Rover found
He was shrinking nearer and nearer the
   ground.
Soon no bigger than a cat
He went indoors and there he sat,
Beside the heater where he could dry.
Then Mum came in and squealed, "Oh,
   my!"
"With Rover now so very small
I suppose you can keep him, after all!"
Now our days are filled with joy
A scaly green dinosaur and his boy.

Flying Carpet

Treacle Tart was tired of riding on her broomstick. "I'll make myself a flying carpet instead," she decided.

She sat on her carpet outside her house and sprinkled flying dust over it. The carpet floated into the sky, taking Treacle Tart along for the ride.

"This is jolly fun?" she thought as she flew over the rooftops. They passed a tall tree and one end of the carpet got caught on one of the branches. Treacle Tart hadn't noticed and as the carpet flew on it began to unravel until there was nothing left but one long piece of wool. Of course, this meant Treacle Tart had nothing to sit on and she fell out of the sky! Luckily she landed safely on a haystack in a field a long way from home.

"I'll stick to riding my broomstick," she sighed, walking along the winding road back to her house. "At least it won't fall to bits on me. . . . I hope!"

Snowball Fight

"Come in at once, children!" shouted David and Melanie's mother crossly as she watched them having snowball fights in the deep snow. "It's too cold to be playing outside."

Melanie and David were disappointed. "Now we can't have our snowball fight," they grumbled.

Back indoors their mother gave them each a packet of cotton wool balls.

"Why don't you have a cotton wool ball fight instead?" she suggested, and threw a cotton wool ball which bounced off David's nose.

"Wahey! This is just as much fun as snowball fights!" the children laughed, throwing the cotton wool balls at each other. "And it's not as cold either!"

The Sparrow

Lucy's favourite time of the day was when she was feeding scraps of bread to the birds outside her flat.

One day a small sparrow came down from its nest to feed but he much bigger starlings pushed the sparrow out of the way and ate all the bread for themselves.

"Something must be done about this," thought Lucy, who was very upset at seeing the poor sparrow go hungry. She asked her friend, Nigel, who lived close by, to build her a wooden box with a small hole in one end.

Lucy placed the box outside her window and filled it with breadcrumbs. The rest of the bread she scattered on the balcony. As usual, the starlings ate all the bread scattered about before the sparrow could taste any. Then they tried to squeeze through the small hole in the box to reach the rest of the bread. But of course they were far too big to get through. Then the sparrow flew down to the window ledge and hopped through the small hole and into the box. It stayed in the box until it had eaten every last crumb of bread, and then flew out again.

"TWEET! TWEET!" it sang as it passed by Lucy's window.

"It's thanking me," laughed Lucy. "But if it carries on eating like that I'll soon have to make a bigger hole for it to fit through!"

The Spy

Big Chief Itchy Nose was out hunting when he came across a set of footprints in the desert sand. "Uggh! Maybe spy from Pongytoe tribe!" he thought, and followed the footprints to see where they would lead him.

"That heapum strange!" he frowned as he passed a cactus he had already seen before. "How that cactus getum here?" He carried on following the footprints until he passed the same cactus a third time. Itchy Nose's nose twitched when he was thinking hard.

"Maybe cactus following Itchy Nose?" he thought. "Maybe cactus is Pongytoe spy in disguise!" Itchy Nose leapt on the cactus and then cried "YEEEEEEEEEEEEE-OOOOOOOOWWW!" as he discovered it was a real cactus and the thorns pricked him all over his body.

Itchy Nose was in a bad mood. "If Itchy Nose catchum Pongytoe tribe. Itchy Nose give him what for!" he bellowed. Then he stepped into one of the footprints in the sand . . . and found it fitted his foot perfectly. The footprints were in fact Itchy Nose's own. The silly Indian had been walking around in circles following his own footprints! That's why he kept passing the same cactus.

"Itchy Nose giving up hunting," groaned the Chief as he hobbled home with the cactus prickles still sticking in him. "It getum too painful!"

Pop-Off

Jimmy had made friends with a magical, blue-spotted gremlin named Pop-Off. Pop-Off had a very special power. He could change himself into any shape he liked. A chair, a car, a wheelbarrow, even a tall building. Every time he changed shape you could hear a loud POP! which is why Jimmy named him POP-OFF.

One day while Jimmy was driving his blue-spotted car (which was really Pop-Off in disguise) through the park, he was stopped by Bully Briggs, the nasty, rough boy from school.

"Give us a ride or I'll tweak your nose!" he threatened Jimmy, holding up his fist to show that he meant it.

A wheel of the car winked at Jimmy. It was Pop-Off telling him to let Bully Briggs sit in the car and he would teach him a lesson.

When Bully Briggs was sitting in the car, POP! the car sprouted a pair of blue-spotted wings. "WAAAAAAH!" screamed Bully Briggs as the car flew high into the air, looped-the-loop, and dived towards the ground. "EEEEEEEK!" he wailed as Pop-Off pulled up before hitting the ground and taking off into the air again. "YAAAAAAAAH!" Bully Briggs squealed as the Pop-Off car turned upsidedown and he fell out!'

POP! Before Bully Briggs could hit the ground Pop-Off turned into a blue-spotted trampoline. He bounced off the trampoline and KER-SPLASH! landed in the park pond.

POP! Pop-Off turned back into a car and drove away with Jimmy. They both laughed merrily. "Ha! Ha! I don't think Bully Briggs will bother us again!" chuckled Jimmy.

The Musical Basset Hound

Willow the basset hound was sitting in the recording studio of Clive, his owner, watching him play an electric guitar.

"Coo! I wish I could do that!" Willow thought wistfully. "Clive is clever. He can play all sorts of musical instruments."

"Clive! Dinner's ready!" called Clive's wife, Mandy, from the house.

"Don't touch anything, Willow," Clive warned his dog, giving him a friendly pat on the head.

"As if I would," snorted Willow crossly. Then he looked at the electric guitar resting against the table. "But surely no one will notice if I just strum a few strings?" Willow picked up the guitar and ran his paw across the strings. TWANG! TWANG! TWANG!

"Cor! That sounded good!" Willow grinned, and did the same again.

TWANG! TWANG! TWANG! TWANG! went the guitar as Willow played. Willow kept on playing until his paws were quite sore.

Suddenly Willow heard Clive returning. He put down the guitar, curled up in a corner, and pretended to be asleep.

"I thought I heard someone messing with my guitar," Clive frowned as he entered the studio. "It wasn't you, was it, Willow?" Then he laughed. "What am I saying? As if a dog could play the guitar! What a silly thought!"

Willow didn't make a sound. It was going to be his secret!

Captain Jim

I have a yellow teddy bear
His name is Captain Jim,
He scares the nighttime
　　monsters away
When I cuddle him.

Water Pistol

Tony was using his water pistol to soak Libby. "Yaah! You can't get me back because you don't have a water pistol!" he sneered. Libby ran into the garden to hide. Then she saw something on the grass that made her smile.

"TONY!" she called, moments later. "Here I am!"

Tony rushed into the garden ready to squirt water at Libby again. SPLOOOOOSSH! A spray of water struck him in the face and he tumbled backwards in surprise.

"I've got a water pistol after all!" Libby giggled, spraying Tony with water from the garden hose.

The Eggs

Helen and Roger were out walking in the forest when they saw a boy trying to steal the eggs out of a bird's nest.

"Be off, or we'll call the police!" Helen threatened, and the frightened boy ran off. Helen and Roger made sure the eggs were safe and then they went home.

A wood sprite in the forest had seen all this and so when the children woke up the next morning, they found a basket of chocolate eggs at the end of their beds. The wood sprite had left them as thanks for looking after the eggs in the bird's nest.

Cleaning Up

Anna was a messy girl. She was always dropping rubbish on the ground and making everywhere look messy

"You'll be for it if Sgt. Smith catches you," Suzi warned Anna as she watched her friend finish eating a banana and drop the skin.

"Rhubarb!" Anna snorted. "He's too slow to catch a tortoise!"

Just then Sgt. Smith's voice roared out from the end of the street. "LITTERBUG! COME HERE!"

Anna turned and ran the other way. "I'll soon escape!" she chuckled. "I'm champion runner at school!"

Unfortunately, Anna had forgotten the banana skin she had dropped. Her foot slipped on the skin and she somersaulted into the air, landing flat on her back. She looked up to see an angry Sgt. Smith looking down at her. "P-Please don't throw me in jail!" pleaded Anna, feeling very scared.

Sgt Smith didn't lock Anna up. Instead she was made to pick up all the rubbish in the town. "That's the last time I drop litter," she groaned, filling another sack with rubbish.

The Climb

There were three animals having an argument over who was the best climber.

"I am the best," said the squirrel.

"No, I am the best," said the monkey.

"No, I am the best," said the ant.

"YOU?" laughed the squirrel and the monkey, looking scornfully at the ant. "Don't be silly!"

"Whoever reaches the top of this tall tree first is the winner," suggested the ant.

"You're on!" said the squirrel and the monkey. "But it won't be you!"

The monkey climbed up the tree, followed by the squirrel. The ant was last to move. He caught hold of the squirrel's tail and climbed onto his back. The ant was so small the squirrel didn't even known he was there.

When the squirrel had caught up with the monkey, the ant leapt onto the squirrel's head and then onto the monkey's tail. Then he climbed onto the monkey's back and clambered onto his head. The ant was so light the monkey didn't even know he was there.

The animals climbed and climbed. The ant sat comfortably on the monkey's head and enjoyed the ride. When the monkey came close to the top of the tree, the ant leapt off his head and landed on the very top branch. The monkey and the squirrel were amazed to see the ant sitting at the top of the tree when they arrived.

"You are the best climber," said the squirrel and the monkey together. "But how did you manage to beat the two of us?"

"Oh, I just used my head," smiled the ant. "Or, should I say, your heads!"

Miss Caterpillar

Miss Caterpillar was standing in the rain getting very wet. Milligan Magpie flew down. In his beak was a large leaf on a stalk. "This will keep you dry," he said, and flew off again.

Later, when Milligan returned, Miss Caterpillar was still standing in the rain, getting wet. "Where's the leaf?" Milligan asked.

"I ate it," said Miss Caterpillar. "But it did no good. I'm still getting wet"

"Foolish caterpillar," cawed Milligan. "You were meant to hold the leaf over your head like an umbrella." Miss Caterpillar did feel silly!

The Rose

There was once a beautiful red rose who was the pride of the garden. Everyone came to look at it and all agreed it was the nicest rose they had ever seen. The rose felt very proud and tried to keep herself clean and tidy.

One day the rose awoke to find dozens of greenfly swarming all over her petals and stalk. They had seen the rose and decided she was the best looking flower to feast on. The poor rose could hear them munching on her beautiful petals and she was very upset.

"Oh, dear," she cried, trying, without success, to shake the greenfly off. "Soon there will be nothing left of me."

A ladybird passed by, looking for a place to live. She heard the rose cry out and flew down to see what was the matter. When she saw the greenfly she was very happy. "These are my favourite food," she said as she ate the greenfly, one by one. It wasn't long before all the greenfly had been eaten.

"You may live with me as long as you wish," the rose told the ladybird when she heard that the insect was looking for a home.

"And I shall protect you from any greenfly that visit," promised the ladybird.

The Pain

One bright sunny day Stubbleback the stegosaur was out walking. As usual, he wasn't really watching where he was going and WHOOOPS! he tripped over his own feet and landed with a BUMP! on his nose. Now I'm sure that if you fell over and landed on your nose you would know about it. However, Stubbleback, who wasn't very bright as dinosaurs go, didn't feel any pain at all. Well, not at first. In fact, it took six whole days before he realised he had hurt himself.

"YEEOOOOOWWCH!" yelled Stubbleback loudly, making the tree quiver. He had finally felt a sharp pain on the end of his nose.

"What's the matter? Why did you cry out?" asked Terry Pterodactyl, who was sunbathing on Stubbleback's tail at the time.

"I don't know why, but my nose hurts," grumbled Stubbleback, rubbing his poor nose tenderly. He couldn't understand what had happened at all!

Hot Air Balloon

The hot air balloon drifted peacefully in the pale blue sky, above the fields of wheat and the large oak tree forest.

"This is the life," it sighed contentedly. "No one to bother me, and so quiet."

"SQUAWK!" cried a very large crow as it collided with the hot air balloon. "Get out of my way, you bag of wind!" the bird snorted rudely.

"You should watch where you're flying," said the hot air balloon indignantly, but the crow wasn't listening. It flew off, muttering angrily to itself.

The hot air balloon had just settled down again when BOOOOOOOOOOOOOOM!! a jet aeroplane flew past, its engines roaring loudly.

"G-Goodness!" quivered the hot air balloon in fright. "What a noisy creature that was! It almost shook me out of the sky!"

The hot air balloon had just settled down for a third time when a big black cloud appeared overhead. "Oh, no! It's not going to do what I think it's going to do?" groaned the hot air balloon. It grimmaced as large spots of rain fell pitter patter onto it. Soon the rain was falling heavily and the hot air balloon became soaking wet.

"I've had enough," it grumbled, and letting its hot air escape it sank to the ground. "I'll go out tomorrow," it decided as it settled down to sleep. "Perhaps the sky will be less crowded then!"

Mr Weatherby's Jacket

Mr Weatherby bought himself a smart new yellow jacket but when he got it home he found it was much too big.

"I'll have to eat and eat until I can fit into my new jacket," said Mr Weatherby, who was rather skinny.

So, starting that very day, Mr Weatherby ate twice as much for his breakfast, three times as much for his dinner and FOUR times as much for his tea! He did this every day for two weeks!

Mr Weatherby grew very fat indeed. When he tried wearing his smart new yellow jacket it fitted perfectly.

"I shall go for a walk to show it off," Mr Weatherby decided, even though it was raining very hard.

The rain made the yellow jacket very wet and it began to shrink. The sleeves shrank up Mr Weatherby's arms. The jacket became so tight around his chest that the buttons popped off one by one. POP! POP! POP!

"Oh, dear," sighed Mr Weatherby when he arrived home wearing the shrunken jacket. "Now I'll have to go on a diet before my jacket will fit me again!"

I Wonder Why

I wonder why
People don't
Listen to what I say.
I talk clearly,
Loud and cheerfully
All the long, long day.
Mummy says, "Pardon?"
Daddy says, "Er? What?"
And Grandma laughs, "Choochie Coo!"
Talking properly
Isn't easy
Especially when you're only two!

The Old Lane

There was once an old country lane that led to nowhere in particular. It was a pretty lane, with a cobbled path, surrounded on each side by a row of chestnut trees. Birds and squirrels lived in the trees, and in the fields beyond lived badgers and foxes, hedgehogs and rabbits. No cars or people travelled along the lane because it didn't lead anywhere.

"It's so peaceful here," thought the old lane happily. "I hope it never changes." But one day it did.

A lorry came and poured hot tar along the old lane. A steamroller flattened the tar until it set into a new road. The lane was extended until it reached a noisy motorway with cars whizzing this way and that at a mad pace. Workmen arrived and put up garish yellow street lamps along the old lane.

"What'a going on?" wondered the old lane, very upset at being disturbed.

Cars started driving up the old lane, leaving clouds of black exhaust as they passed. People wandered along the lane going TRAMP! TRAMP! TRAMP! with their heavy walking boots. The animals and the birds disappeared to hide from the noisy cars and the noisy people, and the old lane felt very alone.

"I'm not putting up with this!" it said crossly. The next time a car drove past the lane wriggled this way and that and soon created a large pothole in the road. BUMP! went the car's wheel as it rode over the pothole. After a few bumpy rides cars stopped coming. Then the lane made lots of smaller potholes all along the road for people to trip in. The people didn't like this much and soon stopped walking along the old lane. Workmen came and dug up the road and blocked the old lane off from the motorway. They replaced the cobbled stones and took down the garish yellow street lamps. Very soon no one came at all. The animals returned and the lane was happy to be back as it used to be . . . an old country lane leading nowhere in particular.

The Fishes

The fishes in the river were hiding from the fisherman who was sitting on the bank with his fishing rod, trying to catch them.

"Fishing isn't fun at all," grumbled one fish. "How would he like to have a sharp hook caught in his mouth? It's very painful!"

The fish decided to teach the fisherman a lesson. The next time he let out his line into the water the fish tied it to a big rock.

"I've got a bite!" cheered the fisherman, thinking it was a fish on the end of the line. He reeled in the line and gave a big jerk to pull out the fish. The rock catapulted out of the water and struck the fisherman on the head.

"OWWW!!" he cried as a large bruise appeared on his head. The fisherman couldn't understand what had happened but he never went fishing in the river again.

Janet's Mole

Janet was surprised to see a mole wearing a business suit and bowler hat, with an umbrella tucked underneath its arm, wandering about in her garden.

"Hello," said the mole politely, raising its hat to Janet." Is this Mr Dewdrop's house?"

"No," replied Janet, somewhat surprised to meet a talking mole, "He lives next door."

"Oh," said the mole, looking somewhat embarrassed at the molehill he had made in Janet's garden. "Sorry about the mess. I visit Mr Dewdrop's garden every morning to feast on his nice, tasty worms." He said goodbye and disappeared down the molehill.

Janet ran indoors to tell her Mummy about the talking mole. Her Mummy said, "That's nice, dear," in an unconvinced way. She didn't really believe that Janet had met a talking mole at all!

Lost Dog

"I've lost Rover!" cried a little girl outside her house.

"I'll find him for you," said Tom. Now Tom knew that many dogs were called Rover but when he saw a stray black dog in the street he thought, "Aha! This could be the little girl's dog!" He tried to catch the dog but it raced away. The dog led Tom a merry chase all around the town and back again. But when it stopped to catch its breath, Tom grabbed it.

"Here's Rover," Tom said to the little girl when he reached her house. The little girl laughed. "Silly! Rover's my dolly." She held up a battered doll for Tom to see. "I found her in my bed."

Tom was quite cross. He was tired from chasing the dog and he thought 'Rover' was a silly name for a doll anyway.

A lady came up to him. "Clever boy! You've found Pumpernickel!" She pointed to the dog. "He escaped from my house this morning." Tom thought Pumpernickel was a silly name for a dog too, but since the lady was so pleased to see her dog again he kept his thoughts to himself.

Three Mice

Timothy Mouse had found his way into a sweet shop. After nibbling on an assortment of chocolate bars he was about to leave when he noticed three other mice nearby. They were all a different colour. Red, green and orange.

"Hello," said Timothy cheerfully, but the mice didn't answer.

"HELLO!," he said again loudly in case the mice were a bit deaf, but still they didn't reply.

"What snooty mice!" Timothy snorted as he left the shop. "Won't even pass the time of day with a chap." He went home to tell his friends about the rude mice.

What the silly mouse didn't realise was that the three coloured mice were only sugar mice for children to eat!

Welly Boots

My welly boots wet passers-by
When in puddles they go SPLASH! SPLISH!
SPLASH!

The people glare and shout at me
And now, I'm afraid I must dash!

King Muddletop's Flag

King Muddletop decided he wanted his own special flag to fly from the top of the royal castle. Of course, Kings don't do any real work for a living. They just sit on their thrones ordering people about. And this is what King Muddletop did.

"Have my flag ready this afternoon," he told the royal seamstress.

When the flag was finished King Muddletop put it in a basket to keep it safe until he was ready to fly it from the royal tower. At the same time a servant entered with a basket of freshly washed clothes for the King to wear.

The King was busy finishing off a game of hopscotch so he called for his royal guard. "Hang this from the royal tower for me," he said, handing the guard a basket. "I'll be out shortly."

When King Muddletop had finished his game he decided to have a change of clothes. Opening the remaining basket he was horrified to find the royal flag inside. Then he heard laughter from the courtyard. Looking out of his window he saw why the people were laughing . . . there, flying from the royal tower, was a line of the King's freshly washed clothes.

King Muddletop felt very embarrassed. "I must have muddled the baskets up!" he groaned.

Pets

My budgie's name is Horace,
My rabbit's name is Fluff,
My tortoise's name is Annie Sue,
My gerbil's name is Muff.
My cat's name is Samson,
My dog's name is Fred
And when I go to sleep at night
They join me on my bed.
Fluff and Samson sleep with Horace,
Fred and Muff with Annie Sue,
When Mummy comes to tuck me in
She cries, "You're bed is like a zoo!"

The Clean House

Milly Mouse liked her house to be clean and tidy. Every day she would dust the furniture, sweep the floor, polish the widows, vacuum the carpet, wash the curtains and replace the flowers in the vase with fresh ones. There was not a speck of dust to be seen in her house. Everything was spotless.

One day Milly's brother, Mucklemess Mouse came to visit. Milly loved her brother but he was rather untidy. In fact, he was extremely messy!

"Hello, Milly!" Mucklemess beamed as he entered her house in his muddy boots. "I've been collecting leaves," he said, emptying a sack of wet and dirty leaves over Milly's spotless table. Creepy-crawly insects scurried out of the leaves and started to climb Milly's spotless curtains.

When Milly served Mucklemess a cup of tea he spilt it over her spotless floor. When he opened the window for a breath of fresh air he left paw prints all over Milly's spotless windows. Mucklemess tried to wipe off the marks and accidently knocked over the vase of fresh flowers. CRASH! went the vase and shattered on the floor.

Milly loved her brother but she was glad when it was time for him to leave. Her spotless house wasn't spotless any longer. "Now I'll have to clean up all over again," Milly sighed. She set to work polishing and dusting and sweeping and cleaning.

Muncher

"No one likes me," sighed Muncher Maggot, poking his head out of a half-eaten apple that grew on Mrs Dilly's apple tree.

"Whenever they see me they pull funny faces and scream a lot."

Just then two naughty children entered Mrs Dilly's garden and approached the apple tree. They began filling a sack with apples until they saw Muncher's head peering out of the half-eaten apple.

"Urrrgggh!" they groaned, pulling funny faces. "A maggot! These apples can't be any good to eat." They didn't know that Muncher had only just arrived in the apple tree that morning and had only tasted one apple. The children ran off.

Mrs Dilly went over to the tree and smiled up at Muncher. "You stopped those children from stealing my apples. Stay in the apple tree as long as you like." Muncher was pleased to have someone who liked him at last.

Floppy Jane

Floppy Jane is a rag doll. She is called Floppy because that's what she does all the time. When Susie, the little girl who owns her, tries to make Floppy Jane stand up she flops flat on her face. When Susie tries to make her kneel she flops on her side. When Susie tries to make her sit she wobbles this way and that and then flops on her back.

"Floppy Jane needs more stuffing," said Susie's Mum. She carefully opened up the doll and filled her with woolly stuffing, then she sewed her up again. Now Floppy Jane can stand up, she can kneel, and she can sit without flopping over. She doesn't really need to be called Floppy Jane anymore. But Susie likes her rag doll to be called Floppy Jane, so she will keep that name anyway.

Caleb is Tricked

Caleb Crocodile was always eating people with his big, sharp teeth.

A man passed Caleb's swamp while returning from a day's shopping. Caleb stopped him and said, "I'm going to eat you!"

"Oh, please, by all means eat me, but don't eat my wife's shopping," pleaded the man. Now Caleb always did what people asked him not to do and the man knew this. So Caleb said, "I WILL eat your shopping and then I'll eat YOU!"

CHOMP! CHOMP! went Caleb's teeth as he ate into the basket full of food. Inside the basket was a large bag of very sticky toffees. Caleb chewed on the toffees and tried to swallow them but the toffees made his teeth stick together instead. Because Caleb the crocodile was unable to open his mouth to eat the man, he went home to his wife quite safely.

Fillmytummy Goes Pop!

Fillmytummy was eating as usual.

"SCOFF! GUZZLE! CHOMP!" he gurgled happily, stuffing a jumbo sandwich into his mouth. This consisted of a filling of green jelly, a carrot, half a chocolate bar, a piece of brown seaweed, and three bananas coated with pickle spread.

"You eat so much you'll go pop one day," said his cousin, Thin-As-A-Rake, who was always on a diet.

"Nonsense," scoffed Fillmytummy and went to make himself another sandwich.

It wasn't long before Fillmytummy was stuffing his face with food again. But as he took one final bite of the sandwich there was an ear-shattering POP!

"Waaaaaah! Thin-As-A-Rake was right!" Fillmytummy shrieked. "I've eaten so much I've burst!" The silly troll ran off home to hide and he didn't eat again all that night.

Of course, Fillmytummy didn't really pop. Thin-As-A-Rake had sneaked up behind him with a large balloon which he burst with a pin!

The Roundabout Horse

Giddyup was a roundabout horse who worked at the fairground. She was a beautiful horse made of strong metal. She was painted a bright yellow, with a fiery red mane and a sparkling orange tail.

Every day children would pay the fairground owner to have a ride on the roundabout and Giddyup was the horse they all preferred. Giddyup went around and around as the music played, bobbing up and down on her pole. Giddyup liked the children but she was tired of going round all day in a circle. "It's boring," she sighed sadly.

One night, when the fairground was asleep, Giddyup slipped off her pole and galloped away. "I'll find another job," she thought. "Something more interesting."

But jobs for roundabout horses are in short supply these days and Giddyup discovered that no one wanted her.

Giddyup had nowhere to stay so she had to live outside in all weathers. When the sun came out her lovely paint peeled from the heat of the sun. When it rained heavily she began to turn a horrible rusty colour.

"Now no one will want me," sobbed Giddyup when she saw her reflection in a puddle and realised what a mess she was in.

A man who owned a junk shop in town, found Giddyup in the street and put her in his shop window to sell. "I might get a few pounds for you," he said, without much enthusiasm. But no one wanted a rusty, tatty ex-roundabout horse. "I'll have to have it melted down for scrap," said the junk shop man. This frightened Giddyup very much.

Just then a man passed by and saw Giddyup in the window. He rushed into the shop and said, "I want to buy that old roundabout horse."

The man took Giddyup home. He cleaned away the rust with a special brush until it was all gone. Then he repainted Giddyup's faded paintwork, this time giving her a royal blue body. He washed her fiery mane and brushed her sparkling orange tail. Then he fixed wooden rockers on the bottom of her feet. Giddyup rocked backwards and forwards. "I'm a rocking horse now!" she thought happily. The man gave Giddyup to his children. They loved her and took great care of her, and she never felt like running away again.

Imp

Bluebottle

I am a little bluebottle
Buzzing around all day,
People don't seem to like me
And shout, "SHOO! GO AWAY!"

Peter's Bike

Peter's dad had bought Peter a brand new racing bike. "Always remember to lock it up whenever you leave it anywhere," his dad warned him.

Peter promised that he would, but that very day when he rode to the sweet shop he parked his bike outside without putting the padlock around it. "I'll only be a few minutes. It'll be quite safe," he thought.

Peter took rather longer than a few minutes to choose his sweets and when he came out his bike had gone. "Someone's stolen it!" he cried unhappily.

Peter's dad was very angry and Peter didn't get another bike until he was much older. He always locked up his new bike whenever he left it anywhere this time, though!

Imp, the little red gremlin, was out looking for mischief to do. Seeing a man carrying a box of rubbish, he thought, "I'll cut a hole in the bottom of the box and all the rubbish will fall out!" Now Imp was very small and so the man didn't feel the gremlin climbing up his jacket to reach the box. With his tiny saw, Imp began to cut through the box.

The rubbish fell through the hole all over the street. You might think Imp was pleased with his naughty trick, but the silly gremlin was still underneath the box when the rubbish tumbled out, and he was buried beneath it. "That wasn't a good trick, after all," groaned Imp. "In fact, it was RUBBISH!"

Timothy's Tooth

Timothy's tooth had fallen out.

"Put it under your pillow tonight and the Good Fairy will exchange it for a silver coin," Mummy told him.

Timothy did this but decided to try to stay awake all night to see if he could catch a glimpse of the fairy when she came to visit him. Of course, he soon fell fast asleep.

The next morning there was no sign of his tooth under his pillow. Instead he found a silver coin.

"It's lucky you went to sleep," Mummy said, after Timothy told her what he had tried to do. "Fairies are very shy. If you had stayed awake she wouldn't have come at all."

The Ice Witch

Sir Bottletop, the brave knight, and his dragon companion, Dewdrop, were flying over a village covered in ice. "This is the work of the Ice Witch," frowned Sir Bottletop. With a beat of her mighty wings Dewdrop flew him to the Witch's Ice Castle.

The Ice Witch saw the two friends approaching and sent out her Ice warriors to fight them. CRASH! SMASH! BASH! sang Sir Bottletop's sword as he struck down the warriors until they were no more than ice cubes. Then Dewdrop took a mighty breath and directed the flame from her mouth towards the Ice Castle.

"AAAAAIIIIEEEEE!" screamed the Ice Witch as, first the castle and then she began to melt. Soon there was nothing left but a very big puddle of water.

Dewdrop melted all the ice around the village. The villagers were very grateful and from that day forward they sang songs about the bravery of Sir Bottletop and Dewdrop.

Spring

Mrs Cherryblossom stood on her doorstep and took a deep breath. "Ahhh, Spring is here at last!" she smiled happily, as she listened to the birds singing in the trees and looked at the snowdrops growing in the garden.

Mrs Cherryblossom decided to hold a garden party to welcome the arrival of Spring. She invited all her friends, who thought this was a wonderful idea.

"No more snow, or sleet, or hail, or cold winds," Mrs Cherryblossom cried happily as she lifted up her glass to toast her favourite time of the year.

Then she felt a drop rain land on her nose. Then another, and another. Soon everyone was running for shelter as the rain poured down. The garden party had to be cancelled.

The rain thought this was very funny. "Mrs Cherryblossom might have seen the last of the snow, and sleet, and hail and cold winds," it chuckled. "But she forgot about the Spring showers that help the flowers to grow."

Summer

Paula and Mick were busy making sandcastles on the beach. Just than a nasty boy came along and kicked the sandcastles down with his bare feet. "Ha ha! I love smashing sandcastles!" he gurgled, and wandered off.

Paula and Mick soon made another sandcastle, even bigger than before. When the boy saw this he ran up and stuck out his foot to smash the new castle down.

CRRUUUUNNNNCCCH!

"YEEEEEOOOOOWW! My toes!" yelled the boy as his foot struck the rock hidden inside the sandcastle. He hopped away, rubbing his sore, throbbing foot. "He won't bother us again," laughed the children, and went back to building sandcastles.

Autumn

The light Autumn breeze blew the yellow, red and brown leaves off the trees and over Treacle Tart's garden.

"Buttercups!" she frowned crossly. "I'll have to clean them up. They're making the garden look untidy."

Treacle Tart cast one of her spells.
"TIDDLEY POM POM
LEAVES BE GONE!"

The leaves swirled around and around the garden and then took off into the air. Soon the garden was clean again.

"I wonder where the leaves went to?" Treacle Tart thought as she made herself a bedtime cup of cocoa. "I never actually told them to go anywhere."

Treacle Tart was feeling very tired, so she pulled back the covers on her bed and jumped in . . . and just as quickly jumped out again, for her bed was full of leaves.

"Daisies!" she sighed, very annoyed. The silly leaves must have flown down my chimney and hidden in my bed!" So Treacle Tart didn't get to bed early that night. She was too busy sweeping up the leaves instead.

Winter

Mr Greenfingers was feeling very unhappy. In the Summer his garden blossomed with all kinds of beautiful flowers.

Everyone agreed his garden was the best in town. But now Winter had drawn in and all his flowers had died off from the cold, his garden was looking drab and dreary.

"My garden doesn't look the best in town now," he sighed. "It looks just the same as everyone else's." Then he had an idea. He went out and bought lots of plastic flowers, which he planted in his garden. People were amazed to see flowers growing in the middle of Winter. "How do you do it?" they asked, but Mr Greenfingers wouldn't tell them. It was his secret.

Imp Again

When Mrs Bumblebee washed her hair in readiness for the Mayor's tea party, Imp, the little red gremlin, swopped her bottle of shampoo for a bottle of hair colour. When Mrs Bumblebee looked in the mirror and saw her hair had turned a bright pinky-orangey-greeny colour she let out a very loud "SHRRRRRRRIIIIIIIIIEEEEEEEEEEEEEKKKK!!" Imp laughed and laughed. He thought it all terribly funny.

Mrs Bumblebee went to the Mayor's tea party wearing a big, floppy hat to cover her hair so no one could see it. The Mayor thought Mrs Bumblebee was very rude not taking off her hat when she met him, but he didn't say so.

Imp had followed Mrs Bumblebee and as she stood with the Mayor he knocked the hat from her head. Of course, as he was so small no one saw him and they all thought the hat had fallen off accidently. The Mayor stared at Mrs Bumblebee's pinky-orangey-greeny hair. Mrs Bumblebee was so embarrassed she didn't know what to say.

Then the Mayor smiled and said, "How clever! Fancy dying your hair in my three favourite colours!" The Mayor was very happy that Mrs Bumblebee had taken so much trouble to please him, and invited her back to the Town Hall for a dinner to be held in her honour.

"Drat!" snorted Imp crossly as he watched Mrs Bumblebee enjoying herself. "My mischief didn't ruin her day after all."

Dylan

Dylan the dachshund was fed up with people tripping over him. "Just because I'm low down and long, people don't see me," he grumbled.

The next day Dylan was seen with a large sign tied to his tail. BEWARE. DACHSHUND BELOW! "I should have thought of this before," he smiled as people steered well clear of him.

Tiny's Trumpet

The safari park where Tiny the elephant lived was organising a carnival procession.

"Can I join in?" Tiny asked the Park Supervisor.

"Sorry, Tiny," said the Supervisor. "This procession's for people only."

The band leader rushed up to the Supervisor, looking very flustered. "My trumpet player is sick. There's no one to play the trumpet in the procession."

The Supervisor smiled, looking down at Tiny. "Yes, there is," he chuckled.

Tiny led the procession along the streets, blowing the trumpet with his trunk as loudly as he could. "This is the happiest day of my life," he laughed.

The Battle

Two Kings had an argument and decided to go to war. But neither liked the idea of fighting in case they were killed.

"Why not have a pillow fight?" suggested the Queen of one of the Kings. "You can't get killed doing that."

Both Kings thought this was a wise idea and decided to have their pillow fight straight away. Soon they were battling it out, striking each other with the large pillows, when POOOUUF! the pillows burst and the Kings found themselves covered in feathers.

"Ha! Ha!" they laughed merrily, realising how silly they looked. "Let's forget our argument and be friends again." And so that is what they did. The Queen was happy because this is what she had planned should happen when she made sure the pillows would burst in the fight.

The Fridge

The ENORMOUS fat black cat saw that Mr Carraway had accidently left his fridge door open. The fridge was full of delicious food and the ENORMOUS fat black cat was hungry. He leapt into the fridge to feast . . . and the fridge door slammed shut tight behind him.

"MEEE-OOOOW!" squealed the ENORMOUS fat black cat, who was very scared. It was cold and dark in the fridge and there was no air to breathe. He thought his end had come.

Luckily Mr Carraway had seen what had happened and quickly pulled open the door again. The ENORMOUS fat black cat was so frightened that he ran off without even thanking Mr Carraway but he never went near an opened fridge again. He felt very guilty about trying to steal Mr Carraway's food, too!

suspiciously.

"Yes, mother," Dimple fibbed, trying hard not to laugh.

"Oh, dear, I'll have to cancel your party then," his mother said.

"PARTY?" squealed Dimple excitedly. "What party?"

"I was going to hold a surprise party for you," his mother told him. "Those letters you delivered were invitations to all the other dragonets to come to the party. But since no one's arrived the party will have to be cancelled."

Dimple's heart sank. "Oooh! I'm such a fool!" he scolded himself after his mother had left. "If I had worked hard instead of being lazy I could be having a great time now." Dimple had learned his lesson. From that day on he always did what his mother asked of him . . . just in case.

Dimple's Lazy Day

Dimple the dragonet lay basking in the warm sunshine. "This is the life," he thought happily. "Doing nothing all day but watch the dandelions float past."

"Dimple, stop being so lazy and deliver these letters to the other dragonets in the village," said his mother.

"ALL these letters?" wailed Dimple horrified. "It'll take me ages."

"You had better get started then," said his mother sharply.

Dimple flew into the air carrying the heavy sack of letters. "I'm not delivering all these, it's too much like hard work," he decided, and dropped the sack into a fast-flowing river. "They're probably not important anyway," he thought as he flew back home.

"Have you delivered all the letters yet?" asked his mother later that day.

"I have," smiled Dimple innocently.

Dimple sat back in the warm sunshine again. "This is better than working," he chuckled.

"Are you sure you delivered those letters properly?" It was some time later and Dimple's mother was looking at him

The Athlete

"I wish I could jump higher than anyone else can," said the athlete, dropping a coin into the Wishing Well.

The athlete had entered the high jump event in the sports arena. He ran, and leapt high into the air. His jump took him so high he disappeared from sight and was last seen heading towards the moon.

"Well, he did want to jump higher than anyone else," chuckled the Wishing Well naughtily. "And no one can jump higher than that!".

The Unicorn

Bambino, the young white unicorn, was feeding in the forest. A young native boy who was out hunting, saw Bambino and decided to kill him for the beautiful horn growing out of his head.

"I will recieve great praise from the elders of my tribe," the boy thought. He crawled towards Bambino and then leapt at the animal, pulling out his long, sharp hunting knife. Bambino galloped away and the boy landed in a prickly bush instead. This made the boy very angry and he chased Bambino through the forest. He was so intent on killing the beautiful unicorn that he failed to see a dangerous swamp until he tumbled into it.

"I-I'm sinking!" he cried as the mud sucked him down. "HELP!" he cried loudly, but there was no one to hear him.

No one, that is, except for Bambino. "Why should I save him! He tried to kill me," he thought. He trotted away, trying not to hear the boy's frightened cries. But it was no use. He was a kind-hearted unicorn and could not bear to see anyone hurt.

"If I allow him to die I am no better than the boy," he decided, hurrying back to the swamp. The boy had already sunk until only his chest and head could be seen. Bambino stretched out his neck for the boy to catch hold of his horn. Using all his strength Bambino pulled and pulled, until, slowly, the boy slipped free of the swamp.

"Thank you," he said, patting Bambino on the head. "For saving my life. I shall tell my father, the chief of our tribe, to make a law that forbids anyone to harm a hair on you head."

The boy did as he promised and from that day forward Bambino was allowed to live in peace.

Captain Bungle

KER-SMASH! Captain Bungle, the super-powered super hero who had the strength of one thousand raging hippopotamuses, smashed through the solid brick wall of a house.

"Hold, Villians!" he cried, flexing his rippling muscles for all to see. "I, Captain Bungle, greatest super hero in the Universe (and the most handsome) have come to bring you to Justice!"

"Oh, Captain!" tittered Granny Grimbles, sitting in her rocking chair. "You are a one. Do I look like a villian?"

Captain Bungle's face went super-red with embarrassment. "Ooops! Bungled again!" he grinned sheepishly. Using his see-through vision to see through the walls of the house, he spotted the real villians next door.

"Aha! They can't fool Captain Bungle!" he cried, and KER-SMASH! he ran through the wall to catch them.

"GASP! Captain Bungle!" quivered Jock, stepping back in terror. "We give up!"

"Oh, fudge!" muttered the Captain feeling very disappointed. "I've been looking forward to fighting you with my super powers. Are you sure you haven't got a multi-dimensional, inter-galactic, ping-pong destructor gun to use against me?"

"No," said Jimmy, stuffing his hand in his pocket and pulling out a paper bag. "But I've got some jelly babies if you'd like one."

As Captain Bungle led the boys away Granny Grimble poked her head out of the hole in the wall of her house. "What dreadful things did they do? she asked. "Rob a bank? Steal the Crown Jewels?"

"Worse than that," growled Captain Bungle. "They drew a rude picture of me on the garden wall!"

Penelope's Travels

"It's too hot in this jungle," complained Penelope Panther as the sun beat down where she lay. "I'm going to live where it is always nice and cool."

She found a raft which had been built by one of the natives and jumped aboard. The raft sailed away and Penelope felt very pleased with herself. Soon she left the jungle far behind. The climate was getting cooler. Some while later she woke up from a deep sleep and found herself feeling very cold. "Brrr! I know I wanted it to be cooler but this is silly!" she shivered, watching ice form on her whiskers. The raft sailed past a huge lump of ice floating in the water. "What's that?" wondered Penelope, never having seen an iceberg before. It wasn't long before the raft struck land and Penelope got off. "I've arrived!" cheered Penelope, stepping onto the icy, snow-covered ground.

"Hello," said a passing penguin. You're a bit far from home, aren't you?"

"Where am I?" asked Penelope, feeling a little foolish for not knowing.

"The Antarctic," replied the penguin.

"Er, it seems a little cold today," Penelope said. "I-I suppose the weather's just having a day-off and it will be nice and warm tomorrow?" she asked hopefully.

The penguin laughed. "This is the warmest day we've had this year. Usually it's twice as cold as this."

The penguin invited Penelope home for tea. "Fish?" growled Penelope ungratefully, looking at the plate of fish the penguin had offered her. "Panthers don't eat fish!"

"They do if they live in the Antarctic," said the penguin. "That's just about all there is to eat."

Penelope was feeling very cold and very fed up. "I want to go home," she said.

So, returning to her raft, Penelope set sail again. Some weeks later she arrived back in the hot jungle.

"What a lovely hot sun," she yawned, stretching out on the ground to sunbathe. "How I've missed it."

Hopeless Baker

There was once a useless baker who made the most disgusting, horrible-tasting cakes.

"Uggh!" cried customers after they had sampled his cakes and lost their front teeth in the process. "They're awful! They're as hard as rock and twice as revolting!" Mr Rolling Pin felt very sad. No one would buy his cakes and he soon became very poor.

One day a king passed through the town. When he heard about Mr Rolling Pin's disasterous rock-hard cakes he was very pleased and ordered three dozen boxes of them. Mr Rolling Pin was amazed and delighted. "Someone appreciates my cakes at last," he thought.

"Oh, they're not for eating," said the king.

"B-But what are you going to do with them then?" asked Mr Rolling Pin, who was feeling very confused.

The king laughed. "I want a rockery in my garden and your rock-hard cakes are just the right shape. They're so hard that the weather won't be able to wear them away."

At first Mr Rolling Pin was very hurt by this but then he had an idea. He began to sell his cakes as part of a rockery. Everyone wanted to have an unusual rockery in their garden and Mr Rolling Pin soon sold out of his cakes and retired, very rich.

The Fast Snail

Sammy Snail lived life in a rush. He always did everything in a hurry. Well, if you or I saw him we would think he was very slow, as snails usually are. But compared to other snails Sammy was always dashing here and there. "Slow down or you'll have an accident," Grandad Snail warned him.

"Silly old duffer," thought Sammy, hurrying past a pond. "Life's too short for moving slowly."

Sammy was rushing so fast he tripped and tumbled into the pond. "I can't swim!" he squealed as he began to sink.

Luckily Grandad Snail was passing and managed to pull him out. "You're right, Grandad," Sammy apologised. "Snails are meant to live life slowly." And from that day on Sammy did slow down.

My Brother

My brother Jake
Pinched the cake
Mum had made for tea,
When Mum found out
She gave Jake a clout,
I'm glad it wasn't me!

Marmaduke's Parachute

Marmaduke Monkey kept falling out of bed, which was a bit of a problem because he lived high in the top of the trees. He had a long way to fall and was always bruising himself.

One day an aeroplane flew overhead and supplies were sent down by parachute to some explorers. This gave Marmaduke's mother an idea. She sewed lots of leaves together until they were as big as a blanket. Using some twine she tied the leaf-blanket to Marmaduke. "What's this for?" he asked, but his mother just said, "Wait and see."

That night, as usual, Marmaduke rolled out of bed. But instead of falling swiftly and landing with a crash, he found himself floating gracefully to the ground. The leaf-blanket had filled with air just like a parachute and gently lowered him to the ground. "How clever," thought Marmaduke. "I'll never bruise myself again."

Lenny's Spots

Lenny the Leopard was always boasting about his wonderful spotted coat. "My coat is the best in the world," he told the other animals.

George Gorilla was fed up with Lenny's boasting. "If you don't shut up I'll knock the spots off you," he said.

"Ha!" snorted Lenny, who believed himself to be the best fighter in the jungle. "I'd like to see you try."

KA-POW! George gave Lenny a good wallop on the end of his nose. "Yeeoow!" Lenny cried. Then he cried even more as, one by one, the spots dropped off his beautiful coat.

"Now your coat's not so wonderful," said George. "In fact it's very plain."

Lenny was upset. He had to get his mother to sew all the spots back on. This took a long time and was rather painful because the needle kept digging into him.

The next time Lenny met the other animals and was ready to boast about his wonderful coat, he saw George approaching and quickly shut up.

"No more boasting for me," he thought wisely.

Hula Hoop

SSSSlither the snake was watching a group of children playing with hula hoops in the park.

"I wish I had a hoop," said a little boy. SSSSlither felt sorry for the boy. He curled himself around until he could catch his tail in his mouth. He looked very much like a hula hoop snake. The boy was very pleased at having a hoop of his own and rolled SSSSlither around the park all morning.

"I'm glad I helped cheer him up," thought SSSSlither after the boy had gone home. "I just feel very dizzy, that's all!"

Cold Weather

I hate the cold
Of a winter's day,
I prefer the warm breeze
That blows in May.
The cold makes me cough
And sneeze and quiver,
And without my gloves
I start to shiver.
Please go away cold,
So bitter and raw,
I'll stay at home behind my door,
Until spring returns
To warm me once more.

Ski-ing

Roger the Rhinoceros wanted to go ski-ing.

"That might be a problem," said his friend, Leroy Lion. "There's no snow here and you can't afford to go on holiday."

Roger was disappointed. Then Leroy saw Albert Alligator riding past on his roller skates. Leroy bought the skates from Albert and fixed them to the bottom of two planks of wood. He fastened these to Roger's feet. "There, now you have your own pair of roller skate skis."

Roger was very excited. Using a pair of broom handles to push himself along, he went ski-ing along the pavement until he came to a steep hill.

"WHEEEEEEEEEE!" he cried happily as he went faster down the hill. Then he frowned. "Er, where are the brakes?"

CRRRAAASSSSSH! Roger crashed through the brick wall of the Mayor's house, through his flower bed, and into the garden fountain, demolishing it. He finally stopped when he landed upsidedown in a dustbin.

"I think I need more practice," he groaned.

roasting fire. "What am I doing in here?" he roared nervously.

"I'm warming you up like you asked," said Mrs Rabbit. "I've never had fox stew before." She was only joking. The only stew she liked was carrot stew, but Mr Fox didn't know this. He leapt out of the cooking pot and ran out of the house, and was never seen again. Clever Mrs Rabbit. She knew what he was up to all the time.

Invited In

Mr Fox wanted to eat Mrs Rabbit so he pretented to be cold, knowing that kind Mrs Rabbit would feel sorry for him and invite him into her house.

"Brrrr!" please let me come in to warm myself by your fire?" he asked Mrs Rabbit, standing shivering outside her door.

"Of course," said Mrs Rabbit. "But I don't really trust you, Mr Fox, and you must promise to wear this blindfold."

Mr Fox put on the blindfold. It was so thick he couldn't see through it at all. "Once I'm in Mrs Rabbits' house, I'll pull this off and gobble her up," he thought.

Mrs Rabbit led Mr Fox by the paw. Mr Fox could feel himself being led into the house and then up a set of steps. "She must be taking me upstairs to tuck me into a warm bed," he thought. "I always did like my breakfast in bed!"

At the top of the steps Mr Fox moved forward, and found himself falling. His feet landed on a cold metal surface. "That's strange," he thought. "This doesn't feel like a nice, comfy bed."

"You may take your blindfold off now," said Mrs Rabbit. Mr Fox did so, ready to pounce on Mrs Rabbit. He found himself standing in a large, metal cooking pot over a

Buffalo

Big Chief Itchy Nose was out hunting.

"Uggh! Buffalo somewhere near," he grunted, and placed his ear to the ground. Indians do this when they are trying to listen for something moving in the distance.

RRRRUUUMMMMBBLE! Big Chief Itchy Nose smiled as he heard the thunder of hooves. "Buffalo very near. I can almost smell um!"

RRRRUUUMMMMBBLE!

"GASPUM!" gasped the Chief as a herd of buffalo stampeded over him in their search for a water hole.

When the buffalo had passed, Big Chief Itchy Nose lay flattened into the desert sand.

"Feel heap run down!" he moaned.

Ben's Surprise

Ben looked out of his window and gasped in surprise. Coming along the road was a cow . . . and it was dancing, it was doing a fox trot!

"I've never seen a dancing cow before," Ben smiled.

He looked again and saw a giraffe following the cow . . . and it was juggling six plates, two cups and a saucer in the air.

"I've never seen a juggling giraffe before," smiled Ben.

Then he saw an elephant riding on a bicycle, a gorilla playing bagpipes, six lions doing somersaults, a zebra balancing a bottle on the end of its nose, and a hippoptamus on a pogo stick!

Ben ran out into the garden . . . and then he laughed as he realised what was happening. "It's a carnival!" he shouted, watching a procession coming along the road. Of course, those animals weren't really animals at all but people dressed in costumes. Ben didn't mind. He enjoyed every minute of the carnival.

Patricia's Nest

It was a blustery day and Patricia Pigeon was fed up. Every time she finished building her nest of twigs, the wind came along and blew it apart again.

A lot of rubbish was being blown along the street by the wind and Patricia saw a cardboard box tumble past. Swooping down, she struggled to lift the box with her beak. This was not easy because she was only a small pigeon and the box was rather big.

Eventually, after much huffing and puffing and dropping the box so that she had to swoop down again to pick it up, Patricia succeeded in carrying the box into the branches of her tree. Once it was secure Patricia began to fill the box with twigs. She fashioned the twigs into a nest. When she had finished, she sat in the nest feeling very happy.

"This box stops the wind from blowing my nest away," she cooed, and settled down to sleep.

Goal!

"Girls can't play soccer!" laughed Derek at his sister when she asked to join in the game he was having with his friends. "It's a boy's game."

"Let Carol play with you," said his mother sternly, so the boys had to let her join in.

"You'll never score a goal," sneered Derek. Carol didn't say a word. She tackled the ball from him, dribbled it around the other boys and kicked it over the goalkeeper's head. The ball landed in the back of the net. "GOAL!" her mother cheered. The boys were astonished but Carol just winked at her mother. "I've been practising!" she chuckled .

Goggles

Dennis was riding his bike in the garden while his sister Kate splashed about in the paddling pool. She wore goggles to keep the water out of her eyes. "You do look funny," Dennis teased her. "Like someone from Outer Space!"

Dennis rode faster and faster. He rode around the trees, past the flower bed and along the garden path.

"Ouch!" he cried as a piece of dirt flew into his eye and made it water. Dennis shut his eyes which, of course, meant he couldn't see where he was going. His bike struck a stone and he tumbled off.

"I won't be able to ride my bike while it's so windy," Dennis said.

"Of course you will," said Kate, handing Dennis her goggles. "If you wear these, nothing can get into your eyes."

This worked a treat and Dennis never teased Kate about her goggles again.

Flying High

Ollie Ostrich didn't like being a flightless bird. He wanted to soar high into the sky with the eagles and doves.

"You're too heavy to fly," said his friend, Koala Kate, but Ollie was determined to make his dream come true. He packed his bags and caught the next train to town.

Koala Kate missed her friend and wondered what had happened to him. One day she heard a loud buzzing in the sky. An aeroplane zoomed overhead and then looped-the-loop. "That's a clever pilot," Kate thought. She was surprised when the aeroplane landed next to her tree. She was even more surprised when Ollie stepped out, wearing a pilot's helmet and goggles. "I've learnt how to fly, after all!" he chuckled.

Where's Granny?

The robin flew down to the bird table for his morning meal of breadcrumbs, but to his disappointment the table was bare.

"The old lady who lives here never misses putting out bread for me in the morning," he trilled. "I hope nothing bad has happened to her."

A little girl approached the bird table, carrying a bowl of breadcrumbs. "Granny's been taken poorly and has gone into hospital," she explained to the robin. "So she's asked me to feed you instead."

The robin was most grateful to the little girl and sang a special song to wish Granny a speedy recovery.

Oswald the Ghost

Oswald the ghost heard a commotion outside his house.

"LIGHTS! CAMERA! ACTION!" shouted a voice very loudly.

"They're making a horror movie!" laughed Oswald. "But I don't think much of the monster!" The "monster" was a man dressed in a rubber suit who kept waving his arms about and saying, "Growl! Growl!" whenever the Director told him to.

"I could do better than that," thought Oswald, who always liked the idea of being a famous movie star. He walked through the wall of his house and into the street.

"Excuse me," he said, tapping the Director on the shoulder. The Director thought Oswald was someone dressed in a white sheet. "Go away!" he snapped. "We've got enough actors. Anyway, you look nothing like a real ghost!" He pushed at Oswald to send him away . . . and his hand went right through Oswald's chest.

"AAAAAAAAAAAAAGGGGGGGHHHH! A real g-g-g-ghost!" screamed the Director and ran off down the road, followed by the rest of the film crew.

"Huh! Bang goes my chance to star in a film," sighed Oswald, going back into his house.

Mr Tremble (1)

"Oh, what a clown you are!" Mrs Tremble roared. Mr Tremble had dropped the plate he was drying and it shattered all over the floor.

"S-Sorry, dear," said Mr Tremble, trembling nervously. Mr Tremble had a hard life. He was rather accident-prone and he had a wife who was always nagging him.

"You clown!" she would bellow if he accidently trod on the cat's tail.

Mrs Tremble always called Mr Tremble a clown because that is what she thought he was. She married him for his money and when that ran out, she didn't have much use for him.

"Go on, out of my way, clown!" she yelled after Mr Tremble had knocked over the coal bucket on the carpet. Mr Tremble decided it would be wise to go for a walk. Then he decided to run away from home altogether. "But where shall I go?" he pondered. Then he had a bright idea.

When Mr Tremble didn't come back home that night Mrs Tremble wasn't worried. Nor did she care when he didn't return the next day, or even the next month. "Good riddance!" she thought.

A Circus (2)

A circus came to town and Mrs Tremble decided to go and see it. She cheered at the high-wire act, clapped at the jugglers. The acrobats were very popular and the trick motorbike rider made the crowd cheer. Then came the clowns, dressed in their baggy trousers, funny noses and painted faces. They chased each other around the ring, throwing custard pies and squirting each other with water. "What funny clowns!" cheered Mrs Tremble.

One of the clowns seemed familiar to Mrs Tremble but she couldn't think why. This clown picked up a large bucket and hopped-skipped-jumped to where she was sitting.

"He'll pretend to throw water over me but really its only paper in the bucket," chuckled Mrs Tremble, who had seen this act before. The clown lifted up the bucket and SPLOOOOSSSH! poured freezing cold water all over Mrs Tremble! "EEEEEEK!" she screamed. She was very angry.

"I've always wanted to do that, dear," laughed the clown. Mrs Tremble stared in amazement. She knew that voice. Looking closely at the clown she recognised who it was under the make-up. "MR TREMBLE!" she gasped.

"Hello, dear," smiled Mr Tremble. "You were always calling me a clown so I became one!" Good for Mr Tremble. He got his own back on his nagging wife at last!

Pirate

If I were a pirate
I'd sail the Seven Seas,
Stealing gold from merchant ships
And keeping it all for me.
I'd bury treasure on an island
That no one knew was there,
I'd fly the skull and crossbones
It's not allowed, but I don't care!
I'd be a rough, tough pirate
So everyone would run away,
But if the navy chased me
I'd hide, to fight another day!

The Lighthouse

Billy's parents had taken him to visit a lighthouse. "This light warns the ships not to come too close or they'll crash on the rocks," explained the lighthouse keeper. He was showing Billy a bright yellow light that swivelled around and around. Billy was fascinated.

That evening his Dad came to tuck him in bed. He found Billy spinning around and around, holding a torch whose yellow beam shone out brightly. "I'm pretending to be a lighthouse!" laughed Billy.

Little Pig

Little Pig was always running off and getting lost. Mrs Pig was tired of having to search for her offspring so she bought a bell and tied it around his neck. "Now I can hear you wherever you are," she said.

When Little Pig went missing again Mrs Pig wasn't worried. She could hear the bell ringing over the hill. But when she climbed the hill there was no sign of Little Pig. Only his bell, hanging from a tree and blowing in the wind. The naughty piglet had taken off the bell so he could run off without anyone finding him.

Morning Dip

Dotty Duck ran to her pond for her morning dip in the refreshing water.

"I wouldn't if I were you," said Gandy Goose, but Dotty wouldn't listen. She leapt over the bushes towards the pond and WHUMP! landed on something hard and very cold to touch. She slid from one end of the pond to the other, ending up with her feet in the air.

"You should have listened to me," laughed Gandy. "It was so cold last night the pond froze over. You'll have to wait until the ice thaws before you can go for your dip."

Catching a Plane

Captain Bungle, the super hero with the strength of a thousand raging rhinoceroses, flew through the air looking for good deeds to do. He was so intent on looking earthwards that he didn't see where he was flying.

SMAAASSSSH! He collided with a jet aeroplane, knocking off one of its wings.

"EEEEEEEEEEEEEEEEEEEKKKK!" screamed the passengers as the aeroplane dropped out of the sky.

"Fear not! I, Captain Bungle, greatest (and most handsome) super hero in the Universe,

will save you!" he cried, flying down after the aeroplane.

Captain Bungle stood on the ground with his arms outstrectched, ready to catch the plane before it hit the ground. Closer, closer it came.

"I'll catch it easily," smiled the Captain.

"Hey, mate, got the time?" asked a little boy.

Captain Bungle looked at the nuclear-powered watch on his wrist. "Yes, it's . . ." KA-BLAAAAAAAAAAAAAAAAAAAAAM! The aeroplane smashed into the ground, breaking into a trillion pieces.

"Oooops! Bungled again" frowned the Captain. "I forgot I was catching the aeroplane!"

"Well, catch this!" bellowed the battered and bruised passengers as they pulled themselves out of the wreckage and started throwing bits of the aeroplane at Captain Bungle.

"Ooow! Ouch! Oooggh! he wailed as the pieces bounced off his super-thick head. "Sorry! Can't stop to chat! Must fly!" and off he dashed.

Bear and Wolf

"Who's been eating my food?" roared Wolf angrily. He had spent all summer and autumn collecting food which he stored in his den for winter. Now it was gone.

"Not me," said Bear, as he passed by. He chuckled to himself. He had eaten all Wolf's food when Wolf was out hunting. "He'll have to go hungry this winter!" he smiled. Now he lumbered home to feast on the food he had stored in his cave. But when he got there his food had gone. Wolf had known that Bear was telling lies and had hurried to his cave to steal all his food before he arrived home. So they both went hungry that winter.

Chestnut Tree

Looking out of his window Glen saw the young chestnut tree in his garden looking bare and forlorn without its leaves.

"It'll catch cold," Glen thought and went outside with a box of his old clothes.

When Glen's father came home and saw the tree dressed in Glen's shirt, coat, hat, scarf and trousers he couldn't help laughing.

Ali and Baba

Diana's mother brought home a black cat. Diana was very happy to have a cat of her own. She called the cat Ali and took great care of him. She fed him twice a day, groomed him when his coat was dirty, and allowed him to sleep on her bed every night.

One night Diana let Ali out for his evening exercise but he didn't come back. Diana was very upset and spent most of the night crying. The next morning she opened the front door and there was Ali, sitting on the doorstep. By his side was another black cat.

"Ali's brought a friend home," Diana smiled. She asked her mother if the new cat could stay. Ali was very happy to have a friend for company.

Diana decided that Ali's new friend would be called Baba!

The Chair

Jake was always rocking back on two legs of a chair.

"If you break that chair you'll be sitting on an orange box," warned his father, but Jake took no notice.

SNAP! went the legs of the chair and Jake tumbled to the ground. Jake's father had meant what he said, and, at the next meal, Jake had to sit on a hard, uncomfortable wooden box that oranges had been delivered in. He had to sit on the box for every meal for a week, and his bottom soon became very sore. Then his father bought him a new chair. "I won't rock back on this one," Jake promised.

The Scarf

Tim and Terry's Granny had promised to knit them both a scarf each. She set to work and her needles went click-click, click-click, all day long. When the twins came to visit next, they asked if the scarves were finished. "Well, one's done," said Granny, looking embarrassed. "But I ran out of wool to finish the other."

"Oh, dear, that means one of us will have to go without," sighed the twins, feeling very disappointed.

Granny fetched the scarf and when the twins saw it they burst out laughing. It was rather a long scarf. In fact, it was very, very, very, very, very, very, very, very long! "I, er, got a bit carried away," Granny said. "That's why I ran out of wool."

"Don't worry," smiled the twins. "This will do for both of us." First Tim wrapped one end of the scarf around his neck, and then Terry wrapped the other end around her neck. "Now we'll have to go everywhere together," they laughed.

Nibbles

Nibbles the donkey was always nibbling things and getting into trouble. One hot summer's day he stood in his field feeling very uncomfortable. "This sun burns my head," he grumbled.

A group of tourists parked nearby. When they saw Nibbles they got out to take photographs. One very fat lady wearing a big straw hat came over to Nibbles. As she got closer he took two big bites out of each side of her hat.

"What a nasty donkey!" shrieked the woman. "He's ruined my best hat." She threw the hat on the ground and hurried away. When the tourists had gone Nibbles picked up the hat. The two holes he had made fitted neatly over his ears. When other tourists drove past and saw a donkey wearing a straw hat on his head, they were very amused. Nibbles didn't care. He had something to protect his head from the sun.

137

idea. "Psssst! Psssst! Psssst!" he whispered into her ear.

That night Treacle Tart rode on her broomstick to the Witch's party wearing nothing but a wooden barrel. "I think I should have just worn my purple clothes instead," she sighed. Back home the ENORMOUS fat black cat spent all evening laughing at the way he had tricked Treacle Tart into making a fool of herself.

"That'll teach her to turn me into an ENORMOUS fat green toad!" he sniggered.

The Purple Dress

Although it is hard to believe, the ENORMOUS fat black cat changed his ways and went to live with Treacle Tart the Witch. Well, actually, Treacle Tart caught him raiding her larder and tried to stop him by turning him into stone. Unfortunately the spell backfired and he found himself turned into an ENORMOUS fat green toad instead. This didn't please him one bit, (for a start he hated water yet now found himself hopping into slimy ponds). He was so grateful when Treacle Tart finally discovered the right spell to turn him back into a cat some weeks later, that he chose to stay with her from that day on.

"MEE-HEE-HEE-OOW!" he sniggered. Treacle Tart's spell for washing her dirty clothes had backfired and turned them a bright purple colour. "If you wear that lot everyone will think you're a grape!"

"Very funny!" scowled Treacle Tart, holding up her purple dress which used to be red. "I can't wear this to the Witch's party!"

The ENORMOUS fat black cat had an

Wooden Horse

The King's magician created for him a magical wooden horse. "This horse won't get tired and doesn't need feeding," he said. The King went for a ride on his new horse but when he returned he was very cross. "I'm going back to real horses," he said. "And you're going to the royal dungeons."

"B-But why?" spluttered the magician. "Don't you like your magical wooden horse?"

"At least with real horses you don't get splinters in your finger!" roared the King.

Pancakes

Mrs Mopp was tossing a pancake in the air when Imp, the mischievous gremlin, sneaked up behind her and shouted, "BOOOO!" very loudly.

Mrs Mopp was so startled she forgot to catch the pancake and it fell with a PLOP! onto the floor and covered Imp. Mrs Mopp picked up the pancake and Imp (who was so small she hadn't see him) and threw them both into the bin.

"YUM!" slurped Imp, tucking into the pancake. "For once my mischief has worked a treat!"

The Frog

The sun had been burning down for many weeks and all the water in the ponds had dried up. "This sun will be the death of me," croaked a poor frog. His once oily skin had become cracked and dry. He was almost too weak to move.

A girl passed by and saw the sad frog. She picked him up and took him home. Once there, she filled a large bucket with water from the kitchen tap, and gently lowered the frog into it. The frog swam happily in the water. He felt much better. "RIBBETT! RIBBETT! he croaked, thanking the girl for saving his life.

Toby's One Man Band

Toby wanted to play in a band, like his big brother.

"You're too young," said his brother, who was busy practising on his drums. Toby did feel miserable.

"Don't worry," said his Dad. "You can start up your own one man band."

"But I don't have any instruments," Toby said.

Toby's Dad pulled out a set of pans from the kitchen cupboard and put them on the table. Then he gave Toby a large wooden mixing spoon. BAM! BAM! BAM! went the pots as Toby hit them with the spoon. "These can be your drums," his Dad said.

Toby's Dad slipped three very large elastic bands around an empty shoe box. TWANG! TWANG! TWANG! went the elastic bands when Toby plucked them. "This is your guitar," his Dad said.

Finally, Toby's Dad wrapped a piece of tissue paper around a comb. He put it to his mouth and began to hum gently on it. HMMMM! HMMMM! HMMMM! went the funny sound. "This can be your mouth organ," he told Toby.

Toby played with his musical instruments all afternoon and everyone agreed his was the best one man band they had ever heard.

Dog, Cat, Rat

There was once a rat who lived in the farmer's barn. It was warm and cozy in the barn and the rat always had plenty to eat. The only trouble was that the farmer had a cat who was always chasing the poor rat so that he could eat him for supper. This made life difficult and dangerous for the rat.

One day the farmer brought home a savage dog to guard the farm from burglars. The dog ignored the rat completely but, when the farmer wasn't looking, he would chase the cat all around the farm. The cat had to hide in the barn and when he saw the rat he said, "Please help me get rid of that dog. If you do I promise I'll never chase you again."

The rat agreed and that night he visited the dog in his kennel. At first the dog ignored him, as usual, but when the rat bit the dog on the nose, he started to bark very loudly. The farmer rushed out in his pyjamas because he thought the dog had caught a burglar. He couldn't see the rat and decided that there was no reason for the dog to bark. The farmer went back to bed. The rat bit the dog's tail next, which started him barking all over again. The farmer hurried out, but of course, no one was there. This went on until daybreak and the farmer had a very sleepless night.

The next morning the farmer took the dog back. "I'll do without a guard dog," he told the man at the kennels.

The cat was relieved that the dog had gone and he kept his promise and never chased the rat again.

The Job

Dreamy Daniel went to a factory to see if he could get a job. When he reached the door of the factory he tried to push it open. He pushed, and he pushed, and he pushed. Then, becoming very annoyed, he charged at the door and tried to burst it open but all he did was bruise his shoulder.

"Stupid door," muttered Daniel, and he went off home again.

The manager of the factory had been watching all this. He sighed with relief as he saw Daniel leave. "What a silly man! I wouldn't have given him a job anyway. The sign over the door says PULL TO OPEN! Poor Daniel. It was a pity he couldn't read!

Sisters

My sister and I
Are always fighting,
Punching and thumping,
Scratching and biting.
I tear up her book
She jumps on my doll,
And sometimes we drive
Poor Mum up the pole.
But then we laugh
And giggle and sing,
We play together
And share everything.
Like other sisters
We do disagree
But really
We're the greatest of pals, you see!

Dally's Bone

Dally, the spotty dog, had unearthed a giant bone in a field. It was at least five times as big as Dally.

"Can I have some?" asked Dilly, Dally's friend.

"Not likely!" growled Dally. "There's only one and it's all for me."

Dilly was disappointed but he couldn't help sniggering when two men came and took Dally's bone away.

"A dinosaur bone," said one of the men, who was a great scientist. "We must have it for our museum."

"GUURRRRR! That's my bone!" snarled Dally crossly.

The second man laughed when he saw how upset Dally was at losing his bone. "Ho! Ho! This little dog deserves a reward for finding it."

That afternoon the two men returned with a large box full of meaty bones which they gave to Dally.

"C'mon, Dilly," Dally called to his friend. "Now there's enough bones for both of us."

Bill and Ben

Bill and Ben, two little brown puppies, were always getting into mischief. One day they escaped from their house and ran into the street. It was getting dark and when they saw two big bright eyes racing towards them, and heard a loud roaring in their ears, they became very frightened and ran back indoors to their mother. "A monster's after us!" they squealed.

"That wasn't a monster!" smiled their mother. "It was a car driven by a human. Those big bright eyes you saw were the car's headlights." Bill and Ben were relieved to hear this, but they stayed with their mother from then on just to be on the safe side.

Magic Umbrella

Pinchapenny the troll was always stealing things that didn't belong to him. Once he stole a lovely yellow umbrella from Mr Weatherby's Umbrella Shop.

"What a fine umbrella this is!" he said, opening it up. "I'll look very grand with this."

What Pinchapenny didn't know was that the umbrella was magical. It knew Pinchapenny was a thief and decided to teach him a lesson.

WWOOOOOSSSH! A gust of wind caught the umbrella and lifted it high into the air. Pinchapenny tried to let go but found his hands were stuck to the handle. "HELP!" he cried as the umbrella flew him high over the rooftops.

"EEEEK! OOOUCH! YOOW!" he yelled as the umbrella swooped down and dragged him through a prickly bush.

BONG! Pinchapenny's ears rattled after the umbrella had flown him into the clock tower bell.

"Please let me down!" Pinchapenny pleaded, sobbing loudly. "I'll never steal anything again!"

The handle of the umbrella came off in Pinchapenny's hand and he found himself falling, falling, out of the sky to land with a SPLOODGGGE! in a dirty, pig's sty.

The next day Pinchapenny saw the umbrella back in Mr Weatherby's Umbrella Shop. But this time he kept his hands tightly in his pockets.

Peter's Rabbit

Peter had caught a rabbit in the field. He took him home to keep as a pet.

"It's cruel to keep wild rabbits as pets," his father said, but Peter wouldn't listen. He put the rabbit in a small hutch and gave it some lettuce to eat. When he returned and saw that the rabbit hadn't eaten he was most upset. "If you don't eat, you'll die," he said, but the rabbit just sat hunched up in a corner of the hutch, looking very scared and miserable.

"I warned you," said his father, when Peter asked his advice. "Wild animals need to be free."

Peter felt guilty about catching the rabbit and the next morning released it back into the fields. "I'll try to persuade dad to buy me a puppy," he thought.

Tails

The lion and tiger had been fighting. When they eventually stopped they discovered that their tails had tangled together. No matter how hard they tried, they couldn't pull them apart.

"Well, I'm off to lunch," said the tiger, and tried to walk in one direction.

"My home's this way," said the lion, trying to walk off in the other direction. Of course, with their tails tangled together they didn't get very far.

"What are we going to do?" asked the lion.

"Cut off your tail," suggested the tiger. "Then we'll be able to go our separate ways."

"Not likely!" snarled the lion, who was very proud of his tail. "Why don't you cut your tail off?"

Neither animal liked this idea so they tried pulling this way and that to see if they could pull free, but it was no use.

Just then a mouse passed by carrying a shopping bag full of groceries. She laughed when she saw the lion and tiger all tangled together. "I'll get you free," she said kindly.

"YOU?" snorted the lion and tiger together. "What can you do?"

The mouse took out a packet of margarine from her bag. She smeared the margarine all over the tails of the lion and tiger. "Now pull!" she told them. They did as she said and FLIIIIP! their tails slipped free of each other.

The lion and tiger were very grateful and always allowed the little mouse to ride on their backs when she went to the shops.

The Egg

Out for her morning waddle Mrs Duck came across an egg in a field. "Who does this belong to?" she pondered. "If it isn't kept warm the baby chick inside will perish." So, picking up the egg in her beak, she carried it home. There she sat on the egg until it hatched and out popped a baby partridge. Mrs Duck was very surprised but she cared for the partridge until it was strong enough to walk. Then she took it to the pond and put it in the water with her other children.

A girl and her mother passed the pond and the mother said, "Look at that baby partridge with those ducks. That mother duck seems to have adopted it."

"Yes, I suppose I have!" said Mrs Duck proudly.

The House

Nitwitty the gnome wasn't very bright. He was always getting things wrong. One day he took a job on a building site where he had to build a house. Nitwitty worked very hard and a few weeks later the house was finished. His boss came out to the site to see how Nitwitty was getting on. When he saw the house, the poor man's mouth dropped open in disbelief. The roof and chimney was resting on the ground while the front door was up in the air.

"You ninny, Nitwitty!" he roared. "You've been reading the plans upside down!"

The Three Bears

Once upon a time there were three bears who did nothing but argue.

"You two take all the blankets," grumbled one bear as he sat up in the bed he shared with his brothers. And he pulled the blankets back over to his side of the bed.

"Now I haven't got any blankets!" growled the bear on the other side of the bed. And he pulled the blanket back again.

"They're my blankets too!" grumbled the bear in the middle of the bed, and he snatched them all for himself.

This went on for some time. First one bear would pull the blankets one way and then another bear would pull them another way. Of course, the bears were very strong and the blankets could not take all this rough treatment.

R-I-I-I-I-I-I-I-I-I-P! they went as they tore into three pieces. But the bears were now happy.

"We've got a blanket each," they smiled, and went to sleep. But each piece of the blanket was very small and only covered the bears slightly, so by morning they woke up freezing and had all caught bad colds.

"This will teach us to argue," they groaned, not feeling at all well.

Pop Star

On his way home one day, a pop star who was feeling very sad because he couldn't sing or play his guitar very well, kicked something on the road. He picked it up and was very surprised to find a strange shaped bottle. He looked closely at the label which had "Genie in a bottle" written on it. "Perhaps my luck will change now!" he thought to himself.

"I wish I could sing better than anyone" said the pop star, releasing the Genie from his bottle. The pop star was hoping the Genie could make him sing so finely he would become very rich and famous.

POOF! The Genie granted the pop star his wish. "TWEET! TWEET! sang the pop star sweetly. To his surprise he found he had been turned into a bird.

"Birds sing better than anyone," said the Genie, returning to his bottle.

Jumping Bean

Titch the troll was out searching for berries when he found a strange-looking bean on the ground. "Hmm! Looks tasty!" he thought, and ate the bean.

Suddenly he found himself bouncing up and down like a rabbit. No matter how hard he tried he couldn't stop.

"OOOER! I must have eaten a jumping bean!" he gasped, bouncing along the field. SPLOSH! he jumped into a dirty puddle. WHUMP! He jumped high into the air and bumped his head on the branch of a tall tree. KRUMP! He jumped face-first into a stone wall and bounced off again to land on the ground. As he hit the earth, the jumping bean popped out of his mouth.

"Phew!" Titch gasped, feeling very scared. "That's the last time I eat something when I don't know what it is!"

Oswald Helps Out

"I'll never win this race," sighed the very slow runner. He was waiting at the starting line with the other runners. "I just can't run fast enough!"

Oswald, the friendly ghost, was passing by as the starting gun was fired for the start of the race. "I wonder what's going on? I think I'll ask someone?" He floated over to where the very slow runner was trying to catch up with the others, who had already left him far behind.

"Excuse me," said Oswald politely, tapping the very slow runner on the shoulder. "What are you doing?"

When the very slow runner saw a ghost behind him he screamed, "A g-g-ghost!" and dashed off leaving a trail of dust behind him. ZOOOOOOOOOOOOOOOOOOOOOOOM! He tore round the track, streaking past the other runners and raced over the finishing line first.

"THE WINNER!" announced the judge, holding out the winner's cup for the runner to collect. But the very slow runner, who was now an incredibly fast runner, didn't stop. He ran out of the sports stadium and away over the hills.

"Funny chap," chuckled Oswald, floating away again. "He acted as if he'd seen a ghost!"

Pulling Faces

"Don't pull faces or one day you'll stay that way," Catrina's mother warned her. But Catrina wouldn't listen and continued to pull rude faces at everyone who passed by.

"Silly old mum," thought Catrina. "She's just saying that to scare me."

A fairy saw Catrina pulling faces and decided she needed to be taught a lesson. "The next face she pulls will stay that way until the end of the day," she said, waving her magic wand.

"BOOO!" shouted Catrina pulling a very rude and horrible face to frighten a little boy. Then she tried to put on her normal face again but found to her horror that she couldn't. She pushed and she pulled, she slapped and she squashed. But the expression on her face stayed.

"Oh, no! My face has stuck!" Catrina wailed.

"I did warn you," scolded her mother. "And now it's too late."

Everyone laughed when they saw Catrina. They said, "Doesn't she look funny!"

Catrina stayed in her room all day so no one could see how awful she was. She cried and cried because she was so unhappy. Finally she fell asleep. When she woke up the next day she ran to the mirror and saw that her face had returned to its normal expression again.

"I'll never pull faces again," she promised, feeling very relieved.

Nurses and Patients

Tim had caught a nasty cold and the doctor had come to see him.

"Nothing to worry about," she told his mother. "He just needs to stay in bed for a few days."

Tim was soon fed up and bored with staying in bed. He wanted to go out and play. But his younger sister had an idea. She went to the toy cupboard and put on her nurses outfit. "I've come to give you a check-up," she told Tim. "Open wide." She looked down Tim's throat the way she had seen the doctor do it. Then she pretended to feel his pulse on his wrist. This made Tim giggle because his sister's little fingers tickled him. After that she read Tim a story and played a game of cards with him.

"This is the best game of nurses and patients we've ever played," Tim laughed.

Eskimo Joe

Eskimo Joe lived in an igloo, a house made from blocks of ice, in a very cold country, far far away. One day he recieved a letter from his friend Jimba, who lived in a very hot country where everyone lived in houses made of mud. Jimba was inviting Joe to visit him. Joe thought this was a grand idea. He had wanted to take a holiday for some time, so he packed his bags and off he went.

When Joe reached Jimba's mud house he was feeling very hot. The sun in Joe's country was never very strong and all the Eskimos had to wrap up warm in fur coats and boots to keep warm. In Jimba's country the sun was always baking hot, so everywhere was hot and sticky, and Joe wasn't too sure he liked it.

"Silly Joe," laughed Jimba, pointing to the fur coat Joe was wearing. "Take off your coat and you'll feel much better." So Joe took off his coat but he was still feeling too hot.

"Silly Joe," laughed Jimba, pointing to the thick jumper Joe was wearing. "Take off your jumper and you'll feel much better." So Joe took off his jumper but still felt too hot.

"Silly Joe," laughed Jimba, pointing to Joe's woolly shirt. "Take off your shirt and you'll feel much better." So Joe took off his shirt but his legs still felt too hot.

"Silly Joe," laughed Jimba, pointing to Joe's thick trousers. "Take off your trousers and you'll feel much better." So Joe took off his trousers but his feet still felt too hot.

"Silly Joe," laughed Jimba, pointing to Joe's heavy boots. "Take off your boots and socks and you'll feel much better." So Joe took off his boots and socks and found that, yes, he did feel much more comfortable.

"In my country it is so hot that we need only wear shorts," Jimba explained. "It is far too hot to wear anything else." Jimba took Joe down to the sea where they splashed about in the warm water all day.

"I'm glad I came on holiday," Joe thought happily.

147

The Robin

Ronnie Robin awoke one morning to find the forest covered in snow. It lay on the branches of the trees bending them with its weight. It lay on the ground where it muffled all the sounds of the forest. The small flowers that grew below Ronnie's nest were now buried under the snow nowhere to be seen. No animals were moving, no birds were singing. Everywhere there was a hushed silence. "The snow makes everywhere look clean," thought Ronnie. "But I miss hearing my friends hurrying, scurrying and flapping about. Most of all I miss seeing the pretty flowers."

The sun heard this and peeked out from behind a cloud. It shone down fiercely and soon the blanket of snow began to melt. It wasn't long before all the snow had disappeared. The animals of the forest came out from their hiding places in search of food and the birds began to sing once more. And the flowers could be seen growing under Ronnie's nest again.

"Thank you, sun," Ronnie said happily.

Baby Sitting

Squirrel enjoyed his batchelor life but now and again he longed to have a wife and lots of little children to care for. Badger saw how unhappy his friend was and went to see Mrs Rabbit. "Perhaps you could help?" he asked her.

Mrs Rabbit was looking very tired and worn out, having to look after her fifteen children all day, and she was glad to hear of Badger's idea.

Next day Mrs Rabbit went to see Squirrel and said, "Would you like to look after my children while I go to the shops?"

Squirrel was very pleased to be asked and had lots of fun playing with Mrs Rabbit's children. When Mrs Rabbit returned he said, "Please ask me to babysit for you again. I had a wonderful time." Mrs Rabbit was only too pleased. She was glad to have some peace and quiet for a few hours.

Ballet Dancing

"Ballet dancing? How soppy!" sniggered Tony, stopping Julie in the street. Julie had just been to her weekly ballet lessons and was hurrying home to watch "SWAN LAKE" on the television. In her haste she left the ballet studio still wearing her pretty yellow tu-tu.

Tony held a handful of mud in his hand. "I'm going to throw this at your silly dress!" he giggled and drew back his hand to throw the mud at Julie. Julie stood on the tip of one foot, spun around in a wonderful pirouette, and kicked the mud out of Tony's hand. SPLAAT! The mud fell back onto Tony's head.

"Ballet dancing comes in useful at times!" Julie giggled, as she ran home.

Litterbug

The Ogre was always eating sweets and dropping his litter. Now, you may not think that was much of a problem (even though you should never drop litter as it makes everywhere look untidy) but when the Ogre's toffee papers are as big as parachutes and his lollypop sticks as large as trees, you can understand why the townsfolk were so annoyed.

"My house has been flattened twice this week by his lollypop sticks!" grumbled one old man.

"And we can't walk down the street without tripping over his sweet papers," complained another. "What we need is a litter bin. One big enough to take his giant-sized rubbish."

A circus was visiting the town and one of the acts was the high-wire. The acrobats always performed with safety nets below to catch them if they fell.

"Could we buy all your nets?" the townsfolk asked the ringmaster, giving him a handful of gold coins. The ringmaster was delighted to sell the nets and the townsfolk took them back home where they sewed them all together until they had made one big net. Then they hung the net over the entire town.

The next time the Ogre passed that way eating sweets and dropping litter, all his rubbish fell into the net instead of onto the town. The Ogre was very pleased to have his own personal litter basket and promised to collect the litter at the end of each week and burn it on the fire in his castle.

Marvo the Magician

Marvo the Magician could turn milk into water, make tables rise into the air, saw a lady in half, then put her back together again. He could do just about anything you can imagine. But he couldn't pull a rabbit out of his top hat.

"Ho hum," sighed Marvo, after trying the trick again and failing. He left his hat on the chair in his dressing room while he went to have a cup of tea.

A little girl called Simone was in the theatre looking for her pure white rabbit, Snowy, who had escaped from his hutch. Simone had seen the rabbit run into the theatre and now she was trying to find him. She searched everywhere but Snowy was nowhere to be found. "I've lost my rabbit forever," Simone thought sadly.

When Marvo returned to his room he decided to have one last go at pulling a rabbit out of his hat. "Alla-Kazam!" he cried, putting his hand into his hat. When he pulled his hand out again he was clutching a pure white rabbit.

"SNOWY!" cried Simone happily as she ran into the room.

"I did it!" Marvo cheered. "I pulled a rabbit out of my hat!" Neither Marvo nor Simone knew that Snowy had hopped into the hat to rest. Simone was just glad to get Snowy back, and Marvo was overjoyed that his trick had finally worked.

New Home

It was the middle of a very cold winter and five little fieldmice were homeless. "I hope we find somewhere warm to hibernate soon," one of the friends squeaked sadly.

They were running through a field when they discovered a glove that someone must have dropped. The glove was very big and fur-lined. The five field mice squeezed snugly into the fingers and the thumb of the glove, where it was warm and comfortable. "This can be our home until winter has passed," they said, and settled down to sleep.

Singing Lessons

Crow wanted to be a famous singer but whenever he opened his mouth all that came out was a horrible CAW! CAW! sound.

"You need singing lessons," said the nightingale, who could sing the most beautiful songs. Nightingale promised to give crow all the help he needed to sing properly.

Crow practised every day and very soon he could sing almost as well as the nightingale. People were amazed when they heard the crow singing so sweetly. "It looks like a crow . . . but it sings like a nightingale!" They were all very confused.

Tinkerbell

Anna's doll, Tinkerbell, sat on a high shelf over Anna's bed. Tinkerbell was Anna's favourite doll and always sat in the best place in the room.

Anna brought home a new china doll one day which was dressed in the finest clothes. Anna placed the doll next to Tinkerbell on the shelf. "Now you have someone to share your shelf," she said.

When Anna came back later that day the china doll was on the floor in a heap. "Now how did that happen?" Anna wondered.

Tinkerbell had a naughty smile on her face. Do you think she was jealous of the china doll sharing her shelf, and perhaps pushed her off when Anna wasn't looking? Well, whatever happened, Anna put the china doll on another shelf. Tinkerbell had the shelf over Anna's bed to herself again.

The Old Man

There was an old man
Who lived in a house,
He had ten cats,
Twelve dogs and a mouse.
He had six parrots,
Two hamsters, and a frog,
Five gerbils and a squirrel
Who lived on a log.
He had twenty fish,
Three hens and a hare,
Seven tortoises, eight owls
And a silver-grey mare.
He had so many animals
As you can plainly see,
But most important was the robin,
For the robin is me!

Winter Coat

Fred the arctic fox had a beautiful brown coat in the summer and he was very proud of it. But in winter his coat turned completely white and poor Fred was very upset.

"Don't be silly," said his father, whose brown coat had also turned white. "There's a good reason for your coat to change colour in winter." But Fred wouldn't listen. He found a mud-hole and rolled in it until he was brown again. Well, it was a sort of muddy brown but Fred preferred it to being white.

Snow began to fall and soon everywhere was covered in a blanket of white. "I hate white," grumbled Fred. He just couldn't understand why the other arctic foxes were so pleased with their new white coats. Then one day hunters came in search of animals to capture and sell to zoos. Fred was very afraid. He tried to hide in the snow but the hunters saw his muddy-brown coat against the white background and chased him.

"Quickly, Fred! Get rid of your brown coat!" said his father, who was almost invisible against the snow in his white coat. Fred leapt into a pile of snow and rolled and rolled until his coat was completely white again. Then he stood with his father against a snowdrift and was amazed when the hunters ran past without seeing him.

"Your white, winter coat allows you to hide from all sorts of hunters, not just humans," his father explained. "It will become brown again in the spring."

Fred was pleased to have his white coat in winter after all.

The Cowboy

"POW! POW!" Jim cried, dressed in his smart cowboy's outfit, shooting everyone with his fingers. "I'm Black Bart, the roughest, toughest, meanest cowboy in the West. No one tells me what to do!"

"Well, Black Bart, I'm afraid it's time for your bath," said his mother firmly. "Or else!"

"Huh! I bet real cowboys didn't have to have baths," Jim grumbled.

Choosing a Husband

Princess Isobel was most annoyed. Her father, the King, had called all the young men, the Princes and the nobles to his palace to choose a husband for his daughter. In those days of long ago a Princess did not have any say in the matter. It was believed that the King was the best person to choose a suitable husband.

"Rubbish!" snapped Isobel crossly. I shall choose whom I wish to marry." She was so angry that the King thought it best to let her do as she wished.

"I am the greatest swordsman in the land," said one man. "Marry me!"

"I am the most handsome man in all the land," said another. "Marry me."

"I am the cleverest man in all the land," said a third. "Marry me."

This went on all day and still Princess Isobel could not find a man she wanted to marry.

A begger came into the palace and took his place in the queue. When the King saw him, he almost threw the poor man out when the Princess cried. "Wait! Let's see what he has to say!"

"You are the most beautiful woman I have ever seen," said the begger. "And the kindest. You do not have to marry me. I wanted to look upon you just once."

"This is the man I shall marry," decided Isobel firmly. "He is the only one who cares for me, not for himself."

The King was most upset by this but he could not stop the marriage and the Princess and the begger, who became a Prince, lived happily ever after.

Lion Cub

There was once a lion cub who was always creeping up on the other animals and letting out a loud "RROOOOAAAARRR!" behind them. This startled them so much they tumbled over backwards with fright.

The lion cub saw a rhinoceros close by. He sneaked up on him and gave a "RROOOOAAAARRR!" very loudly. The rhinoceros thought he was being attacked. He spun round and tossed the lion cub into the air with his horn. The lion cub was so startled and so afraid that he ran off and never tried to scare anyone again.

Flowers?

Libby Ladybird was out looking for a greenfly to feed on. Suddenly she saw a girl in the street carrying a bunch of flowers.

Swooping down, Libby landed on the flowers and looked for some greenflies. "That's strange," she thought. "There's no pollen on these. And where is the beautiful perfume which flowers usually have?"

Libby didn't like these flowers at all and so she flew off to look elsewhere. The girl was surprised to see a ladybird on her flowers. "Why would a ladybird want to visit my silk flowers?" she wondered.

Cleaning Up

Professor Noodle, was a nutty professor whose inventions were always going wrong. His latest creation was a machine that would do all the housework at the press of a button. "It will clean out a house in minutes," he told the mayor. Professor Noodle had been invited to demonstrate the machine at the Town Hall.

The Professor switched on the machine, and then he and the Mayor left the room, which was full of the Mayor's most prized possessions.

When they returned and looked into the room, they couldn't believe their eyes. Apart from the machine, the room was empty. Not a table, chair, ornament or painting was left. The machine was still working busily away. They watched as it pulled down the curtains and threw them out of the window. The rest of the furniture was piled up in a heap under the window.

"Buffoon!" roared the Mayor at Professor Noodle. "Your machine cleans out rooms all right — until there's nothing left!"

Making Friends

Danny was a very quiet boy who didn't have any friends. He was too shy to talk to other children. He always stayed on his own at playtime while his classmates played their games together.

One day Danny was at home reading a book and feeling bored when he heard a dog barking in the garden. Rushing outside he found a small, brown puppy digging up his mother's flowers.

"Hello," he said, patting the dog on the head. "You don't belong here. Lost, are you?"

"Excuse me," said a voice over the garden fence. It was a boy the same age as Danny. "That's my dog. We've just moved in and he escaped through a hole in the fence into your garden."

Danny was disappointed that the dog had an owner. He was hoping to keep him as a playmate. When he passed the dog back over the fence, the boy said, "Since I'm new here I don't have any friends. Would you like to play with me?"

"Oh, yes! I'd love to!" said Danny excitedly. Soon he and the boy, whose name was Simon, were playing happily together. "It's good to have a friend," Danny smiled.

Flying South

"Huh! I'm not flying south for winter!" honked Gandy Goose, as all her friends took off for warmer climates to escape the harsh weather. "I'm staying right here in my pond."

Winter arrived and it soon became very cold but Gandy refused to move from her pond. "Who cares about a bit of cold?" she snorted and went to sleep. When she woke up she found she couldn't move. It had become so cold that the water had frozen around her. Poor Gandy. She had to stay where she was until the ice melted. She was very hungry and there was no food to be found. Luckily people passing by gave Gandy bread to eat to keep her alive. "Next year I'll fly south for winter with my friends," she decided.

The Cheeky Parrot (1)

Percy Parrot was very cheeky. Whenever anyone visited old Mrs Tingle's house he would stand on his perch, flap his wings and squawk, "HELLO, YOU LOOK LIKE A PRUNE! SQUAWK!" Or, "WHO'S A SILLY BOY THEN? YOU ARE! SQUAWK!"

Now this was very embarrassing, especially when Mrs Tingle was serving tea to the vicar. Percy would shout, "HELLO, BALDY! SQUAWK!" Well, it's true the vicar didn't have much hair left, but it's not something you go around shouting about, is it?

"Percy, what am I going to do with you?" sighed Mrs Tingle, after the vicar had hurriedly left. Percy didn't care. He was thoroughly enjoying himself.

No More Fun (2)

Mrs Tingle decided Percy should be taught a lesson. She knew he loved to be in the company of people, so that he could show off. So she took him upstairs and locked him in an empty room, where he could be as cheeky as he liked and nobody could hear him.

"SQUAWK! THIS ISN'T FUN!" Percy grumbled after a day of seeing no one but Mrs Tingle, who brought him his dinner. Percy soon became very bored at flying around the room and not meeting anyone. When Mrs Tingle visited him that night he cried, "SQUAWK! I'M SORRY!"

The next day Mrs Tingle allowed Percy to come back downstairs. The next time the vicar paid a visit, Percy squawked, "HELLO, BAL. . . ." and then stopped himself in time. Instead he said, "HELLO, VICAR! NICE DAY! SQUAWK!" very politely. The vicar was pleased that he hadn't been insulted and gave Percy some of his current bun as a treat. As for Percy, he was never cheeky again.

Hugo's Toys

The toys in Hugo's room were fed up with being left scattered on the cold floor each night when Hugo went to bed. He was too lazy to put them away properly.

"Let's show him how upset we are," they agreed. One by one the toys climbed, bounced, hopped, skipped, rolled and jumped onto Hugo's bed. There was Hugo's favourite bear, his best fire engine, his three pretty coloured balls, a spinning top, four walking, talking robots, a rocking horse, cowboys, indians and soldiers of all different shapes and colours, and his very heavy tricycle. They pushed, wriggled, pulled and wiggled until they had managed to push the sleeping Hugo out of bed. He fell to the floor with a bump, but didn't wake up. Then the toys pulled the covers over themselves and went to sleep. Hugo was surprised to find himself on the floor when he woke the next morning. He was even more surprised to find his toys in his bed.

"I'll always put you away each night from now on," he promised them. The toys were pleased to hear this!

Measles

"I've got measles," groaned Molly one morning. Her face was covered in red spots.

"No school for you today," said her father, tucking Molly into bed.

Later that morning he brought up a bowl of water and placed it on the bedside table. "We'd better give you a wash for when the doctor comes," he said.

"Er, that's not a good idea," said Molly, and tried to hide inside the bed, but her father pulled her back up again. As Molly's father wiped her face with the soapy flannel a strange thing happened. The red spots came off her face!

"These aren't measle spots at all!" her father shouted. "You painted them on your face so you could have the day off school!"

Molly's father was very cross and made Molly go to school and explain why she was so late. Her teacher was also cross and gave Molly extra homework as punishment.

Jam Tarts

Ernie the fox looked hungrily at the plate of delicious jam tarts his mother had made.

"They're for tea so don't touch!" his mother warned him. Ernie promised that he wouldn't. But he kept looking at the plate and couldn't resist having a small bite of just one tart. "Hmmm! Yummy!" he smiled, and ate it all up.

"I'll be in trouble if Mum finds out," he thought, so he quickly fetched his play dough. Rolling it out, he cut it into a jam tart shape and put some red play dough inside for the jam. "No one will notice the difference," he said hopefully.

At teatime Mum brought out the jam tarts. "Good boy, Ernie," she said. "You haven't taken any." Ernie chuckled to himself for fooling her.

His mother gave him one of the tarts from the plate, and Ernie, being greedy, popped it into his mouth without waiting. Then his face turned a pale green. "Uggh! It's my play dough tart!" he groaned, and ran out of the room to spit it out. His mother had known all the time about Ernie pinching a tart and had given him the play dough one to teach him a lesson. Poor Ernie felt so sick he couldn't face eating another jam tart all that evening.

Reindeer

Dreamy Dan was visiting a country park with his sister.

"Look, reindeer!" shouted his sister. She had seen a beautiful reindeer grazing in the park.

Dan pulled out his umbrella and opened it up. His sister was puzzled. "Why have you put your umbrella up on such a lovely, sunny day?" she asked.

Dan frowned at her crossly. "Well, you said, 'rain, dear'!"

Isn't he the silly one!

Piano

Imp, the little gremlin, watched two delivery men pushing a grand piano up a very steep hill. "If I trip them up they'll let go of the piano and it'll roll down the hill again!" he sniggered.

The two men had just reached the top of the hill when Imp wrapped a piece of string around their feet and they fell over, letting go of the piano. The piano rolled away down the hill.

WHUMP! It ran straight into Imp who was standing in the way and he was carried down the hill. The piano crashed into a wall, squashing poor Imp between it. The very flattened Imp pulled himself off the wall and staggered away. "I'm feeling a bit flat!" he groaned.

The New Suit

Andrew had given Patch, his one-eyed teddy bear, a smart new suit to wear. "Take care of it," Andrew warned him.

Patch did look grand in his new suit. "I'm the best dressed bear in town," he chuckled.

Andrew took Patch to see his cousin Sue. They found her playing with her doll, Betty. Patch and Betty were left in the house while Andrew and Sue went out to play. "Let's have a game," Patch suggested, and started kicking Andrew's ball in the house.

"I wouldn't if I were you," warned Betty, but Patch ignored her. The ball bounced onto the table and knocked over a vase of flowers. SPLAASSH! The water poured all over Patch and his new suit was ruined. When Andrew came back he was very cross.

"You can't wear your suit home now," he said. Then Sue had an idea. She dressed Patch in one of Betty's old dresses.

"Ahhh, don't you look sweet!" Andrew laughed but Patch wasn't amused.

"I feel such a fool!" he grumbled.

Gran

My granny is quite ancient,
At least one hundred and three,
She remembers Queen Victoria
And all sorts of history.
Her face is covered in wrinkles
Reminding me somewhat of prunes,
She's good at telling stories
And sings lots of different tunes.
When I go to visit
She's always sitting in her chair,
It rocks this way and that
But Granny doesn't care.
I once sat in Granny's chair
And rocked more and more,
Then to my surprise, I was
Sitting on the floor!
Granny always bakes me cakes
Or buys me bags of sweets,
Mummy does get cross with her
But I like my little treats.
When I leave, we kiss goodbye
And she says, "toodle-oo!"
You may be old and frail, Gran
But you're special and I love you.

Watching the Stars

It was a clear night and young Albert was in the garden looking at the stars through his telescope. "Ooooh! There's the Great Bear! And there's Orion's Belt!" he cried excitedly. A big, black cloud passed overhead and blocked Albert's view of the stars. "Bother!" he said crossly. "I can't see a thing!" He ran indoors to tell his mother about the cloud. In his hurry he tripped over the step and knocked his head as he fell. Albert's fall had left him dazed and he could see sparkling stars floating around his head. "Ouch! I can see plenty of stars after all," he groaned. "But this time they're not in the sky!"

A Million Wishes

"You may have one wish," said the fairy to Pinchapenny the troll.

"One wish won't get me much," Pinchapenny grumbled, so he decided to cheat. "I wish I had another ONE MILLION wishes!" he said, thinking of all the wonderful things he could have with a million wishes.

The fairy waved her magic wand. PING! The flabberghasted Pinchapenny found himself surrounded by one million dishes, all dirty and cracked.

"I said wishes, not dishes!" he roared crossly.

"Sorry, I must be going deaf!" laughed the fairy and flew away.

Saving the Prince! (1)

Bambino, the young white unicorn, was bathing in the forest pool. A frog jumped on his back and said in a croaky sort of voice, "Dear unicorn, help me, do! I am a Prince who has been turned into a frog by a wicked witch. Help me reach my castle and I shall reward you for your kindness."

Bambino was always willing to help anyone and so with the frog-prince on his back, he galloped through the forest. But the wicked witch had seen them and she cast a spell. "I'll kill the unicorn with my magic," she cackled. "Then I shall capture the frog-prince and keep him in a cage!"

Bambino was hurrying through the forest when he was stopped by a tree-monster that the wicked witch had brought to life. "GRRRRRRRRRRRRH!" snarled the tree-monster and it tried to crush Bambino with one of its thick branches. Bambino lowered his head and charged, spearing the tree-monster with his horn. Bambino's horn was filled with good magic and so the tree-monster became an ordinary tree again.

With night falling, the wicked witch lost sight of them. "I'll find you tomorrow!" she screeched!

Safe at Last! (2)

The wicked witch was very angry. She had searched all night for Bambino and the frog-prince. She finally caught sight of them as the sun rose in the forest. She cast a spell which shook a huge boulder from the top of a hillside. The boulder came crashing down and Bambino was in its path!

"We'll be crushed!" cried the frog-prince, but Bambino lowered his head and charged at the boulder. As his magic horn struck the boulder it split in two, and one piece flew through the air to fall on the wicked witch, killing her at once. As the witch died, her spell was broken and the frog became a handsome Prince once more.

"Thank you, dear Bambino!" he said, patting him on the head. "I will always remember your kindness." From that day Bambino always found a box of fresh fruit beside the forest pool every day, a present from the Prince.

The Sandstorm

Clarence the camel had the hump. Well, actually he had two humps, but he was fed up with sand. This presented a bit of a problem because Clarence lived in the desert and the desert is FULL of sand. In fact, apart from a few prickly cactus plants and the odd tree growing here and there, deserts don't have much else.

"Sand, sand, sand!" snorted Clarence, and then snorted again when he accidently inhaled some sand up his nose. This made him sneeze uncontrollably for a few minutes and gave him the hump even more. At that moment Sheikh Yaleg, the leader of a tribe of Arab bedouins, was passing by on his horse. He saw Clarence and said, "I must have that camel for my zoo!"

"He must have sand in his head!"

Clarence thought, having overheard the Sheikh. "As much as I hate sand, I hate being locked up even more!" He decided to run off but Sheikh Yaleg gave chase. While Clarence could run fast when he wanted to, the Sheikh's horse was much faster.

"Oh, coconuts!" wailed Clarence as the Sheikh drew closer. "He's going to catch me!"

The Sands of the Desert heard Clarence's cries. They liked him a lot, even though he complained a lot, and decided to help. Softly at first, and then becoming more fierce, the sand began to blow across the desert.

"Oh, Yakabee!" cried the Sheikh, which is what he always cried when he was upset. "A sandstorm!" He didn't want to get lost in the sandstorm so he turned back, leaving Clarence to escape safely.

"Thanks, sand," said Clarence later. "I think I like you after all!"

Bella

Rosalita always enjoyed her Uncle's visits for he always brought along his dog, Bella, to see her. Rosalita and Bella would play in the garden until it was time for her Uncle to leave. Rosalita hated this as she missed Bella very much and would sit up in bed for hours thinking about the dog. This worried her mother and father, who thought that Rosalita would be too tired to go to school, and sometimes she was.

Then one day Rosalita's Uncle paid a visit with Bella . . . and a baby Bella, too!

"Yap!" cried the little dog, leaping into Rosalita's arms.

"Bella's had puppies," explained her Uncle. "And since I know how much you love dogs I thought you would like to care for one."

Rosalita was overjoyed at this and took great care of her puppy, which she named Belladonna.

A Home for Wesley

RAT-A-TAT-TAT! went Wesley Woodpecker's beak as he pecked on the trunk of a tree.

"Who's that knocking on my door?" said Nutcracker Squirrel, coming out of his tree-house to investigate.

"Only me," said Wesley. "I'm looking for grubs to eat."

"Well, look elsewhere!" grumbled Nutcracker, slamming his door. "I want some peace!"

Wesley flew away to find another tree. "I'm always being told to move on," he sighed. "No one likes my pecking noise."

"If you'll do me a favour, you may stay in my tree," said Simon Sparrow. A large branch has snapped and was blocking Simon's entrance to his nest.

Wesley's beak went RAT-A-TAT-TAT! on the branch until it broke away and fell crashing to the ground, allowing Simon back into his nest.

Simon was very pleased and he invited his new neighbour in for a cup of tea.

Long Hair

Sally Sheepdog was very proud of her long, thick, shaggy coat. It was so long it fell over her eyes and she couldn't always see where she was going.

"You should have your hair cut," said Heidi Dachshund, Sally's friend. "You'll have an accident one day."

"Nonsense!" scoffed Sally, accidently colliding with a tree. "Things should get out of my way when they see me coming. Then I wouldn't walk into them."

Sally and Heidi went out for a walk. They liked playing a game of chase. Heidi ran off first and Sally chased after her. If Sally managed to catch Heidi's tail it was Heidi's turn to give chase.

Heidi ran past a decorator who was up his ladder, painting a house, Sally, whose long hair flopped over her eyes, ran INTO the ladder. THUMP! The decorator dropped his pot and the pink paint fell all over Sally's thick, shaggy coat.

All the other dogs laughed when they saw Sally's now-pink coat. She had to scrub and scrub her coat very hard in hot water before the paint was washed off.

The next morning when Heidi went to visit, she found Sally with her hair cut short and neat.

"I still like long hair," Sally told her as they went for a walk. "But short hair's safer!"

The Birds' Plan

Slinky Stoat was becoming an unbearable pest. He kept sneaking into the birds' nests and stealing their eggs.

"Something must be done," declared Barnaby Blackbird when the birds held a meeting. They all discussed the best way to protect their eggs, and decided to put their plan into action straight away.

When Slinky went to the nests the next day there was no sign of the birds. "This is too easy," he thought happily, reaching out to take a thrush's egg. BONK! BONK! BONK! He jumped back as three large stones hit him on the head.

"Leave those eggs alone!" screeched the birds, swooping out of the sky. Each bird carried a stone in their claws which they dropped on Slinky.

BONK! BONK! BONK!

"OOOOOUCH!" yelled Slinky, running off. The birds chased him for a long time before they ran out of stones and flew back home. Slinky was so frightened he just kept on running and decided to look elsewhere for his supper.

Leaf Trouble

Captain Bungle, the super-hero without fear, (or any brains) had offered to help Granny Grimble clear her path of fallen autumn leaves.

"Have no fear, Granny. I, Captain Bungle, greatest, (and most handsome) super-hero in the Universe, will soon rid you of these pesky leaves!" So saying, Captain Bungle took a deep breath and gave a super-blow!

WHOOOOOOOOOOOOOOOO-SSSSSSSSSHHH! His super breath blew away all the leaves in Granny's garden. Unfortunately it also blew away Granny's cottage, too. Of course, Granny was most upset. She kept hitting Captain Bungle on the head with her rolling pin until he had built her a new house. As for the cottage, it was nowhere to be found. But if one day you visit the moon and you come across a quaint cottage with roses growing up the walls . . . well, you'll know where it's come from, won't you?

Birthday

Tim and Terry were twins, which means they both have their birthday's on the same day.

"I must get something special for Terry's birthday," thought Tim.

"I must get something special for Tim's birthday, said Terry.

Tim and Terry both went shopping to buy each other a present. When they returned home they wrapped the presents in pretty paper and put them on the table.

"Happy birthday, Tim," said Terry.

"Happy birthday, Terry," said Tim.

They were both eager to find out what their presents were and quickly opened them. Tim had bought Terry a box of his favourite sweets, jelly bears.

Terry had bought Tim a box of his favourite sweets. Yes, you've guessed it. Jelly bears!

"Ha! Ha! What a funny pair we are!" they laughed, tucking into the sweets. "Fancy buying each other the same present!"

The Dolls House

Victoria owned a lovely dolls house which her Granny had given her. It had yellow coloured walls, and a bright red door. When Victoria opened it up she could see the living room with its tiny armchairs and television, and the kitchen with its miniature cooker and sink. Upstairs there was a bathroom with a bath and a bedroom with a wardrobe, a cupboard and a nice soft bed for the dolls to sleep in at night. It was the most wonderful dolls house Victoria had ever seen . . . but it didn't have any curtains!

"It doesn't look right without curtains," Victoria told her Mother.

"I'm too busy to make any now," her Mother said, pulling the freshly washed clothes out of the washing machine. Then she gasped, holding up four tiny green handkerchiefs. "Oh, dear! They must have shrunk in the wash. I'll have to throw them out."

"I'll have them," said Victoria eagerly. She sewed the handkerchiefs into two pairs of curtains and put them up in her dolls house. "Now my dolls house is complete!" she said happily.

The Helpful Whale

Eskimo Joe had been out for a walk in the icy wastes where he lived. He was just crossing a piece of ice when he heard a cracking sound and discovered that the ice he was standing on was floating out to sea.

"Oh, no! If I jump into the water it's so cold I'll freeze into an icicle before I reach land," he groaned as the ice took him further and further from his home.

Luckily a large whale was passing by. "Hop on my back," he said. "I'll give you a lift back to your igloo."

Eskimo Joe was very grateful to the whale and always waved to him if he saw him in the water.

Slimming

Treacle Tart the witch was fed up with being plump, so she made a potion that would help her loose weight.

"This will end in disaster," said the ENORMOUS fat black cat, who knew all about Treacle Tart's magic.

Treacle Tart drank the potion, but instead of making her slim, it made her shrink until she was no bigger than a toy doll.

"Bubbling cauldrons!" she wailed in a tiny voice. "I've lost so much weight there's hardly anything left of me!" Poor Treacle Tart. She had to live in her old doll's house until the potion wore off!

Broken Glass

Ray and Lyn were in their garden having a quiet game of catching the ball. Lyn threw the ball high into the air. Then their faces fell as they heard the sound of breaking glass coming from Mr McDoogle's house. SMAASSSH!

"Ooer! The ball must have broken a window!" groaned Lyn.

"It's your fault for throwing it so hard!" Ray grumbled.

"Huh! You should have caught it!" Lyn grumbled.

They decided they had better own up, so they went to Mr McDoogle's house, feeling very nervous. Mr McDoogle was in his garden looking very cross.

"What a silly billy I am!" he muttered, looking down at the broken glass beside his feet. "I was in such a hurry to get home, I dropped my new vase!"

"Whew!" smiled Ray and Lyn, very relieved. "We didn't break a window after all!"

Changing Ways (1)

Mrs Jolly was a very happy, cheerful woman. She laughed at everything there was to laugh at in life, and always looked on the bright side.

"Oh, my!" she chuckled when her dog knocked over her best china pot and broke it. "Not to worry. Accidents will happen! Ho! Ho! Ho!" She patted her dog on the head to show she wasn't at all cross with him.

Next door lived Mrs Not-Very-Jolly-At-All. She was a miserable and depressed woman. She moaned at everything there is to moan at in life, and always looked on the black side.

"Drat!" she snapped after she had spilt her cup of tea over her best tablecloth. "Trust that to happen. It's going to be a rotten day, I can tell!"

Mrs Jolly could not understand how Mrs Not-Very-Jolly-At-All could be so miserable all the time.

"You should try to laugh your troubles away," she said to her unhappy neighbour one day.

"And you should take life more seriously!" retorted Mrs Not-Very-Jolly-At-All. This gave Mrs Jolly an idea.

"If you promise to spend a whole day being happy, I'll try hard to spend the day being miserable. Then we can see how the other half lives." She was hoping that Mrs Not-Very-Jolly-At-All would find being happy wonderful and she would stay that way all the time.

"We'll start tomorrow!" they both agreed.

The Change Over (2)

Mrs Jolly got up early the next day. She quickly put on her clothes, only to find she had put her jumper on back-to-front. "Ho! Ho! Silly me!" she chuckled merrily. Then she remembered her promise to be miserable for a day. Trying hard to look annoyed she snapped crossly, "Bother! How angry I am now!" Actually she didn't really feel angry at all but a promise was a promise, and Mrs Jolly always kept her word.

When she broke a milk bottle on the doorstep, instead of laughing she stamped her feet and made lots of grumbling noises. When she missed her bus, and then arrived at the shops only to find she had left her purse at home, she bellowed and roared and looked very miserable indeed.

"What's the matter with Mrs Jolly?" asked a shopkeeper. "She's usually so happy."

Mrs Not-Very-Jolly-At-All woke up late. But instead of being angry, she tried hard to put on a smile. "What a silly-billy I am!" she said, struggling hard to give a chuckle. When she burnt the toast, stubbed her foot on a large stone in the garden, and tore a hole in her best skirt, she almost exploded with anger, but remembering her promise, she laughed out loud instead.

"What's the matter with Mrs Not-Very-Jolly-At-All?" wondered a neighbour. "She's usually so miserable."

Mrs Jolly met Mrs Not-Very-Jolly-At-All that evening. "I'm worn out, said Mrs Jolly. "I never knew being miserable could be such hard work."

"I can hardly stand," said her friend. "All that laughing has made me weak."

The two women realised they could not change each other's ways after all.

"I think I'll stick to being happy," smiled Mrs Jolly.

"And I'll stay miserable," frowned Mrs Not-Very-Jolly-At-All.

"It's best to accept people the way they are," the two women agreed.

Money

Mr Moneybags was so rich there were not enough banks to keep his money in, so he kept it in his incredibly big mansion instead. One day his nephew, Donny, visited him. I'm going to dive into the pool," he said. "I love to hear the loud SPLASH! when I hit the water."

Donny ran to the edge of the pool and jumped in. But instead of a SPLASH! there was a muffled sound instead. Donny had landed in a pool full of paper money.

"Silly uncle," he laughed. "You do keep your money in the most unusual places!"

Granny's Kettle

PEEEP! PEEEP! sang the kettle, singing out that the water inside was boiling. But when Granny went to look, the water had not boiled at all, so she went back to her sewing.

PEEEP! PEEEP! sang the kettle again. Granny went to look, but still the water hadn't boiled, so she went back to her sewing.

PEEEP! PEEEP! sang the kettle a third time but Granny ignored it and carried on sewing. But this time the water in the kettle really was boiling, and when Granny finally went to look, the kettle had boiled dry. The kettle's insides were black and it felt very poorly.

"That will teach you to play tricks," said Granny.

The Kindest Fairy

There was once a magical fairy whose name was Joice. Now Joice worked very hard to make sure everyone was happy and contented. She could weave spells to make the sun shine, the birds sing, and the flowers grow. All the people, animals, pixies and elves loved her dearly. "You are the nicest, kindest fairy in the world!" they all agreed.

One day a nasty wizard decided to capture Joice and then use his bad magic to turn the whole world black and rotten.

When Joice heard a voice cry out, "HELP! HELP!" she raced to the rescue, as she always did. The wizard caught her in a wooden box and locked the door. Joice was trapped! But luckily she still had her magic wand and she changed the box into daisies. Then she flew after the wizard and cast a spell that sent him spinning into the air, over the mountains, never to return. As for Joice, she brought love and happiness to everyone who met her, and she will always be remembered as the nicest fairy of them all.

Bee

BUZZZ! BUZZZ! went all the bees in the bee hive. All except one. He went PUTT! PUTT!

"That's no way to buzz," said the Queen bee. "Like this. BUZZZ! BUZZZ!"

"BRUUM! BRUUM!" went the bee, sounding like a motor car.

"Look here," said the Queen. "All bees buzz! They don't PUTT! PUTT! and they don't BRUUM! BRUUM!"

The bee tried again. "OOOOGAA! OOOGAA!" he went, sounding like a foghorn.

"Flap your wings harder," said the Queen. "Then you'll go BUZZZ! BUZZZ! like the rest of us."

The bee flapped his wings harder. He went, "POP! POP!" Then, "DINGLE! DINGLE!" Then, "BING! BONG!" And finally, "ZZZUB! ZZZUB!"

"Well, that's a little backwards but it's better than nothing," sighed the Queen. So the bee went, "ZZZUB! ZZZUB!" all day long.

Sweeping

Mrs Springclean was always sweeping up. Sweep, sweep, sweep went her broom on the living room carpet. She swept so hard she created a cloud of thick dust which she could hardly see through.

Mr Jumpy was passing by and saw the cloud of dust. Being a nervous sort of fellow, he thought it was smoke. "Mrs Springclean's house is on fire!" he squealed. Seeing a bucket of soapy water which Mrs Springclean had left outside to clean her windows, he picked it up. "Hold on, Mrs Springclean! I'll save you!" he shouted, and chucked the water through the open window. SPLOOOSH! The water struck the startled Mrs Springclean, bowling her off her feet.

"Ooops! S-Sorry," Mr Jumpy apologised when he realised what he had done. He expected Mrs Springclean to be very angry but she found the whole episode quite funny. "I won't sweep up so hard from now on," she laughed.

Lost

A little fox was lost in the forest. He was trying to be brave but was feeling scared.

"Hell-oooo!" said a voice above him. The little fox jumped into a bush to hide. An owl swooped down from its tree.

"Lost your way?" he asked, when the fox poked his head out of the bush. "I'll help yoooooou!" The owl flew into the air and started shouting directions to the fox. "Left, right a bit, down this path, over this bridge." This went on for some time but eventually the fox had found his way home. "Never be afraid to ask for help," the owl told him. "We forest folk look after one another." The little fox promised to remember this.

Vagrants

There were strange noises coming from downstairs in Oswald the ghost's house.

"Ooer! Vagrants!" said Oswald, as he popped his head through the living room ceiling to see who was there. Two scruffy men had broken the window and climbed in.

"This place has been empty for years," said one. "We'll set up home here and invite all our friends to stay."

"I'm not having that!" snorted Oswald crossly. "This is my house. I don't want a lot of dirty old vagrants living here!"

The men went into the kitchen to make a cup of tea. They turned on the tap to fill a kettle with water.

GURGLE! GURGLE! went the tap but no water came out. "Must be blocked," said one of the men, and gave the tap a good thump . . . and out popped Oswald.

"Hello," he said. "I'll have my tea black with no sugar. I must watch my weight, you know!"

"EEEK! A g-ghost living in the tap!" cried one of the vagrants. "I'm not staying here!" He ran out of the house, quickly followed by his friend.

"Funny chaps," Oswald laughed. "They didn't even stay for tea!"

172

Tiny's Trunk

Tiny the elephant was having one of his naughty days. He would fill his trunk with small pebbles and then blow hard so that they would shoot out and hit passers by.

"OUCH!" yelled the monkeys and the lions and the antelope. "Wait until we catch you!" But Tiny was so small he easily escaped from them in the undergrowth.

The safari park warden heard about Tiny's tricks and went out to tell him off. Tiny saw him coming and sucked up more pebbles in his trunk. But one pebble was rather big and it became wedged half way up his trunk. No matter how hard Tiny tried, he couldn't blow it out again.

"Oh, help!" he cried, going bright red in the face. "I can't breathe!"

The warden saw what had happened and gave Tiny a sharp slap on his trunk, knocking the pebble out. Tiny was very grateful and promised not to do such a silly trick again.

Moving House

Picklenose the elf lived in a deep valley. It was so deep that the sun's rays never reached the ground, and it was always cold and grey.

"I want to live up there on the mountain top," said Picklenose, looking up to the top of the mountain where the sun always shone brightly. But I can't move house because there are no houses up there."

A giant overheard this. He told Picklenose to go into his house. When he was inside, the giant lifted the house off the ground and put it onto the mountain top.

"What a funny way to move house," laughed Picklenose.

Toadstool Umbrella

Lippityskip, the troll, was resting under his toadstool umbrella. "Hmmm. I feel thirsty," he thought, and went off to get a drink of water. While he was away a great big bear came lumbering past. He saw the toadstool, and promptly ate it. When Lippityskip returned he was amazed to find his toadstool umbrella had gone. He searched everywhere for it. "Who could have taken it?" he wondered. We know, don't we!

Squirrel

There was a little squirrel
Living in a tree,
Scampering from branch to branch
Collecting nuts for tea.
Suddenly she saw a face
floating in the air,
It had a big, green smiling face,
It gave her such a scare!
"Oh, please don't eat me!"
Said the squirrel, thinking it would bite,
"Don't be silly!" said the face,
"Can't you see, I'm only a kite!"

Magic Pencil

Kim owned a magic pencil. Whenever she drew a picture and said the magic words "ZIM-ZAM-ZOP!" the picture would come to life!

Kim had drawn a picture of a monkey. "ZIM-ZAM-ZOP!" she said, and the monkey leapt off the paper. It ran around the room, pulling down the curtains, knocking over the grandfather clock, scattering the ornaments, smashing a vase and knocking over the table.

"Help! I must stop him!" cried Kim. Using her rubber, she rubbed out the monkey. When her father came in and saw the mess, he bellowed, "What have you been up to?"

"Drawing," said Kim. Of course, her father didn't believe her and she had to stay in her room all day.

The Sack

Clever Tricks, the pixie, visited his cousin, Slow-To-Catch-On, with a large sack.

"I have to go away," Clever Tricks said. "Please look after my sack until I return — but whatever you do, don't look inside."

Slow-To-Catch-On promised that he wouldn't look inside the sack and Clever Tricks went away. But Slow-To-Catch-On couldn't resist having just a tiny peek inside the sack to see what Clever Tricks had brought to his house.

"That's strange," he frowned, looking into the empty sack. "There's nothing here at all."

Just then Clever Tricks returned. "You've looked in my sack!" he shouted.

"B-B-But there's nothing there!" spluttered Slow-To-Catch-On.

"Yes, there was," said Clever Tricks. "There was an invisible food fairy who gave me as much food as I wanted. Now she's escaped!"

Clever Tricks went to Slow-To-Catch-On's cupboard and filled his sack with all the food that he found there. "You lost my food fairy so I'll take all your food instead," he said. Poor Slow-To-Catch-On. He was very hungry that night, while Clever Trick had a very big meal.

Boastful Badger

There was a race to be held at Billy Badger's school. "I'll win easily," he boasted to his friends.

The next morning, before school, Billy did some extra exercises to make sure he was really fit for the race. He did fifty press-ups, a five mile cross-country run, touched his toes one hundred times, ran-on-the-spot for twenty minutes, jumped up and down thirty times, and jogged up and down the lane three times!

"WHEW!" he gasped as he hurried to school. "No one will stand a chance against me now!"

The race was run that afternoon and the winner was — Freddy Ferret! As for Billy, he didn't even enter the race. He had exercised so much, he had fallen asleep at the starting line!

Bittern Bert (1)

Bittern Bert was a funny-looking bird. He had a long neck, long legs and even a long, pointed bill. He was usually found skulking in the reeds and when he spoke, his voice was so loud it sounded like a distant fog-horn. He was also something of a collector. He would keep whatever he found. Old bottle tops, pieces of string, cardboard of all sizes and colours, rusty bikes, broken fridges, bits and bobs of every kind. His home looked like a rubbish tip.

"I wish you'd tidy up," said his neighbour, Harriet Heron. You make everywhere look untidy."

"You never know when this stuff will be worth something," is all Bert would reply. Actually, he always meant to sort through the rubbish but somehow never got around to it. But something happened to make him change his mind.

Too Much Rubbish (2)

One day Bittern Bert woke up to discover that he couldn't find his way out because of all the rubbish that cluttered his house. "AAAARK!" he cried, and then "WOOOOMP!" which he usually did when he was upset. "I know the front door's here somewhere but I just can't find it!"

He tried to push the rubbish aside but found it wouldn't move. He tried climbing over it but it was too high to climb. He tried burrowing under it but only ended up with a bottle top stuck on the end of his bill.

"HELP!" he cried, hoping that someone would hear him. Luckily, Harriet Heron was passing by. She fetched her broom and spent the next hour brushing the rubbish from the house. Bittern Bert was very relieved to be free at last. "Perhaps it's time I had a clean out," he said.

"What a good idea!" Harriet agreed.

Clean Town

"I'm going to clean up this town!" said Sheriff Blowhard after seeing the roads covered in litter. He saw Black Jake and his gang dropping their sweet wrappers all over the place. "Pick them up!" shouted the Sheriff.

"Make us!" laughed Black Jake.

The Sheriff took his garden hose and connected it to the tap beside the horse trough, and turned it on. WHOOOOSH! The water spurted out of the hose and knocked Black Jake off his feet. "I surrender!" he spluttered, holding up a white handkerchief in surrender. Sheriff Blowhard soon had Black Jake and his gang sweeping up all the litter. "I said I'd clean up this town!" he laughed.

Wet Cement

Dreamy Dan arrived home to find that his father had cemented the garden path. "The coment's still wet so don't walk on the path," his father said. "I won't," Dan promised.

Dan ran along the path, his feet going SPLODGE! SPLODGE! in the cement.

"Aaaggh! My path!" roared his father. "I thought I told you not to walk on it?"

"I didn't," Dan said. "I ran on it instead!" Silly Dan. His father made Dan cement the path again, on his own!

Moving

A tortoise decided to move house. He crawled out of his shell and went to find somewhere else to live. He found an old box but a weasel was sleeping there and chased him away. He saw an abandoned mouse hole but could only fit his head through the front door, so that was no good. He discovered an old piece of drainpipe but it was full of insects and bugs, so he decided not to stay there. Then he came across a chicken coop but the chickens made such a noise a-clucking and a-squawking because they thought he was a fox, he quickly ran off again. "I'll go back to living in my shell," he thought wisely.

The Park Keeper

Murray the park keeper was always in a bad mood. If someone walked on the grass he would shout, "GET OFF MY GRASS!" If someone rode a bicycle into the park he would shout, "NO CYCLING IN MY PARK!" And if someone tried to laugh, he would shout, "NO LAUGHING IN MY PARK!" He was a thoroughly ill-tempered man and everyone was afraid of him.

"Perhaps if we sang him a song he'd be better tempered," they thought. But when they tried this Murray shouted, "NO SINGING IN MY PARK!"

"Well, let's tell him a joke then," the people decided. "That should cheer him up. But Murray didn't find the joke the slightest bit funny. "NO JOKING IN MY PARK!" he shouted.

"Why are you always so bad-tempered?" a man asked Murray.

"Huh! You would be too if you hadn't had a swing since you were a little boy," said Murray.

"Well, why don't you have a go on the park swings?" the man suggested.

"Oh, I couldn't," said Murray bashfully.

"Of course you could. Go on!" So Murray, feeling rather foolish, sat on one of the swings. At first he swung backwards and forwards. Then he swung a little bit harder. Soon he was swinging high in the air and loving every minute of it.

Murray had a swing every day before opening the park and was never in a bad temper again.

Footprints

Alex's mother had shown him how to make footprints on paper. He put his feet in a tray of blue paint and walked backwards and forwards over sheets of paper. "Carry on while I make some tea," his mum said.

When she had finished, Alex's mum went back to see how he was getting on. She had quite a shock to find blue footprints all over the carpet, the table, and even the walls!

"I got bored with walking on paper," the naughty Alex said.

Flea

Phineas Flea was looking for a dog to bite. He saw Sally Sheepdog and Heidi Dachshund walking towards him. "The dachshund's coat is too short to hide in properly," Phineas thought. "But that sheepdog is perfect." So he hopped onto Sally's back.

"OOOW!" Sally cried when Phineas took a bite of her. She tried to scratch Phineas off but he held on tightly.

"If it's a flea pestering you, come with me," said Heidi. Sally followed Heidi home, taking Phineas with her. "They won't get rid of me," he chuckled.

Once home Heidi took a tub of powder from a cupboard and sprinkled it over Sally's coat.

"A-A-A-AAA-CHOOOO!" Poor Phineas. The powder made him sneeze and sneeze. "I can't stay here!" he grumbled, and hopped away.

"I thought this flea powder would do the trick!" laughed Heidi, showing Sally the tub of powder.

Two Cats

B.J. and Foxy were two cats who lived in the same house, and they were always fighting!

"Meeoow!" snarled B.J., who was a black cat with a white patch under his throat, and white paws. "I want to sleep in the armchair today!"

"Meeoow!" hissed Foxy, a ginger cat with a white patch under his throat and white paws. "You'll do no such thing! I'm having the armchair!"

B.J. and Foxy started fighting again. When their owner came in he shouted, "If you two don't stop fighting, I'll sell you to a pet shop!"

B.J. and Foxy didn't like the sound of that at all.

"Why don't we share the armchair?" B.J. suggested.

"Good idea!" said Foxy. And that's what they did.

Photographer Peter

CLICK! CLICK! CLICK! went the shutter of Peter Porcupine's new camera. He took a picture of Sally Squirrel hanging upsidedown by her tail, from a tree. He took a picture of Arnold Alligator bathing in a swamp. He took a picture of Belinda Butterfly fluttering from flower to flower.

"You're a jolly clever photographer," said Mrs Hedgehog. "Perhaps you can help me. Someone's pinching the food from my cupboard."

"That's easy," Peter smiled. He went over to Mrs Hedgehog's house and waited in the dark, beside the cupboard. Soon he heard someone enter the house and sneak over to the cupboard. FLAASSH! went the flash-gun on Peter's camera. The startled thief ran away. When the photograph was developed there was the picture of Maurice Mole trying to break into the cupboard. Maurice had to give back all the food he had stolen, and Mrs Hedgehog gave Peter a special supper to thank him.

Officer Clink's Mistake

Mr Swizzlestick had planted a scarecrow in his garden to stop the birds from eating his seeds. The Scarecrow stood in the garden, through rain or mist or snow. After a while he began looking rather weather-beaten so Mr Swizzlestick pulled him out of the ground and took him indoors. He undressed the scarecrow and replaced his old clothes with those he had bought at a jumble sale.

"You look almost real!" chuckled Mr Swizzlestick, looking at the scarecrow in his new clothes.

Mr Swizzlestick went into the kitchen to make a cup of tea before he replanted the scarecrow. Officer Clink passed by the house. When he looked into the window and saw the scarecrow dressed in its new clothes, he thought it was a burglar who had broken into Mr Swizzlestick's house to rob him.

"I'll have to arrest the fellow before he escapes," he thought.

Officer Clink burst through the door and threw himself at the scarecrow. CRRASSH! They fell to the floor in a tumble.

"Goodness! What's going on?" asked Mr Swizzlestick, as he ran into the room. When he saw Officer Clink wrestling with his scarecrow, he couldn't help laughing. Officer Clink wasn't amused when he discovered he'd tried to arrest a scarecrow. But Mr Swizzlestick gave him a cup of tea and both men had a jolly good laugh.

The Pests (1)

Mandy and her dog, Toby, were always getting into mischief. While Mandy filled her dad's boots with cold custard, Toby chased the postman out of the garden and down the street. They had already upset the neighbours' dustbins, run through Mrs Glockenspiel's rose garden, crashed the scooter into Mr Pippen's apple cart upsetting all his apples. They dug a large hole in the park and filled it with water.

"Something's got to be done about these pests!" their neighbours decided.

The Trap (2)

The next day Mandy's neighbours worked hard to set a trap. They filled a bucket full of soot and balanced it in the branches of a tree which grew beside Mr Spooner's garden gate. Then they tied a piece of string from the bucket to the gate, and put a sign outside the house: FREE FOOD. "When those two pests rush in to eat the food, they'll open the gate and pull the bucket down onto themselves!" the neighbours chuckled.

"Ooh! Free grub!" Mandy grinned, when she saw the sign outside Mr Spooner's garden. "Let's get it, Toby!"

"WOOF!" Toby agreed excitedly.

Mandy and Toby ran to the gate and were just about to pull it open when Officer Truncheon came along. He growled crossly at them. "Up to more mischief, no doubt! Be off with you!"

Mandy and Toby went off, grumbling. Then Officer Truncheon saw the notice. "Free food, eh? I am feeling rather hungry!" And he pulled open the gate! CRRASSH! The bucket of soot was pulled out of the tree and spilled over his head.

"Oh, no!" cried the neighbours. "Our trick's backfired!"

"You're worse than Mandy and Toby!" Officer Truncheon roared.

Mandy and Toby laughed and laughed. "We couldn't have done better ourselves!" Mandy giggled.

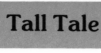

Tall Tale

There was once a giraffe who was always telling unbelievable stories. This is one of them.

"I had taken a trip down the river in a boat when all at once a sea monster appeared," the giraffe told his friends. "He was an ugly sea monster and he had a very long neck."

The sea monster growled, and said "You're neck is not as long as mine!"

"Huh!" I said. "My neck is longer than anyone's! So we decided to have a neck stretching contest. The sea monster went first. He stretched his neck higher than the trees, higher than the mountains, higher than the birds flying in the sky, so high, his head almost touched the clouds."

"Try to beat that!" he challenged me. So I began to stretch my neck. I stretched it higher than the trees, higher than the mountains, higher than the birds flying in the sky, until I reached the clouds. But I didn't stop there. I stretched my neck higher than the clouds, higher than the moon, higher, even, than the stars in the sky!"

"You win!" the sea monster said when I pulled my neck back down again. "You have the longest neck in the world!"

"And the biggest cheek!" laughed his friends. "Fancy expecting us to believe such a tall tale!"

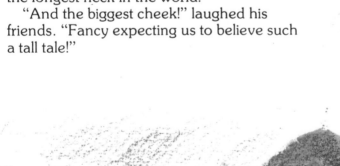

Banana Skin

A banana skin was lying on the pavement waiting for someone to slip on it. "Heh! They'll go down with such a bump!" it chuckled.

Lots of people passed by the banana skin but no one was silly enough to step on it. Then a man came along. He did step on the banana skin, but his boots were so heavy he didn't slip up at all, he just squashed the banana skin flat. Then he picked it up and dropped it into a nearby dustbin. "Huh! It's not my day!" grumbled the disappointed banana skin.

A Birthday Day

Baa Lamb munched the rich green grass in her field, and wondered when it would be her birthday.

"Your birthday is on the day you were born." said Rodney Redstart when Baa asked if he knew. "When were you born?"

Baa thought for a moment. "I don't know," she said. "I was too young to remember."

"Silly lamb!" snorted Rodney crossly, and flew away.

Baa asked Rabbit if he knew when it was her birthday.

"Yesterday. Today. Tomorrow," he said. "Why not have a birthday every day. At least one of them will be right."

Baa didn't like this idea. "Birthdays are meant to be special occasions. They wouldn't be very special if I had one every day."

She decided to choose a day for her birthday by looking through a calender. "Eeeny, meeeny, miny mo! I'll have this one. Why, January 24th. That's today!"

"HAPPY BIRTHDAY, BAA!" shouted all her animal friends, running up with armfuls of presents. "We thought you'd choose today!" Baa was very happy and had a lovely surprise birthday.

Beautiful Swan

There was once an ugly duckling who grew into a beautiful swan.

"Am I not the most beautiful swan you have ever seen?" she boasted to her friends. The other swans had to agree there was not another more beautiful than she, but they soon grew tired of their friend's boasting. The swan didn't care. Every day she would scornfully tell the others how plain they looked compared to her. The other swans were very hurt by this and decided not to have anything more to do with their friend.

The beautiful swan just sneered and said, "You're all jealous of me!" The other swans wouldn't go near her so she had to swim, eat, and sleep all by herself. This went on for many days and the beautiful swan soon grew tired of having no one to talk to. "What is the point of being beautiful if I have no friends?" she sighed.

"There is nothing wrong with being beautiful," said a frog which was sitting on a lily pad. "It is your constant boasting that has chased your friends away."

The swan realised that this was true. The next time she saw the other swans, she complimented them on how beautiful THEY looked. The swans were pleased to see that their friend was changing her conceited ways and started to talk to her again. "Having friends is more important than being beautiful," the swan thought happily.

Space Ranger

Steven was playing his favourite game, Space Ranger. "ZAP! POW! Take that, you alien monsters!" he cried, leaping over the furniture and shooting his toy gun at the cat. "I, Space Ranger, will soon sort you out and save the Universe! ZAP! POW! KA-PING!"

Steven was so carried away by his game that he didn't see his mum coming in with a tray of dishes. He jumped backwards to escape the alien monsters and bumped right into her. CRRAASSH! The tray of dishes his mum was carrying fell to the floor and broke into tiny pieces. "Right, Space Ranger! I'm the Queen Alien and I've caught you!" said his mum, grabbing Steven by the collar. She sent him to his room to stay there all morning.

Tale of a Tail

Penny Pig didn't like her curly tail. "It's not grand like a peacocks or long like a monkeys," she grumbled.

Penny fetched her feather duster from the cupboard and pulled all the feathers off the stick. There were red and green feathers. Orange and yellow feathers. Purple and blue feathers. Penny tied all the feathers to her tail. "Now I have a lovely feathered tail just like the birds," she thought happily.

She went for a walk to show off her new tail, but a strong wind was blowing and one by one the feathers blew away, until there was only one left. "You do look silly!" laughed Penny's friends when they saw her.

Penny ran back home, very cross. She found a length of rope which she painted pink, and tied it to her tail. "Now I have a long tail like the monkeys," she said. But the tail was so long that she kept tripping over it, so she pulled it off in disgust. "I'll have to keep my silly curly tail after all," she moaned.

Peter Pig arrived at Penny's house with a lovely bunch of flowers. He heard Penny moaning and said, "I think you have the prettiest tail I've ever seen." This made Penny feel much better. "Perhaps it's not such a silly tail after all," she said.

Holiday

Sitting in my deckchair
Soaking up the sun,
On the beach, beside the sea
Is my idea of fun.
Building castles made of sand
And playing with my ball,
Jumping in and out of water
Helps to keep me cool.
Daddy says it's time to go
But I don't really care,
"Goodbye, sand! Goodbye, sea!
"We'll be back again next year!"

Weather Man

The Weather Man was sitting on his cloud deciding what weather to give the people on Earth. "Sun!" he thought, and taking a handful of sunshine rays from his bag he threw them to Earth. "No," he said, changing his mind. "Snow, I think." And he threw down a handful of snow. Then he changed his mind again. "Hail," he said, tossing a handful of hailstones down onto Earth. But he still wasn't happy. "Thunder and lightning, mist, strong winds and rain!" he shouted and emptied out his entire bag over Earth.

Down below, the people could hardly believe their eyes when they saw the sun shine, quickly followed by snow, hail, thunder, lightning, mist, strong winds and rain.

"I wish the Weather Man would make up his mind!" they grumbled.

Motorbike

BROOOM! BROOOM! roared the motorbike very loudly as it sped up and down the road.

"What a noise!" cried the trolls, covering their ears. "It gives us such a headache!" The motorbike didn't care. "I love being noisy!" it laughed. And it went BROOOM! BROOOOM! twice as loudly to prove it.

That night, while the motorbike was asleep, the trolls sneaked up to it and fitted a special round metal pipe, called a "silencer", onto its exhaust pipe. The next day when the motorbike started up instead of going BROOOOM! BROOOOM! it made a quiet putt! putt! The silencer was muffling the noise of its engine.

"This is no fun!" moaned the motorbike but the trolls didn't care. They had peace and quiet at last!

The Island

A sailor was shipwrecked on a desert island. He clambered ashore and was surprised to find a large plug on a chain stuck in the ground. "Perhaps pirate's treasure is hidden beneath it," thought the sailor. He pulled and pulled on the chain and PLOP! the plug popped out of the ground.

WHOOOOOOSSH! A large fountain of water gushed up through the hole and the island started to sink. Soon it was completely under water and the sailor found himself swimming home. "No one will ever believe my story," he said.

Bucket

An old woman was collecting water in a bucket from a stream, but the bucket had a hole in the bottom, and, by the time she reached her home, all the water had leaked out. Tackingstitch the pixie saw this and her heart went out to the old woman. Gathering reeds from the stream, she stitched and stitched until she had fashioned a wicker basket. She then lined the basket with leaves to make it waterproof. She filled the bucket with water and took it back to the old woman's house. The old woman was very surprised and delighted to find the water, and would have liked to thank her mysterious helper, but Tackingstitch had already gone. Like all pixies, she didn't expect thanks for her kindness.

The Flowers (1)

Henrietta the horse loved flowers. She enjoyed sitting in her field, smelling all the beautiful flowers that surrounded her. Tulips, daffodils, marigolds, roses, flowers of all description. "Flowers make me feel happy," she thought. "I don't know what I'd do without them."

One day Henrietta woke up and some of her flowers were missing. She was most upset. "Who could have taken them?" she wondered, but there were no clues to who the thief might be, she couldn't do anything about it.

The next morning Henrietta awoke to find more flowers had gone, and even more the day after that. "If I don't catch the thief soon there won't be any flowers left!" she wailed.

That night Henrietta lay in wait behind a bush. Just after midnight, a dark figure crept into the field and began to pick the flowers until he had filled a large sack with them.

"It's that old Mr Miserly," frowned Henrietta, peeping through the bush. "He's too mean to buy flowers so he comes along and pinches all mine!" Henrietta decided to teach Mr Miserly a lesson that very next night.

Henrietta's Trick (2)

The following morning Henrietta went into town and bought a large packet of pepper from the supermarket. When she returned to her field, she sprinkled the pepper all over the flowers. Then she settled down behind the bush to wait.

That night, on the stroke of midnight, Mr Miserly crept into the field and began filling his sack with the flowers. But every now and then he kept sneezing loudly. "ATISCHOOO! A-A-A-TISCHOOOO! Drat! I must be coming down with a . . . a . . . a . . . TISCHOOOOO! . . . cold!" he grumbled.

Mr Miserly filled his sack and hurried home sneezing all the while. When he had gone, Henrietta chuckled to herself as she went to sleep.

The Elephant

Daniel found an elephant crying in the street. He took him home, and, knowing that his parents wouldn't approve of him bringing an elephant home for tea, disguised him in a hat, coat, scarf and sunglasses.

When Daniel's mother saw the elephant eating at the table she thought, "My, Daniel's friend is rather fat!". But she was too polite to say this out loud. When Daniel's father saw the elephant he thought, "My, Daniel's friend has a rather long nose!" but he was too polite to say anything either. So the elephant had a grand supper, thanks to Daniel.

Hay Fever (3)

The next morning Henrietta passed by Mr Miserly's house. She could hear him sneezing very loudly. "Not feeling well?" she asked politely, when Mr Miserly came out with his nose red and his eyes watering.

"I can't understand it!" Mr Miserly muttered. "Ever since I, er, bought some flowers yesterday," he fibbed. "I c-can't s-stop s-s-sneezing! AAAAACHOO!"

"Oh, my! It sounds as if you're suffering from hay fever!" said Henrietta. "Lots of humans do. The pollen in the flowers makes you sneeze. If I were you I'd get rid of all the flowers in your house and keep well away from flowers in future."

Mr Miserly took Henrietta's advice and never returned to her field to pinch any flowers again. Henrietta laughed as she sat down to smell her favourite flowers. "Poor Mr Miserly. He didn't know it was the pepper I sprinkled on the flowers that made him sneeze! That'll teach him not to take things which don't belong to him."

McDingle McSquirt

Billy and Ann
Were very big fans
of McDingle McSquirt,
The wrestling man.
They watched him fight
Every night,
Beating his opponents
With all his might.
"Hurray! Hurrah!" Billy and Ann shout
As McDingle McSquirt, the great big lout,
Flattens his opponent
And wins the bout.
"I'm the greatest of them all!"
Boasted McSquirt, standing tall
Watching his opponent
Start to bawl.
But one day when McSquirt got old.
And this is the story, so I'm told.
Wearing nothing but shorts
He caught a chill and then a cold.
Weak and sick and feeling blue,
And I assure you that this is true,
He ran from the ring and the fight,
And so Ann and Billy chose someone new
To shower all their attention on.
This wrestler being Roaring Ron,
They never spoke another word
Of McDingle McSquirt or where he had
gone.

War-cries

Big Chief Itchy Nose decided to practise his war-cries to scare his enemy.

"WHOOOO-OOO-OOOAAARRR!" he wailed, dancing around his totem pole. Then "TOOOW-AARRRR-OOOAARRR!" he cried even louder.

The medicine man rushed up to the Chief, pulled open his mouth, and poured a nasty tasting medicine down his throat.

"YUCK!" Itchy Nose growled. "What you wantum do that for?"

"With all that wailing you were doing I thought you had a stomach-ache!" said the medicine man. Big Chief Itchy Nose decided not to practise his war-cries after that!

The Bungalow

King Stephen and Queen Karen were bored with living in their big, drafty castle. "Let's go and live in a comfortable bungalow instead," suggested Queen Karen. So they packed their bags and went off to find a bungalow, followed by their ten servants, twelve maids, six chefs, four cleaners and two butlers.

They found a pretty bungalow in the country, away from anywhere. "Perfect!" King Stephen said happily, and they moved in straight away. But a bungalow is much smaller than a huge castle and there was such a tight squeeze with all the servants maids, chefs, cleaners and butlers that no one had room to move. "This is hopeless!" cried Queen Karen. "We'll have to go back to living in the castle!"

Neither she nor her husband liked this idea, but then King Stephen came up with a plan. He ordered his servants to dismantle the bungalow brick by brick and then made them rebuild it INSIDE the castle! When it was finished the Queen and King were able to live in their nice, warm bungalow while their servants, maids, chefs, cleaners and butlers went back to living in the rooms of the big, drafty castle.